The Midnight Aviary

Books by Eleanor Fitzgerald:

Novels

The Ministry of Supernatural Affairs

Night People

The Black Carnation

Children of the Rat

The Midnight Aviary

Other Works

Oxford Junction

The Forest

Anthologies

Hymns for the Gallows, Volume One: The Trial

Hymns for the Gallows, Volume Two: The Last Meal

Hymns for the Gallows, Volume Three: The Hanging

Anima, Volume One: The Signal

This is a work of fiction. Names, characters, places, and incidents either are the product of the author's imagination or are used fictitiously. Any resemblance to actual persons, living or dead, events, or locales is entirely coincidental.

First paperback edition June 2024

ISBN: 9798865339052

Published Independently

Contents

Author's Note and Content Warnings

I have drawn from my own experiences and knowledge to create this novel as well as some fairly extensive research, and have taken some creative license with the geography of Oregon and certain aspects of history.

I hope that you will forgive me my little tweaks in light of the tense and frightening narrative that I have produced.

There are also some content warnings that I would like to point out in advance, although I will not be too specific; I do not wish to spoil the plot, after all! This will be the last mention of these warnings so that the story may unfold uninterrupted.

- **Body Horror**
- **Medical Horror/Surgery**
- **Torture**
- **Graphic Violence/Bloodshed**
- **Institutional Violence**
- **Mind Control**
- **Transphobia**
- **Kidnapping**
- **Suicide/Self Harm**
- **Child Abuse**

Thank you for choosing this novel, dear Reader. I hope you enjoy reading it as much as I enjoyed writing it.

THE MINISTRY OF SUPERNATURAL AFFAIRS

Pugnamus In Obumbratio

For Frank, my Gramps.

You always ask about my writing whenever we speak, and I feel that you'd appreciate the sentiment behind this book more than most.

If you get to read it, I hope you enjoy it.

Part One: The Exclusion Zone

Chapter One – The Body Remembers

Ivy

Ivy Livingston dozed quietly in her seat, one hand on her wakizashi; she'd eschewed the sleeping area of the Bombardier Global 6000 in favour of staying near an emergency exit. The rumble of the jet engines was muted, but it still touched the edges of her dreams and coloured them with thoughts of fiery crashes and mass casualty events.

The therapist turned Ministry Agent twitched slightly in her sleep, a frown twinging her lips as she did so. She murmured softly and her fingers unconsciously tightened around the ray skin-wrapped hilt of her sword. Her eyes moved rapidly beneath her eyelids as her mind wandered.

The trees creaked loudly in the prevailing easterly wind and heavy storm clouds blanketed the late afternoon sky.

"Something is about to happen," Ivy muttered as she walked slowly through the mossy trunks, following the gentle incline of the slope towards civilisation. There was a damp chill to the air and she shivered slightly as she made her careful path across the forest floor.

Ivy turned up the collar of Edgar's flight coat to guard against the cold and tucked her cane under one arm; though she was unsteady without it, misplacing her walking aid would send her crashing down the steepening hill.

"I should've brought a scarf," she said to herself. A squirrel bounded across the ground before darting up a nearby fir; the flash of red in its tail gave her pause. *We don't have many reds nowadays.* Ivy took a moment to consider the bird song that filled the air around her and frowned. *I don't recognise any of these.*

"Where am I?" she asked the forest creatures, only half expecting silence as a reply. When no answer was forthcoming, however, she quickened her pace and trotted down the hill. "Head to the bottom of the valley, find water, and follow it to people."

Her foot caught in a root and sent her falling forwards into a towering trunk. The impact knocked the wind from her lungs and the rough bark scraped her face, leaving several small cuts on her cheek. She groaned and pushed herself upright only to find that the entire forest had fallen silent.

That's not good, Ivy thought, and reached to her hip for her swords; instead, her hands met only empty air.

The unnatural stillness of the forest, save for the distinctive sound of the wind bent trees, made Ivy's skin creep with trepidation. Only the presence of an apex predator could bring such a supernatural hush over the wildlife, and Ivy was all too aware that without her folded steel claws she was not at the top of the food chain.

A flash of movement caught her eye; it was only the gentle rustle of a fern as something passed through it, but it was enough to send her heart racing. She dropped into an uneasy crouch and held her breath as she stared up the slope, scanning for further movement.

Another sound in the undergrowth; closer this time.

Just stay calm, Ivy, she thought as she reflexively reached to her hip once again. *Just keep it together.*

You've faced down far worse than this.

Her fingers relaxed as she let out a low steady breath and rose to her full height. A sense of tranquillity replaced the fear as she squared her shoulders, defiantly facing down the forest.

"Show yourself," she said. Her words were firm, with only a scant trace of threat in the tone. "Come out and face me."

There was a scrabbling sound followed by an excited yowl, and a fox hopped on to a fallen log before her. It blinked once and then regarded her with an uncanny boldness. Ivy smiled, almost overcome with the silliness of it all; she had always liked foxes and this one, whilst large, was not a threat.

Still, she pondered, *there's something strange about this one.*

Although her dreaming brain did not notice it, the fox was a curious mossy green colour instead of the typical russet red, and had eyes that shone like polished jade. It cocked its head to one side, as if it was studying her, and she suddenly felt afraid.

This is all wrong, she realised. *This is very fucking wrong.*

Foxes did not behave like this one did, and the unnatural colouration finally registered in her mind. Whatever this creature was, it was not native to the forest; the reaction of the birds and small animals should have told her that.

"What do you want from me?" Ivy demanded.

The fox remained silent, although she was certain that it was by choice.

"Who, or what, are you?"

The fox glanced back up the slope, and only then did Ivy notice the lurking creature behind it; a silver lupine creature that was as large as a horse. Its fur glittered in the gloom, casting an almost crystalline light show on the nearby trees.

"Go away!" Ivy screamed, losing control of her fear. "Get away from me!"

The mossy fox continued to watch her impassively.

"I said get away!" Ivy yelled. Her hands moved reflexively, drawing her wakizashi into a horizontal strike that whipped through the cabin of the Bombardier. She panted heavily as her eyes came into focus and she realised where she was.

Mallory Marsh stood before her, his eyes wide. Noor Turner had one hand on his shoulder, having just yanked him backwards out of the path of Ivy's perfect strike. She looked at them both before sheepishly sheathing the blade. Mallory let out a low whistle.

"Bad dreams?" Noor asked gently. Ivy tried not to look at the young woman; her freakish golden iris flashed and glimmered in a way that made the therapist extremely nervous.

"I, uh, I had a nightmare."

"Then maybe don't sleep with your sword?" Mallory said testily as he inspected his tie; Ivy's strike had damaged the embroidery. "If our resident Seer hadn't been on the ball, you'd have cut my whole body off."

"Sorry, Mal." Ivy let go of the hilt of her sword and went to nervously run the fingers of her hand through her sleep-tousled hair. Instead, she froze in place when she saw her left wrist.

Oh my god, she thought, unblinking and shocked, *it's back.*

On her wrist was a stylised tattoo of an ishi-doro; a Japanese stone lantern. Inked beneath it was the number one hundred and twenty three in elegant calligraphy. Mallory Marsh stared at her and she extended her arm to show him.

The colour drained from his face as Noor peered over his shoulder.

"What's that?" she asked.

"A nightmare," Ivy murmured, "or maybe a ghost."

"A mistake," Mallory said decisively. "Something that should never have existed in the first place."

However they felt about it, there was no denying that Ivy Livingston's long dormant abilities had reawakened to their fullest extent and her once destroyed Lamplight tattoo had returned with them.

My eyes are finally open, Ivy realised, *for the first time in almost thirty years.*

Ivy splashed her face with water, gasping at the chill, before straightening up and looking at herself in the mirror over the bathroom sink.

"Spacious, especially for an aircraft," Michaela said softly from behind her. Ivy could see her other self grinning at her in their shared reflection. She tutted disapprovingly as Michaela clipped her cigar and picked up a torch lighter to toast the end. "What?"

"You can't smoke in an aircraft, Michaela," Edgar said tentatively from the other edge of the mirror. "You'll get us into trouble."

"Firstly," Michaela said testily as she went about her smoking ritual, "this is a Ministry owned jet, so I doubt they'll care. More importantly, however, is the fact that I'm not actually here, am I?"

Ivy glanced over her shoulder; the bathroom behind her was empty.

Despite their lack of physical forms, the reflections of her companions persisted. This had been the only way that the three of them could see each other in the real world, although they could enter their headspace, the Parlour, whenever they wanted.

I've got a feeling that that's about to change, she though, equal parts excited and nervous.

Ivy wrinkled her nose at the ticklish savoury scent of dried tobacco and tried not to sneeze. Michaela rolled her eyes.

"Must you insist on smoking that thing? Can't it wait?" she asked, almost pleading.

"This thing," Michaela said, pausing to savour a mouthful of smoke, "is a Cohiba Behike 52, and I am smoking it in celebration. This is a momentous occasion, Ivy."

"Our first overseas case or flying in a private jet?" the therapist asked warily.

"Neither," Edgar said quietly. "She's talking about the tattoo; you remember now, don't you?"

Ivy nodded wordlessly.

"Marvellous!" Michaela said cheerfully. "At least we can stop skirting around the subject now; Charity will be so pleased!"

"She knew!?" Ivy asked, shocked. Before either of her alters could respond, there was a sharp tap on the door. She turned her head when a voice followed.

"Dr Livingston, Ivy, are you nearly done in there? Agent Marsh wants to discuss the case before we land."

"We'll be there in a minute," Ivy said, looking back at the mirror. Her reflection stood alone in the bathroom. "Or I will be, rather."

She finished up her ablutions before returning to the main seating area of the Bombardier where Noor and Mallory were sat. The latter had papers and a map spread out over the table in front of him; his hat was tilted precipitously far forward as he studied the documents with a careful eye.

"I'm back now, Mallory," Ivy said as she settled in her seat. "You can start the briefing."

"If you're certain you're ready?" He eyed the newly returned tattoo pointedly. "We can take another hour or two to rest if you need."

"I'm fine," she said tersely. "Let's get on with it, yeah?"

He nodded and motioned for the two women to join him at the table. Noor settled into the chair next to Mallory and Ivy leant against the gently curving wall; her looming position afforded her a much clearer view of the map.

Look once, a voice in her head said, *see everything.* Ivy shook her head at the thought; it wasn't one of the others. *An old memory, perhaps.*

Noor was staring at her with her mismatched eyes, the worry plain on her face. Ivy met her gaze before pointedly looking at the map. *Pay attention, kid; something said here could save your life later.*

"This is a map of the Cascade Mountains, specifically the part of the range that's in Oregon. This circle here is our eventual goal," he said, pointing to a grey blotch on the map. "Dead in the centre of this area is the town of Galaxy.

"On the surface it's a fairly unremarkable location; just another mountain town with a broken down diner and a dwindling population. However, there are three points of interest that are worth making a note of."

He unfolded another map; this one was focussed on the town. He pointed out the important locations, describing them as he did so.

"The first is the community radio station, which is here. If our information is good, this has a large antenna that is visible throughout the entire zone; if you get lost or separated when we're out there, head for the radio station and wait for the rest of us to regroup with you there."

"What are the broadcasts like?" Ivy asked, but Mallory seemed to ignore the question.

"Next we have the Galaxy Observatory. The entire town is a designated Dark Sky Sight, so it is going to be difficult to navigate after sunset; as such, we should move only during the daylight wherever possible."

"Is the Observatory linked to whatever is happening there?" Noor asked.

"Assuming that you're going to tell us what we're walking into..." Ivy remarked, irked at his refusal to even acknowledge her earlier query.

Mallory sighed heavily and looked at her pointedly.

"I'm getting to all that, but please let me go through the lay of the land first." He frowned as he spoke. "It's going to be cold, Ivy; below minus ten Celsius, especially at night. I've been cross country skiing since I was a teen and I know how to deal with navigating in the snow.

"Knowing your landmarks, especially buildings where you can take shelter, can save your life, so please let me finish or hand over to Edgar; I know he understands how dangerous this is going to be."

"Go on, Mallory," Ivy said after a moment, sufficiently cowed.

"Thank you. The final point of interest is here." He jabbed his finger at a collection of structures on the map that were surrounded by red cross-hatching. "These buildings make up Galaxy Applied Physics;

the information concerning whether they're a private company or government institute is unclear.

"Honestly, so many of the details surrounding this fucking town are murky at best." He looked at Noor and Ivy. "Want to talk through the lay of the land any more, or are you ready for things to get weird?"

"I'm good," Ivy said as Noor nodded in agreement, "so bring on the supernatural angle."

"So," Mallory said, referring to the earlier map, "the entire shaded area here was cut off from the outside world on the Twenty Second of March, Nineteen Eighty Six. It seems like it happened instantly, but I don't have anything certain.

"The entire area is impenetrable," he said, handing them a sheaf of photographs. "No attempt to photograph or image the town has succeeded since. No phone calls, broadcasts, or any other kind of signal have come out for almost thirty eight years.

"The Americans have sent people in, of course, but no one has ever come back out. The place is a fucking black hole." He sighed heavily. "The Ministry can't have something like this just sitting out in the open, however, so we sent in two of our Ravenblades, my brother and his partner, three months ago.

"They haven't been heard from since."

"Why don't we ask the Americans to help us?" Noor asked. "Surely they've got their own version of the Ministry, right?"

"They do," Mallory said slowly, "but Francis and Midori were working under the radar; they didn't have permission to be operating on American soil."

"It was a black op?" Ivy asked. Mallory nodded.

Fucking great.

"What does that mean?" Noor asked.

“Well, rook,” Mallory said softly, “it means that we're on our own.”

Chapter Two – Heaven Come Down

Noor

Noor shifted in her seat; the luxurious cabin of the Ministry's private aircraft suddenly seemed impossibly cramped and she felt her heart rate skyrocket as the claustrophobia set in. She glanced around, panicked both by the sheer riskiness of the mission and the dispassionate reactions of her colleagues.

"We're going to die," she blurted out, unable to hold her tongue. "We're gonna cross over the fucking boundary and we're never going to come back out!"

Mallory glanced at Ivy, who regarded Noor for a moment before shaking her head. He sighed and pinched the bridge of his nose in frustration as the burned woman moved to kneel beside her.

"It's okay to be frightened, Noor," Ivy said gently. "What we're walking into is strange and unnatural, but we'll figure it out and put it right. Maybe you should have a little lie down?"

"I..." Noor began as she felt a sense of calm suffusing her body. She yawned slightly, but fought back the sudden wave of tiredness. "I want to stay awake. I want to go into this as informed as I can."

"Alright then," Ivy replied and the tiredness dissipated as quickly as it had come on. Noor frowned at her.

"Did you do that to me?" she asked quietly. Ivy nodded. "How?"

"It's part of my gift," Ivy said. "I'm kind of a universal transmitter and receiver for psychic energy; it makes my skills extremely versatile."

“That's one way of putting it,” Mallory said with a grim chuckle. “She made one of my former colleagues brain himself with a medical implement, all whilst she was strapped to a chair.”

“One of your colleagues?” Noor's voice was small, but her sizeable concerns were conveyed nonetheless.

“He'd gone rogue after he was bitten by a vampire,” Mallory clarified, as if that would make it alright.

“Nightwalker,” Ivy corrected, seemingly speaking as a reflex.

What the fuck is happening? Noor wondered, her head spinning. *These people are fucking crazy!*

“Rude,” Ivy said sharply.

“Stay out of my head!” Noor yelled, getting to her feet. “No more reading my thoughts or making me feel things!”

“I'll try,” Ivy said, “but it's not quite as cut and dried as that. I'll do my best, though; you have my word on that.”

Ivy held up her left hand as she placed her right on her chest, and Noor's eyes settled on the tattoo that had spontaneously formed on the strange woman's wrist.

“Seeing as I want to be informed,” Noor said, “what the fuck is that? And don't give me some hyperbolic bullshit this time; just be honest with me.”

Or else I'll make you show me, she thought, fully intending Ivy to hear. The other woman looked at Mallory Marsh, who shrugged.

“Your call, Livingston; you've got the clearance, after all.” He settled back in his seat, adjusting his hat as he did so. “She's gonna find out eventually, so you might as well be the one to tell her.”

“So tell me,” Noor said as Ivy moved from the floor

into one of the comfy chairs.

"There's an island," Ivy began, "in the Thames Estuary. A little under thirty years ago there was an experiment carried out on the island that involved one hundred and sixty four supernaturally gifted children.

"This was called Project Lamplight."

Noor stared into the middle distance, absolutely horrified at what Ivy had told her. If she had realised that the Ministry had been involved in such nightmarish programmes, she would never have signed up.

But that isn't true, is it, Noor?

The twisting voice in her head wasn't Ivy, as much as she tried to wish it so; no, it was Noor's own conscience. She flushed with shame as she tried to avoid admitting the truth, but it was no good.

Noor Turner was already addicted to the adrenaline and power that came with working a supernatural case. It was such a marked difference from the dull humdrum of her previous life that she scarcely thought of herself as the same person.

I would turn a blind eye to almost anything to keep doing this, she realised without a scrap of shame. *Even experimenting on little children.*

"Your honesty is refreshing," Ivy said, "and there's no need to feel guilty now; it was almost three decades ago and things have moved on considerably. Hell, there's even one of our own in the upper echelons of the Ministry trying to set up some accountability!"

"That there is," Mallory said with a proud smile. "She might not write as often as I would like, but Commander Holloway is doing good work that will benefit us all in the end."

“A friend of yours?” Noor asked, before she felt a gentle ripple in the Tangle. “No... She's your girlfriend, isn't she? You and her and... hmmm, that's strange.”

“What is?” Mallory asked, his tone implying that he knew exactly what her answer would be.

“It's like there's a third person, but instead of the Tangle having any information, there's just a man shaped hole.”

“That would be Thaddeus,” Mallory said with a grin. “You'll meet him soon enough, I'm sure.”

“So you're a throuple?” Noor asked, intrigued. Images of her, Elsie, and Finley filled her mind, completely unbidden.

“We are, but there's been a bit of distance between Jess and the two of us; Thad and me, that is.” Mallory smiled at her. “I may be face blind, but I can tell that you've just had a bit of a lightbulb moment; care to share?”

“Are we all gay?” Noor asked. Mallory chuckled heartily as Ivy snorted slightly. “I mean it; almost every Exception I've met so far has been gay or bisexual or a lesbian or trans or-”

Mallory held up his hand, silencing her for long enough to answer her question.

“Queer people are considerably overrepresented amongst Ceps,” Mallory said. “Take being trans for example; we occur in the general populace at an instance of one in every two hundred or so, but amongst Ceps that number is closer to one in fifty, with a few caveats.”

“Such as?” Ivy asked, genuinely interested.

“The number is higher amongst those with certain types of gifts, especially those who can impose their will on the world."

Like Elsie, Noor thought.

"Of course, those Ceps tend to be more powerful, which is another contributing factor. The final one that I've noticed is that trans Ceps are almost guaranteed after a certain number of generations in supernatural dynasties; the Marsh and Cherry families are evidence of this, and I would bet good money that if Charity had any offspring they'd be sporting the pink, white, and blue before too long."

"But why?" Noor asked, her earlier discomfort all but forgotten at this point.

"If I may venture an explanation," Ivy said, "once the regular societal rules around what is normal and, indeed, possible are subverted or even shattered by the presence of supernatural abilities and non-humans, all the other social rules suddenly look all the more arbitrary. In the light of all that, I feel that most Ceps toss them out in order to be themselves in the most authentic, fulfilling way possible.

"In short, if you can already see through time, how much more of a leap is it to finding someone of the same gender attractive? If you can ignore gravity, why not ignore the convention of monogamy? If you can change the world with a thought, why not change your gender?"

"Well put, if a touch lengthy." Mallory said. "We are because we know that anything is possible, Noor. Does that answer your question?"

"Yes, thank you." She smiled at her new colleagues, suddenly hopeful for her Ministry career. "I was so worried that all of you would be like Archer!"

"I am nothing like Archer fucking Treen," Mallory said, clearly wounded by her momentary comparison.

“Furthermore, I-”

Mallory's words were cut off as a jet fighter roared past the Bombardier. The three of them turned to watch it soar into the clouds, but their attention was drawn to the opposite window as three more military aircraft formed up around them.

“What's happening?” Noor said, her earlier fear returning with a vengeance.

“We must be in American airspace,” Mallory said, far too calmly for Noor's liking. “So, I'd hazard a guess that they're about to force us to land at the nearest airstrip.”

“To assist us?” Noor asked.

“I doubt it,” Mallory said. “I'd say that an arrest is far more likely.”

I should've stayed at home.

The jet fighters escorted the Ministry Bombardier across the continental United States before guiding it in to land at Portland International Airport. Noor remained in her seat even after the aircraft had taxied off the runway and come to a stop inside a dimly lit hangar alongside a small helicopter. The other aircraft had a strange logo emblazoned on it; some kind of stylized bird over a pyramid, which was topped with a blinded eye. The text that surrounded it was too small for her to read, but she'd seen enough similar iconography on the television to know that they were dealing with the American government.

This is not going to end well.

The three Ministry operatives sat quietly for ten minutes or so as soldiers and two people in identical grey suits bustled around the hangar. Noor looked at Ivy, hoping for some reassurance, but she seemed just as perturbed as the young Seer.

"Are they going to hurt us?" Noor asked quietly.

"No," Mallory said after a moment of consideration, "that would be very foolish and I doubt that their superiors will give them enough leeway to allow something like that to happen. Most likely they'll want to talk to us, followed by some diplomatic dick waving and then they'll either let us continue or send us home.

"The latter, however, isn't an option; we aren't leaving this country without my brother."

"Well, at least we've not done anything wrong, so they can't charge us with anything, right?" Ivy asked, her fingers resting on the hilt of her sword.

She's like a coiled snake, just waiting to strike. Noor shuddered at the memory of the doctor's impossibly fast slash as she woke from her nightmare. *She scares the shit out of me.*

"We did register a flight plan," Mallory said slowly, "and as long as nobody brought any illegal drugs or..."

He trailed off as he stared at the weapon in Ivy's hand.

We are going to fucking Alcatraz.

"Alcatraz isn't a prison any more," Ivy said, trying to keep her voice light.

"They might reopen it just for us!" Noor snapped.

"Everyone just calm down," Mallory said evenly. "Ivy, are your blades the only weapons you brought with you?"

Silence.

"Okay then," Mallory said after a considerable pause. "How many guns are on this plane?"

"Two Taylor & Bullock Giantslayers, a Serpentine with a suppressor and long range scope, and three specialist weapons from Reichardt Arms Limited."

"Reichardt?" Noor asked, excited to hear Elsie's name. "As in Elsie Reichardt?"

"Why the fuck," Mallory asked before Ivy could answer Noor, "would you bring so many weapons with you? Especially the Serpentine, Livingston; are you planning on shooting the fucking President whilst you're here?"

"Maybe let's not joke about that right now," Noor said quietly. She looked through the window, suddenly afraid. "They're coming towards us."

"I wanted to be prepared!" Ivy said, her voice growing louder with every word.

"They have guns," Noor continued.

"They're Americans," Mallory said dismissively, "they always have guns!"

There was a screeching sound from outside as one of the people in the grey suits switched on a megaphone. After a few tries, she managed to make her voice heard.

"This is Agent Miranda Salt of the Bureau," she said. "We have your aircraft surrounded by the National Guard; please do not attempt to start your aircraft or otherwise leave the hangar. We will use deadly force if required."

Noor's stomach turned sour as Mallory got to his feet and tidied his appearance. He fixed a small eye-shaped medal to the lapel of his loden jacket and took a deep breath.

"Mallory, what are you doing?" Noor whispered.

"Could the Agent in charge of this operation please exit the aircraft for questioning." Agent Salt said through the megaphone.

"The pleasure of my company is requested,"

Mallory said with a smile. "Let's see if I can't sort all this out."

"Good luck," Ivy said.

You're going to need it.

Chapter Three – The Federal Bureau of the Weird and Eerie

Mallory

Mallory straightened his hat and buttoned his jacket before one of the flight crew opened the door of the Bombardier and lowered the retractable staircase. The red dots of dozens of laser sights danced over his chest as he carefully descended the steps into the hangar; he was sure that the weapons trained on him were loaded with silver rounds.

Calmly, Mallory, he thought as he walked with slow and deliberate precision. *Remember, all this is beneath you.*

When he reached the hangar floor he nodded curtly at the woman with the megaphone, Agent Salt. She took a moment to appraise him, looking up and down his stylish if eccentrically dressed frame, before ordering the soldiers to stand down.

"You're not what I expected," she said once the weapons had been aimed back at the entrance to the aircraft. "Follow me, please."

She led him into a small office and gestured for him to sit down. He took a moment to get comfortable and drank in the appearance of his American counterpart.

Miranda Salt was in her early forties and her chestnut hair was beginning to show the first few hints of grey. Her eyes, although intense, were an inviting warm brown in colour, and her face was set in a stern frown; the laughter lines around her mouth and the gentle upward turn at the corner of her lips hinted at a humorous disposition, however.

Mallory Marsh saw none of this; instead he saw an unrelated collection of features. He blinked, and it was as if he'd never seen Miranda Salt at all.

"Are you alright?" she asked as he shook his head sadly.

"I'm face blind, Agent Salt; I was merely wondering what you looked like. I also believe that more formal introductions are in order." He removed the glove from his right hand and extended it across the table to her. "Lord Marsh, the Viscount Rutland; it's a pleasure to meet you, Agent Salt."

"Is that supposed to impress me?" Salt scoffed, leaving his hand hanging awkwardly in the air. "Am I supposed to get dewy-eyed and start cooing over the fact that you're an aristocrat? I think not, *Mister* Marsh."

"Well then, Agent Salt," Mallory said, withdrawing both his hand and any semblance of warmth from his voice, "we'll just use our professional titles then. By all means, please go first."

"Agent Miranda Salt, Special Liaison from the Federal Bureau of the Weird and Eerie to the Ministry of Supernatural Affairs." She smirked at him. "You might not know this, Marsh, but I know all about you."

"Is that so?" Mallory asked softly as he reached out to a withered plant on the desk between them. Before Salt could speak again, he gently stroked the leaves and stem. Instead of snapping under his touch, the plant was revitalised; it stood tall and verdant before bursting into blossom.

"How are you doing that?" Salt muttered, suddenly confused.

“I thought you knew all about me?” Mallory asked, his tone both playful and venomous, but not too much of either.

“Our background check should've flagged this,” Salt said, pulling out a folder from a briefcase underneath the table. Her face flashed with anger. “I'm serious; how are you doing that?”

“I'm the Viscount Rutland,” Mallory said, as if this would explain everything. He let her stew for a few seconds longer before continuing. “Shall we start over?”

He extended his hand across the table once again, and this time she shook it, although she did not remove her own gloves.

“Agent Mallory Marsh, Recipient of the Eye of Empire and an Inspired of the Order of the Third Eye.” He withdrew his hand as Salt's suddenly went limp. *That got your fucking attention, didn't it?* “Is everything alright, Agent Salt?”

“That was also not listed in your file, Agent Marsh.” He noted that her voice had an almost reverential note to it.

As it should. Mallory did not throw his professional clout around often, but he did not hesitate when the occasion called for it. *Point, Marsh.*

“Professional honours aside,” she said after regaining her composure, “you are not authorised to be on American soil, Agent Marsh.”

“The flight plan was approved and the Ministry Agents aboard have the necessary paperwork to be here; that sounds authorised to me.” He smiled at her, carefully watching her body language; whilst faces were a still a mystery, Charity Walpole had taught him plenty when it came to reading people.

"We know why you're here, Marsh! Are there weapons on that aircraft?"

"Yes," he said calmly. "They're not on the ground yet, however."

"And why would you bring arms into this country?"

"Our Seer said that we would need them," Mallory lied. Whilst he tried to stay away from untruths, his technique was second to none; the years spent living a lie did come with some benefits, after all. "I'm sure that your Seers can quite easily corroborate such a prediction."

Not that you have any.

"Or sit her in front of an Inquisitor; you'll find out that we're being completely honest with you." Mallory saw her stiffen in her seat. *Oh, the Bureau is rather thin on the ground these days, isn't it?* "I would normally say at your convenience, Agent Salt, but as you're aware my brother has been missing for almost three months and I am quite anxious to start looking for him."

"Your brother entered this country illegally to carry out an unauthorised operation!" Salt yelled, getting to her feet. She slammed one hand down on the desk. "I am tired of playing fucking games with you, Marsh!"

"There's no need to get angry," he said, still sitting comfortably in his chair.

"The actions of the Ministry have no place in this country; in my country!" Her eyes flicked to the American flag that adorned the wall.

"Are you some kind of patriot?" he asked leaning forwards, his smile broadening.

"I love my country, Agent Marsh!" Salt said angrily, leaning down so that her face was mere centimetres from his. Instead of flinching, he merely cocked his

head to one side, a curious expression on his face.
"But do you, though?"

Golden leaves fell through the air in a gentle cascade as a chilly autumn breeze cleared the early fallers from the trees of the Marsh Estate. Mallory smiled at the elegance of it all and picked up an appropriate hawthorn handled brush before deftly adding several tumbling leaves to his canvas.

"It's no wonder you've got such an eye for that!" Francis said with a chuckle as he strolled over to where his younger brother was painting. "You're tied to this land, Mallory; no doubt about it."

"We all are," Mallory said as he firmly loaded the brush with yellow ochre oil paint.

"This is true, but you more than most."

The two men, one standing and one perched on a stool, were silent for a few minutes as they listened to the rustle of the trees.

"I always feel close to her out here," Francis said wistfully, before looking at the graves that were scattered throughout the trees. "Close to both of them."

Mallory nodded silently as he looked at the stones that marked the resting places of his father, grandfather, and great grandfather; all the Marsh men, in fact, going back to the founding of the estate.

"We belong here, Mallory," Francis said, "and even if we wander for years the root rich earth will always call us home."

"You're leaving again, aren't you?" Mallory asked without looking up from the graves on the canvas. Francis did not need to answer. "I suppose that you can't tell me where you're headed?"

"You know I would if I could." Francis put a hand on the painter's shoulder, giving it an affectionate squeeze before sighing heavily. "Sometimes I wonder if I should just jack it all in, Mal. Just come home for good and spend my time tending the house, wandering the forest, and just living quietly; in the deep darkness of the night, it always seems like a better way."

"Then do it," Mallory said. "Maybe if you stand still long enough, she'll finally come to you."

"I'm not sure I'm the marrying type."

"That's what he said," Mallory replied softly, "the day before he met her. Clearly minds change."

"They may well do, but the song still remains the same."

The trees creaked as the men looked wordlessly through the boughs and into the leafy canopy. The low autumn sun glinted slightly as it caught one of the many sharp iron structures that dotted the Estate. Along with the fence that ringed the grounds, the beautiful spires of razor edged metal were stark reminders that the forest hadn't always been peaceful.

"Here," Francis said, holding out an ornate charm on a necklace. Mallory took it, looking over the details with fascination; the complex design was carved from hawthorn heartwood. "I hereby name you, Mallory Marsh, as the Viscount Rutland and Lord of the Wood."

"I gladly accept Stewardship of these lands in your stead, Lord Marsh." Mallory slipped the necklace over his head and felt a gentle rush of power run through him. "Take care, Francis."

"Likewise, Mallory." He smiled softly at his younger brother before he walked away through the falling leaves. Mallory watched him go, his gaze lingering for a moment before turning back to the graves.

"I hope I'm up to the task," he muttered, taking care not to look at the dozen or so creatures that stood at the edge of the forest.

"Of course I do!" Agent Salt said hotly. "I'm insulted that you think I don't!"

"What about it do you love?" Mallory asked, sitting back in his chair.

"We're the land of the free and-"

Mallory held up his hand, silencing her.

"I don't care about the hot air and empty politics, Salt." His voice was hard, creaking slightly at the edges like an old tree in the wind. "Tell me about the country; the land that you call home."

"There's more to America than the geography, Marsh!"

"Spoken by someone who sees herself as an owner of the land, rather than someone in deep symbiosis with it." He was silent for a few seconds, introspective. "You really believe that all this is somehow separate from you, don't you?"

"What are you, some kind of pagan?"

"I am a *patriot*, Agent Salt. A true one, who loves the soil as much as he loves the people." Mallory smiled sadly. "I miss England already, Miranda. I love the dense copses and the golden fields; shaped in tune with nature, rather than against it. I miss the little rivers that run through Oxford, like capillaries to some great heart; the city is shaped by the water, defined by the bridges.

"Even the roads that run between towns are hemmed by the trees, limbs dangling over to form arboreal tunnels so that we, the lifeblood of the country, can go safely on our way. I love my country, Agent Salt; it's where I'm from, where I was *grown.* There's beauty in the working of the earth and the tilling of the soil.

"If God lives anywhere, Agent Salt, he lives in England," Mallory said, his voice cracking slightly. "My father used to say that a lot."

Miranda Salt sat quietly in her seat. Mallory could not read her expression, of course, but if he could have he would've seen the total bewilderment on her face.

"I love the land I'm from," Mallory said after a pause, "it's more in me than anyone alive knows; except for my brother, that is. My kin, blood and those that I've chosen, are the only thing I love more.

"I can't leave Francis lost on a distant shore, Miranda." He sighed sadly. "His bones belong to the woods; our woods."

Mallory got to his feet and stared at the seated woman.

"Where do you think you're going?" she asked. "We're not done here."

"Yes we are." Mallory's shoulders slumped slightly. "I have made it clear to you just how important my brother is to me; will you please just let that be enough?"

"I'm sorry, Mallory."

"I'm not leaving Oregon without him." Mallory's voice took on a hard, almost sharp edge. "I'm not going to let you or anyone else get in my way."

"You and what army?" Salt said, her face smug. Mallory reached across the table and sought out Ivy's dossier. He flipped it open and grinned; it was almost completely empty. He tapped her picture to draw Salt's attention.

"She's Lamplight," he said softly. "Ivy is one of the most powerful Séances that we've ever seen, and you think that a handful of squaddies are going to stop her?"

"There's still me and Agent Roebuck," Salt said tersely. "You have no idea what we can do."

"True," Mallory said, "but I know that the Bureau doesn't give its Agents any kind of training to resist mind control; she'll make fucking mincemeat out of you."

Salt sighed heavily and rubbed her eyes.

"Drop the threats, Marsh." Her voice was tired. "This is too big for both of us."

"Then let us at least come into the country and cast our eyes over this thing," Mallory said softly. "Maybe we can figure this thing out, if we work together."

"Fuck it," Salt said, "why not. Sending you back would be a serious diplomatic headache and I know that I was only sent here from Savannah to let you know that the Bureau is calling the shots, not the Ministry.

"I fucking hate politics."

"Likewise," Mallory said, his face sympathetic. "We'll see what we can work out together, and then our respective Directors can argue about what happens next."

Salt nodded and Mallory went to return to the Bombardier.

"Marsh," she said as he reached the door, "if anyone asks, this whole thing was my idea, okay?"

"Of course," he said with a smile. "You're in charge, after all."

He didn't wait for a response, quickly crossing the hangar back to the plane. Salt must've radioed her men, as they lowered their weapons as he passed. Mallory was too distracted to notice, however; the mention of capillaries and lifeblood earlier had set his heart racing.

Not now, Mallory thought nervously, *especially not around Livingston.*

He paused at the bottom of the stairs to the aircraft and took a moment to compose himself. Once he was certain that his thoughts would not betray him, he rejoined his colleagues.

"Gather your things," Mallory said with a smile as he strode into the cabin, "guns included; we're heading to the Oregon Field Office."

<u>**Chapter Four** – Airborne Once Again</u>

Ivy

He's thinking about blood again, Michaela whispered to Ivy as she placed her swords into a protective case. *It's getting more and more frequent.*

"He'll be fine," Ivy muttered. "He had control of it then, and he has control of it now. Trauma just takes a little while to heal."

Trauma, yes, but this is vampirism! Ivy could feel Michaela stamp her foot to punctuate the point. *We are in uncharted territories.*

"And what should we do about it?" Ivy asked softly. "Shoot him?"

No, Michaela responded evenly, *but it would be prudent to keep an eye on him. He's hiding something, that's for sure.*

Ivy was about to respond when Noor tapped her gently on the shoulder.

"Dr Livingston-"

"Ivy," she said firmly, "please."

"Ivy, are you alright?" asked the young Seer. Ivy smiled and nodded. "It sounded like you were talking to yourself."

"I was," Ivy replied carefully, ignoring Michaela's increasingly shrill voice in her head. "Sometimes it's easier to reply to the others by speaking out loud."

"That's Edgar and Michaela?" Noor asked. Ivy gave her a thumbs up. "It must be so strange to share your head with other people."

"It's all I've ever known."

"But surely there was a time before, when-"

"Michaela might have a memory like that," Ivy said, cutting her off. "I'm not the original, you see."

"What is that even like?"

"What, being someone's imaginary friend?" Ivy asked with a chuckle, deliberately using Charity's words.

"Yeah."

"It's pretty fucking weird at first, but once you accept it, it's downright liberating." She turned to look at Mallory. "Hey, Mal, what would you give to be not real?"

"Sometimes, Ivy, and I say this with love, you sound crazier than Ed." Mallory chuckled softly as he shrugged on a heavy, fur lined coat, and in her head Ivy could hear Edgar laughing along with him. "Once your swords and guns are stowed in their cases, you need to give them to Agent Roebuck; he'll give you a receipt."

"Is he the huge hulking one?" Ivy asked and Mallory nodded. "He looks like he should be a quadruped; maybe someone stole the back half of him?"

"People don't like people that used to be centaurs, Ivy; there's a racism about it." Mallory grinned as he spoke, whilst Noor just stared blankly at them both.

"I don't know what's a joke and what's serious any more," she muttered. Ivy put an arm around the young woman's shoulders and gave her a reassuring squeeze.

"It gets easier; you'll be surprised at just how fast you leave the ordinary world behind," Ivy said. She thought for a moment and then leant in to whisper to Noor. "Just between you and me, will you let me know if you catch anything about a green fox through the Tangle?"

"Sure," Noor said quietly.

"Thank you." Ivy snapped the clasps of the case shut and muddled the combination lock. She looked at the lock for a heartbeat or two before turning back to Noor. "Open that."

"I don't know the combination."

"True," Ivy said, "but you should be able to lift it from the case or find it in my history. You have forty five seconds."

"But-"

"Forty four." Ivy looked at her watch as Noor ran her hands over the case. She saw the seconds count down and only looked up when a sharp click filled the air. "Well done..."

Her voice faded when she saw Noor's head twisted at an unnatural angle, her hands in the shape of rigid claws. Only the whites of her eyes were visible as she toppled backwards and began to convulse on the carpeted floor of the cabin.

"Mallory!" Ivy yelled as she dropped to her knees, her hands supporting Noor's head as the seizure rocked her body. "Mallory, get a fucking medic in here!"

Noor was muttering something over and over again. Ivy leant in to listen to her words.

"Snow and steel," she said, her words hollow and distant. "Blood everywhere."

"What's wrong with her?" asked the fresh faced National Guard medic as he entered the aircraft.

"She's having some kind of seizure," Ivy said. "I don't know what caused it; there weren't any strobe lights or high pitched sounds."

"Is she an Exception?" the medic asked. He saw Mallory and Ivy give each other a look. "I trained with the Bureau; everyone outside knows what you folks are."

"Yes," Ivy said after a pause. "She was combing the Tangle for the combination to my suitcase lock."

"Why?" Mallory asked.

"I just wanted to see how quickly she could manage it," Ivy said sullenly. Mallory shook his head. "What?"

"She has had her gift a few weeks, Ivy! Did you read her file?"

"No," Ivy admitted. *I've become too reliant on my powers already,* she realised.

"She's barely in control; the few deep dives into the Tangle she's actually managed nearly killed her." Mallory shot her a disappointed look. "What were you fucking thinking?"

Ivy did not respond. Instead, she looked down at the trembling young woman, her heart heavy with guilt. Michaela chastised her sharply, but Edgar's voice was strangely absent.

"It can take people years, if not decades to master their gifts," Mallory said quietly. "Don't let your experiences warp your expectations, Ivy; the level of progression you underwent in Project Lamplight was... well... unnatural."

The medic managed to administer a syringe of medicine, probably an anticonvulsant, to Noor. Her spasmodic movements faded soon after and Ivy let out a sigh of relief. She let go of her head and carefully got to her feet.

"She should go to a hospital," the medic said, although the look on his face suggested that he already knew their response.

"She'll be fine," Mallory said after swiftly checking her pulse. "We can't afford to have her on the bench for this; she's coming with us."

"I really must advise against it," the medic said, drawing himself up to his full height.

It must be terrifying to be so ordinary, Ivy thought. *Makes him that much braver for standing up to us.*

"What's your name?" Ivy asked, as warmly as she could manage.

"Captain Jennings, ma'am." Ivy tried to gauge his accent, but couldn't place him more concretely than somewhere in the south.

"Do you know where we are headed, Captain?" she asked.

"I believe that you're headed to the Forward Command Post, around twenty miles outside the Easy, ma'am."

"The Easy?" Mallory asked, clearly confused.

"Exclusion Zone, sir. Echo Zulu, but everyone calls it the Easy."

Mobile, Alabama, Edgar whispered in Ivy's mind. She smiled; as soon as he said it, she knew he was correct.

"Well, Captain Jennings," Ivy said, "how about we split the difference? Instead of taking Noor to the hospital, we bring you with us? You seem like a plenty capable young man, after all."

"I'd have to clear it with Agent Salt," Jennings said slowly, his accent becoming more apparent with each passing syllable, "but I would accept that compromise."

He gave her a quick salute before heading out of the aircraft, most likely to confirm Ivy's suggestion with his commanding officer. Mallory gave her a sideways look.

"What?"

"You're a physician, Ivy. We don't need him."

"I'm not here to be a doctor, Mal. If he can look after Noor, I can actually do my job."

Mallory paused for a moment, then nodded reluctantly. Ivy didn't gloat or grin; she was far too occupied with Noor. The Seer's pulse was strong and her breathing was even, but she showed no signs of waking.

What if she never comes back? Michaela asked fearfully.

"We'll burn that bridge when we come to it," Ivy whispered.

The Sikorsky Black Hawk rocked in the turbulent snowy sky as they hurtled towards the Forward Command Post. Captain Jennings was tending to Noor, who was still unconscious, and Mallory was staring wordlessly at Agent Salt. Ivy was tempted to probe the mind of the dour woman to take her nervous thoughts off their flight, but decided against it; Mallory had worked hard to get them this far, and she wasn't going to let an intrusive impulse ruin everything now.

The helicopter dropped suddenly and Ivy let out a slight shriek.

"Afraid of flying?" Salt asked, a sneer on her lips. Her voice came through the headset in Ivy's helmet, cutting through the roar of the rotors.

"Falling," Ivy replied as she regained her composure with a little help from Michaela. "I know what happens when you die, after all."

Ivy saw Mallory smile slightly in the corner of her eye.

"I'm surprised that neither of you has asked me what my gift is," Salt said after a few minutes of silence.

"I'll give you three guesses."

Oh god, Michaela said, already exhausted, *she's one of those people.*

"Go on," Salt said playfully. "I'm waiting."

"Playing the odds," Mallory said, "I'm going to say Tracer."

"Nope. Two left."

"It's a trick question," Jennings suggested, looking up from Noor's still form. "You're as ordinary as I am."

"No dice, Captain." Salt grinned at Ivy. "Just one guess left, and I feel we should let Dr Livingston have it. Maybe she will illuminate us all."

Fine, Ivy thought angrily, *let's play, bitch.*

Ivy sat back in her seat and truly looked at the woman opposite her. *Note the posture; open and unguarded. She's leaning forward and is being deliberately antagonistic,* Ivy thought, *which would suggest an offensive gift rather than a defensive one.*

"We're all waiting for you, Doc," Salt said. "Surely I can't have stumped you?"

The gloves are important. Ivy thought back to the moment they climbed into the helicopter, just as the snow was starting. *None of it settled on her,* she realised. *It all melted too quickly.*

"Take off your gloves." Ivy's voice was firm. "Show me your hands, and then I'll make my guess."

"That wasn't part of the game!"

"Then I know what you are," Ivy said with a smirk. "Underneath those gloves are hands that are so badly burned that there's little left, besides charred bones. You're an Inferno, albeit not an especially powerful one."

Salt was silent.

"You did ask," Jennings said quietly.

"Yes, I did." Salt's voice was full of venom. "Truth be told, I can't wait to drop the lot of you in the middle of fucking nowhere so I can get back to Savannah. It's far too cold here for me."

If you were even slightly talented you wouldn't even feel this, Ivy thought smugly, but she kept her snide words to herself.

"Well, now that we're done with that we can..." Mallory's words trailed off. Ivy followed his gaze and her mouth fell open.

Before them, in the distance, was an enormous mirrored hemisphere. It would've been completely invisible in clear skies, but the perfect reflection of the falling snow made it stand out like the unnatural phenomenon that it was.

"Is that it?" Ivy asked.

"Sure is," Salt said. "Having second thoughts about going in?"

"It's massive!" Mallory said, clearly in awe. "How have you kept this under wraps?"

"We've had to dissuade a few people," Salt said, "but truth be told, most ordinary folk just don't want to know. There's something to be said for a simple life, after all."

"Where's the forward command post?" Mallory asked, frowning as he peered through the frosted glass of the window.

"We're just coming down on it now. Why?"

Mallory didn't reply; the shrieking sound of alarms could be heard over the roar of the Black Hawk's rotor blades. Ivy followed his gaze and saw dark shapes lying motionless on the ground. Many of the were surrounded by red patches in the snow.

“What the fuck is going on down there?” Salt yelled through her headset. “Forward Command Post, this is Agent Salt! Somebody tell me what the fuck is happening!”

“The Green Fox!” Noor screamed as she sat up, wild eyed and awake. She grabbed Ivy's wrist in a vice-like grip. “The Green Fox! Blood in the snow!”

Ivy was speechless as the helicopter touched down. Salt glared at both of them.

“What is she talking about?” Salt yelled into the headset once again. “Forward Command Post, are you there!?”

Mallory opened his mouth to respond, but a sudden splash of blood across the window silenced him. There was a rattle, followed by a metallic shearing sound, as the door was ripped open. Ivy stared at the figure in the swirling snow and felt her blood run cold.

I thought I'd left you behind.

Chapter Five – The Keeper of the Dead

Noor

The combination lock on Ivy's case began to waver and shake as Noor's vision blurred. She felt nauseous and something deep in her mind urged her to stop, but she did not want to disappoint the older woman.

I'll show them just how powerful I am.

She grasped at more and more threads, desperate to prove herself. The potential futures, past, and ever changing present all merged into a mad kaleidoscopic whirl. Deeper and deeper she went; at no point did she notice that the single thread tying her to the present had slipped from her grasp.

I can't even feel my body any more, she thought dreamily. If her mind had not been completely obsessed on solving the puzzle Ivy had given her, she would've realised how similar her current trance was to the one Finley Carmichael had inflicted on her less than a month earlier.

Noor's mind slipped slightly, shifting the focus from Ivy's luggage to the woman herself.

Suddenly, the timeline split sharply into three, tearing Noor's mind asunder with it. Fragmented and completely helpless, Noor tumbled through memory and time.

"Help me!" she screamed, unaware that in the physical world her body was convulsing and twitching violently. She continued to fall, flailing madly for any thread that could ground her or slow her descent.

She looked down and her terror was renewed by what she saw.

The endless shining mass of the Tangle was before her, undulating like some great glittering ocean of possibility.

If I hit that, she realised, *I'll be lost forever!*

The waves of probability seemed to rush hungrily upwards to meet her; to consume her, even. Colour pulsed and rippled through the surface, faster and faster as she drew ever closer. She closed her eyes, determined to think of Elsie one last time before she died.

Something grabbed her wrist, almost wrenching her arm from its socket with the force of bringing her to such an abrupt halt. She opened her eyes and looked up at who, or what, had saved her. A powerful hand clung to her arm, with pale fire dancing around the white knuckled digits.

"I'm going to pull you up," the strange man said. He groaned with exertion before moving her as if she weighed no more than a kitten. She felt solid ground under her feet once again and looked around; they were in the little kitchen of a modest sized house. Sunlight streamed in through the windows, warming her skin.

"Where are we?" Noor asked.

"This was a house I once lived in," the man replied. He wore a flight coat that looked a lot like Ivy's, and his facial hair was groomed into a stylish beard. His eyes were hidden from hers behind dark sunglasses. "It's gone now, like so many things; that's why it's mine."

"Who are you?" Noor asked. He smiled at her.

"I'm the Keeper of the Dead."

"But I'm alive!" Noor protested.

"In body, yes, but you sure seemed intent on

throwing your soul into the void." He pulled up a chair and gestured for her to sit. He then busied himself in the kitchen, making something on the stovetop. "I tend to the dead that end up down here, and I can bring them back to the world of the living as ghosts, but only once."

"What happens then?" Noor asked quietly.

"They move on, I guess." The man turned to look over his shoulder. "I'm not really sure what happens, but it's on purpose, whatever it is; there are no coincidences."

Noor felt her blood run cold at his words.

"Most importantly," he said, turning back to the stove, "how do you like your hot chocolate?"

"My what!?" Noor asked, floored by the mundanity of his question. "I need to get out of here! Why the fuck would I want hot chocolate?"

"Hot chocolate is nourishing, warming, and it will lend vigour to your soul," he replied. "You'll need to find your strength if you're to get out of here."

"Can't you just summon-"

"Conjure," he corrected.

"-conjure me back up like you do your ghosts?"

"Are you a ghost?" he asked, setting a steaming mug down before her. Noor hesitated, then shook her head. "Then we'll have to go the long way."

"Are you an angel?" Noor asked quietly.

"No. Just a friend." He smiled at her. "Drink up; it's a long way to the top."

"Have you made the journey before?" Noor asked before taking a tentative sip. She blinked in surprise; it was the best hot chocolate that she'd ever tasted. *The ideal hot chocolate, in fact.*

"I go back and forth all the time, but we can't take

my short cut."

"Why not?"

"It only has room for one," he said with a sigh. "Whether down to Gehenna, or up to the Throne, He travels the fastest who travels alone."

"Is that from the Bible?" Noor asked after draining her cup. The Keeper shook his head.

"It's Kipling, and a favourite of a friend of mine." The man smiled at her. "Still, better to move slowly and safely in good company than carelessly by oneself."

"More Kipling?" Noor asked, running her finger around the inside of the mug.

"No; that one is all me." He got to his feet. "Would you like a little more before we go?"

Noor contemplated his offer; on the one hand, she certainly had not had her fill, but on the other, she was eager to get back to her body. The Keeper grinned and refilled her cup.

"Never pass up the chance to drink something warming, eat something nourishing, or take a piss."

"Words to live by," Noor said with a confident grin. She downed the mug in a single long gulp. "Now I'm ready, Mr Keeper. Lead the way!"

"Are these all going to be places that you've lived?" Noor asked as they passed from the sunlit kitchen to a chintz covered lounge with a crackling fireplace.

"At first," the Keeper said, "but soon they'll give way to other memories; then you'll have to navigate for us."

"Me?" Noor said, her eyes wide with panic. "But I don't know how to get out of here!"

"Neither do I," the Keeper said, dropping into an

armchair. "Don't you have the Sight?"

"Yeah, but-" Noor stopped abruptly as the Keeper raised his hand.

"Please don't try to tell me that your powers don't work without your body, because it's not true. How else could you be down here?"

Noor opened her mouth to protest, but try as she might, she could not find fault in his logic. He looked at her through his dark glasses, almost challenging her to contradict him. Eventually, she just shrugged at him.

"I'll take confused disbelief over denial," he said quietly. He gestured to the room around them. "This was my flat when I was your age. I'm hoping that if we can align ourselves with your current body's level of experience, we can find an easier path back."

"You really think that will work?"

"No, but I don't think it will hinder us any." He smiled as he lovingly stroked the worn armchair he sat in. "Besides, I always adored this chair."

"I'm going to kill Ivy when I get out of here," Noor muttered.

"Why?" asked the Keeper.

"She sent me down here!"

"Is that so?" he asked, eyebrows raised.

"Yes! She asked me to find a code to that stupid lock and-"

"And you decided to plunge into the Tangle to solve such a puzzling conundrum?"

"Yes, and-"

"What's the combination?" the Keeper asked. Noor shrugged. "Don't think about it, Noor Turner; just open your mind and realise that you already know."

Noor closed her eyes and relaxed. Her mind filled

with the case and she reached out for Ivy's memories, but her focus was shattered by the Keeper clicking his blazing fingers in front of her face.

"What the fuck?" she cried, stepping back in shock.

"Why are you going into Ivy's past?" he asked.

"Because she locked the case and knows the combination!"

"She does," he said patiently, "but so do you. You were in the same place as it, weren't you?"

"Yes."

"It was in your eyeline, wasn't it?"

"Yes," Noor said almost sulkily, "but I wasn't paying attention to it!"

"Doesn't matter," the Keeper said. "You still saw it, and that information is in your past; your memories, which are so much easier to access. So, Noor Turner, what is the code?"

"Three, seven, seven, five," she said after a heartbeat of introspection. "I know you're trying to teach me something, but I can't quite see what it is."

"Sometimes it's better to think before acting. A moment of serenity and contemplation before you commit to a path." He smiled at her once again. "There's a place between the world and the Tangle; an infinitesimally small place where time stands perfectly still.

"You can, with practice, find it and step into it when you need to. You can take as long as you like because in the still place you will have forever to think before acting." He placed a careful hand on her shoulder. "You don't have the Sight like a normal Seer does, Noor.

"What you can do is much more akin to something like time travel, rather than reading threads. In time,

I'm sure you'll find all sorts of incredible uses for your gift."

"Who are you, really?" Noor asked. The Keeper smiled and raised his eyebrows.

"Another thing that you already know, Noor."

She closed her eyes once more, hoping that he wouldn't startle her again. A quick peek showed that he had retreated to his favourite chair and she relaxed a little.

Start at the beginning, she thought. *You were sifting through Ivy's past when it all went wrong.*

"A good start," the Keeper said softly.

"Can you hear my thoughts?" Noor asked, opening her eyes.

"Only if you think particularly loudly," he replied with a smile. Inside her head, the final piece of the puzzle fell into place.

I was fine until Ivy split into three; three timelines for three people! He isn't Ivy or Michaela so he must be...

"Edgar," she said softly. "You're Edgar, aren't you?"

"At your service," he said with a slight bow. "You hamstrung yourself slightly by closing your eyes, however."

He stood up and walked in front of an ornate mirror that hung on the nearby wall. His reflection was joined by two others; Ivy, and a stern looking bespectacled woman who must be Michaela. *She looks frightening.*

"She's not unpleasant," Edgar said, "although she doesn't suffer fools kindly."

"Do you really think I can get out of here, Edgar?" Noor asked sadly; it was as if the warmth and vigour that she'd gained from the hot chocolate had suddenly been stolen away. Edgar frowned at her tone and took her hand in his.

“Do not lose hope; lingering too long in this place will fill your mind with morbid thoughts, so we must hurry.” He lowered his glasses with his other hand and looked her in the eye. “You are not alone; take heart in that, Noor Turner.”

“I'll try,” she said softly.

“You will succeed,” he countered, his words suddenly full of power. She felt his certainty pour into her. “We are not the only ones here, Noor; Michaela stands at the threshold and she will help us find the way.”

Noor went to reply, but she caught sight of a moss green fox darting past the window. Hope was kindled from the ashes of her despair as her grip on Edgar's hand tightened. He smiled and pushed his glasses back up.

“You've found the thread back to your body.” It was not a question.

“We'll lose it if we don't hurry!” Noor said, leading him towards the window. Edgar grinned at her like a madman.

“Then let us run!”

Chapter Six – Massacre in a Snowstorm

Mallory

This is going from bad to worse, Mallory thought as he saw the woman standing in the bloodstained snow. He could not recognise her face, but the green hue of her clothing, the pearl pendant at her neck, and the swords she carried were unmistakable. She was Midori Aoki; a Ravenblade, and his brother's partner. He was too stunned to move, and his colleagues were either struck silent or raving with visions.

Agent Salt, however, was not.

Mallory felt the heat before he saw the flames spew from the Inferno's charred hands. He leant back in his seat, kicking Ivy out of danger as he did so. Midori moved so fast that she was almost a blur, nimbly stepping out of harm's way.

Mallory grabbed Salt's collar as she rushed past, wincing at the searing heat that radiated from her body.

"Salt, no!" Mallory roared, desperate to make himself heard. "She'll kill you!"

Mallory had almost succeeded in pulling her back inside when a fist crashed into his jaw, sending his vision flashing white. He lost his grip on Salt, who leapt into the snow and sent another tide of flame towards the woman.

Salt had chosen a broad arc this time instead of a targeted blast, and Midori's heavy winter coat burst into flames. She yelped in pain and shed it as quickly as she could, dropping her blade as she did so.

Mallory's vision cleared enough for him to see the

dark stains on Midori's green leather armour; she was already hurt, badly. A jet of fire sent her leaping back, her weapon still on the damp ground and now out of reach.

The Ministry Agent reached down and unbuckled his harness, ready to jump to Midori's assistance, but as soon as he moved he felt a powerful arm lock around his chest, holding him in place.

"You aren't going anywhere, Marsh!" Agent Roebuck said, grunting as he held the struggling Artist. "Salt will deal with her and then we'll deal with you!"

Mallory squirmed in his grip and turned to face the hulking bear of a man. He took a deep breath, hoping to summon every ounce of authority that his upbringing could lend him. Instead, when he spoke he found that he'd summoned up something quite different indeed.

"Let me go," Mallory commanded, his voice coloured with just enough of the Master's power to push Roebuck's will in the direction he wanted. The large man's arms slackened slightly, and Mallory, ever the opportunist, slipped free. His hat, which had been on his lap for the entire helicopter journey, now plopped to the ground, landing squarely in one of the puddles left by Salt.

Mallory did not even notice as he leapt from the helicopter and charged at the Bureau Agent.

She reflexively sent a wave of fire at him. It flashed through the air at head height, and Mallory dropped down, rolling beneath it. The flames grazed the back of his loden jacket, but it did not catch.

"Wool doesn't burn," he said as he rose up, delivering a swift punch to her stomach, knocking the wind out of her. “At least not that easily.”

In a blur, Midori was by his side, her sword in her grip once again. With her free hand she traced a complex pattern in the air before Salt's face, leaving a green haze around the Inferno's eyes. Salt looked left and right, her panic rising.

She's blinded her, Mallory realised. He saw the woman angle her blade, preparing for a killing blow, and shoved Salt out of the way at the last moment. The sword plunged into his shoulder and he screamed in pain.

Salt, unable to see but with intact hearing, sent a fireball hurtling at them and Midori leapt back, snatching her blade from Mallory's flesh. He groaned and staggered back, clutching his wound in a feeble attempt to stop the bleeding.

Midori manoeuvred in the snow, her footsteps nearly silent, as she closed in on her prey once again. Mallory tried to get between them, but was too slow. Instead, he cried out, drawing both their attention.

“Stop it!” he yelled, pain colouring the tone of his words. “Stop fucking fighting!”

Whatever wellspring he had drawn the vestiges of the Master's power from only moments ago was now dry, and they both ignored his plea. He was on the verge of screaming in frustration when a different sensation overcame him.

SLEEP.

He felt, rather than heard, Ivy's words as they surged out from her to all those around the helicopter; she was pushing her gift to its very limit, but the effort was successful. Mallory's vision darkened and he was unconscious before he hit the ground.

The first thing he was aware of was the gentle beeping of medical equipment. He shifted slightly in the bed, wincing at the pain in his shoulder. *It's always the fucking shoulder,* he thought moodily. *I'm going to get arthritis by the time I'm forty.*

He slowly opened his eyes and looked around the room.

He was in some sort of makeshift hospital. Someone had cleaned, stitched, and dressed his wound before putting him to bed. An intravenous drip ran into his arm, yet his mouth felt bone dry. He groaned as he sat up, and caught sight of Ivy sitting beside his bed.

"How long was I out?" Mallory asked.

"About three days," Ivy said sheepishly as she handed him a glass of water. "I didn't mean to lay it on so strong."

"Is everyone alive?" Mallory continued after downing the glass in a single parched gulp.

"Yes. Midori was touch and go for a while; we had to get her into surgery. It's been a long time since I last scrubbed in for something like that, but it was all hands on deck. She's wounded, but she'll heal in time." She gestured to Mallory's bandaged shoulder. "You can thank Jennings for patching you up."

"You didn't put the whammy on him?"

"He shrugged it off," Ivy said, almost proudly. "If he's still breathing when all's said and done, we should try and recruit him."

"He'd make a hell of a Martinet," Mallory agreed. "How's the kid?"

"Alive," Ivy said, "and more importantly, not completely insane."

"At least she found her way back to us."

"She had help; Edgar caught her on the way down."

Ivy smirked a little at Mallory's shock. "What's that look for?"

"You take multitasking to a new level, Livingston," he said with a pained chuckle. "Is Salt still blind?"

"No; it seems whatever Midori did was only temporary." Mallory nodded as she spoke, relieved. "Any more questions, Mr Magnusson?"

"Just the one," Mallory said, exhaustion washing over him like a wave. "Give it to me straight; how fucked are we?"

"Less than you might think," Ivy said with a smile.

"But all those bodies-"

"Were killed by something else." Ivy's eyes glinted in the fluorescent light as a look of triumph crossed her face. "Or someone else, to be more accurate; the Bureau is not without enemies, it seems."

"But the blood on the helicopter door!" Mallory said.

"It was hers." Ivy settled back in her chair. "She was coming to warn us away; the entire Forward Command Post was on lockdown as we came in."

"Did they find whoever it was?" Mallory asked, suddenly fearful.

"No, but the tracks in the snow suggest a Ghost or Tracer." Ivy sighed heavily. "You think it could be Carmichael again?"

"No; Thad would've given us a heads-up. Can I have another glass of water, please?" Mallory thanked her as she refilled his glass, and took a small sip before continuing. "I was actually stunned to see Midori, truth be told; Francis never went anywhere without her."

"Goes," Ivy corrected, not unkindly. "Don't lose hope yet, Mallory. Come, tell me about Francis."

“What's to tell?” Mallory replied after a moment. “He's my older brother and one of the three remaining Ravenblades; what more do you want to know?”

“How did he meet Midori?” Ivy asked, her words unnaturally casual.

“She was his mentor; he's been with her since his first day in the Ministry.”

“She wasn't a Ravenblade back then?”

“No. He actually pushed her to take the assessment.” Mallory sighed. “What you actually want to know, however, is if she was involved in Project Lamplight.”

Ivy said nothing.

“Your silence betrays you, Ivy; you should really talk to Charity and ask her to train you to lie.”

“That's not a skill I want; I value honesty in those closest to me, Mal.” Ivy rubbed her eyes, clearly tired. “And yes, as soon as I saw her I knew that she was involved.”

“She gave you those blades, didn't she?” Mallory asked, gesturing to the pair of swords next to Ivy's chair.

“I assume so.”

“I thought you remembered everything?”

“I remember as much as Michaela and Edgar do. There are parts that are just completely blank, or have been blurred so that it's impossible to make out any details.”

“That's worrying,” Mallory said quietly. “There are a couple of kinds of Exceptions that can mess with memory, but they are few and far between; who fucking knows what else is lurking in those redacted files. Did you ask Midori about it?”

“So, when I said that we were less fucked that you might expect, there's a reason I didn't say not at all;

Midori is under armed guard. They aren't letting anyone in to see her."

"Fuck." Mallory slumped back in his seat as the fragile plan that had been forming in his mind crumbled into dust. *She was the last person to see Francis alive; she has to know something!* "I need to speak to her, Ivy. Is there any chance that you could-"

"Sorry, Mallory," Ivy said, gesturing to the slender cane next to the two swords, "but the combined effort of stopping the fight and Edgar rescuing Noor has left me barely able to stand; if I do any more without resting, I think it might kill me."

Mallory sighed heavily and Ivy opened her mouth to apologise again, but he stopped her.

"It's okay, Ivy; it was wrong of me to ask you in the first place. This isn't something we can brute force our way through."

"What are you going to do?"

"First, I'm going to try and find something approaching a passable cup of tea." Ivy grinned at him. "Then I'm going to start making phone calls; the time has come to play politics, it seems."

"Let me know if I can help in any way."

"Get as much information as you can about what we're walking into; how many went in before us, any updated maps, anything that you think is important." He winked at the ashen faced therapist. "You're an excellent strategist, Livingston, and it's one of the reasons I wanted you with me on this one."

"I half expected you to ask for Teaser instead of me, truth be told."

"Tea's skilled, to be sure, but she's not as brave as you; whatever we face in there, I know you won't break." He gave her a dark look. "I also want you by my side in case Francis is dead; you can help me talk to him one last time."

"Hopefully it won't come to that," Ivy said, getting awkwardly to her feet. "I knew you were worried about him, but I didn't realise just how all consuming it was."

"Reading my thoughts again, Dr Livingston?" Mallory asked with mock sincerity.

"I don't need to," Ivy replied. "You haven't asked about your hat."

Mallory's hand immediately shot to the top of his head, where he found nothing but his own hair. His eyes were wide as he looked around and Ivy chuckled.

"Panic not, Mal," she said as she opened a little locker beside the bed.

He peered inside and saw his clothes in a neatly folded pile, with his favourite hat perched safely on top. He let out a long sigh of relief as Ivy hobbled towards the door, swords tucked neatly under her arm.

"Thank you, Ivy."

"For rescuing your hat?" she asked playfully.

"For agreeing to come on this mission with me." He looked at the floor for a moment, almost shamefaced. "I know that you'd rather be at home, helping Charity recover. So, thank you."

She turned to face him, and there was a beat of silence between them.

"That's what friends are for, Mallory," Ivy said evenly before walking out of the room.

Mallory busied himself with getting dressed; he had a lot to do. If he had been able to see Ivy's face as she turned around, however, he would not have let her leave without questioning her about her expression.

For as she looked at him for the last time, Ivy

Livingston's face had been a mask of absolute terror.

Chapter Seven – The Price of Power

Noor

"I can't believe that we're going in there," Noor said quietly as she stood in the whirling snow. The huge mirrored dome of the Easy loomed in the distance. Even the thought of it sent shivers down her spine, but seeing it with her waking eyes turned her very heart to ice in her chest.

Edgar mentioned time travel, she thought as she bounced lightly on the balls of her feet, trying to keep the circulation in her legs moving. *I wonder if he was right?*

"Can I change things?" Noor asked the flurry filled air. "Can I fix my mistakes?"

Can I save James? Make things right with Dee?

She wiped the tears from her cheeks before they froze in place, and another thought flashed into her mind, completely unbidden.

Can I save Elsie from herself?

"You shouldn't be out here by yourself, you know."

Noor turned at the voice and frowned slightly as she saw Miranda Salt walking towards her. The American offered Noor a cigarette.

"No thank you, I don't smoke."

"Suit yourself." Salt placed the slim cigarette in her mouth and took a drag as the end flared orange. She winked at Noor. "Being a pyro has its perks."

"I've heard it's a rare gift," Noor replied carefully.

"It's a fucking curse, that's what it is, but you know what they say about life and lemons." Salt gestured to Noor with the cigarette. "I meant what I said;

hypothermia sneaks up on you, or so they tell me. I'd be more worried about the wolves, however."

Noor laughed.

"I mean it. There are something like six known packs up here." Salt took a moment to savour Noor's terrified expression before grinning at the young woman. "No need to look so afraid; I was just yanking your chain. I don't think there's ever been a wolf attack a human that wasn't rabid."

"What brand do you smoke?" Noor asked, desperate to change the direction of the conversation.

"Mavericks." Salt took a deep breath and grimaced. "Cheap and nasty, that's how I like them."

"My father used to smoke Sobranies; he got a taste for them when he was in India for a while before I was born."

"Is that where you're from?" Salt asked.

"No," Noor replied with a laugh, "I'm from Dartford!"

"That's in England, right?"

"It's in Kent," Noor said, with an affected posh voice. Salt chuckled and Noor reverted to her natural accent. "Nowadays, though, it's practically in London. I lived in the same house all my life. My parents, however, are from Pakistan, if that's what you're actually asking."

"Did you know that Agent Marsh is a Viscount?" Salt asked. Noor shook her head. "Neither did I, until he brought it up."

"Why are you telling me?"

"Just commenting on the diverse range of social standings in your little group."

"My girlfriend's ex is a billionaire," Noor said after a pause. "I met him once."

"Was he decent, or an asshole?"
"He poisoned my home town, and then he tortured me," Noor replied matter-of-factly. "Still, he made me a more powerful Seer, so in a weird way I'm grateful."
"He tortured you for shacking up with his ex!?" Salt sounded appalled. "I've had some rough romances, but fuck me, that's another level!"
"No, that wasn't the reason." Noor gestured to her golden iris. "I got exposed to some chemical that supercharged my powers; he just wanted to realise my potential."
"I'm not sure how to respond to all that, if I'm being honest with you." Salt took another long drag on her cigarette. The two women were silent for a few minutes, and they stood and watched the snow fall in chaotic eddies around the mirrored edge of the Easy.
It was Salt who broke the silence, almost startling Noor.
"So, what's your Janus setup?"
"I'm not sure I follow," Noor said. *I'm sure Silas mentioned something to do with this, but I can't for the life of me remember.*
"Can you see the future, the past, or both?"
"Both. There are so many possible futures, though, that sometimes it feels like a shot in the dark."
"Possible futures?" Salt asked, frowning in confusion. "You can look at variant timelines?"
"Yeah... Is that not normal?"
"It's fucking unheard of!" Salt dropped her cigarette into the snow as the burning end finally reached the filter. "In fact, it sounds downright impossible! That isn't how the Janus gene works at all.
"So, if you're not a Seer, what are you?"
"I am a Seer," Noor said, backing away slightly, "but

I don't think I have the Janus gene. I got my gift recently, in an accident, so I don't think I'm like other Seers."

"Induction," Salt said in a hushed voice, "it *is* possible!"

"Can we talk about something else, please?" Noor asked. "I lost some of my best friends in the accident and the awfulness that followed."

"Yeah, sure. Sorry." Salt shuffled her feet awkwardly. "Sometimes I can be a bit much for people, so I get it."

"It's okay. I'd be curious too."

"I'm sorry about your friends. I hope they're in a better place, if that's what you believe in."

"I'm not sure what I believe any more," Noor said quietly. She thought for a moment before continuing. "I've seen the Tangle with my own eyes, and I can feel it around me, always. A friend of mine said that it might be alive and that my gift is only as helpful as the Tangle wants to it be."

Salt placed an unnaturally warm hand on Noor's shoulder. The younger woman smiled sadly at the touch.

"Even with all the shit it's put me through, I'm grateful that my gift is an uncomplicated one." Salt stared out into the whirling snow and shuddered. "I fucking hate the cold."

"I didn't think someone like you could get cold."

"I won't ever *be* cold, but I can feel it all the same." Salt's voice was bitter. "I can feel it leeching the heat from me, always hungry and wanting more. It drains you of the very life in your veins and the light in your soul.

"The cold, to me at least, feels like a cancer." She

was digging her fingers into Noor's shoulder without realising it, but the Seer remained silent. “I hate it. I've always hated it. I spent the first ten years of my life in Alaska, before the Bureau caught up with me, and it was like living in hell.”

“Did they identify you early?” Noor asked, and Salt shook her head.

“Not early enough. By that point I'd already burned my family home to the ground, along with two orphanages and six foster homes.” She laughed darkly. “They took special care to keep matches and other such things away from me, not that it would make a lick of difference.”

“They were accidents, though.”

“At first,” Salt said ominously. “That's what they never tell you about the really powerful Ceps, Noor; their true power lies in restraint. It's so easy to become a slave to the flames.”

Salt removed her hand from Noor's shoulder and the two women stood in silence for a few more minutes. Noor soon started shivering, however, and moved towards the nearby building. Salt caught her hand as she moved; it was almost unpleasantly hot.

“Remember to control your power, or it will end up controlling you. If you find that it's taking too much from you, don't just stop using it; that will only weaken your resolve even further.”

“What should I do?”

“Find a way to focus your energy. Ground yourself. Some people use music, others prayer or meditation.” She held up the crumpled packet in her other hand. “I prefer cheap cigarettes, personally, but whatever you choose, make sure you've always got access to it.”

“Thanks for the advice, Miranda.” Noor stepped

back as the Bureau agent released her hand. "Enjoy your cigarettes."

"You're welcome, kid." Salt muttered as she watched Noor walk away. "I just hope you're smarter than I was."

Noor stretched and took a deep breath as she settled back on the small bunk she'd been assigned at the Forward Command Post. She put the noise cancelling headphones Elsie had made for her over her ears.

"Wow," she said with a gasp as the hustle and bustle was drowned out in an instant. She smiled, not a little pridefully, at just just how skilled the woman she loved was. *I hope that she's getting on okay.* Noor let out a wistful sigh. Even though they'd only met a little over a month before, she already missed her dreadfully.

I am the worst kind of lesbian stereotype.

She looked through the music that Elsie had loaded on to the little digital player she'd brought with her; Nick Cave, First Aid Kit, Kate Bush, and countless others. Noor smiled when she saw a playlist entitled 'Miss Me Yet?' and set it to shuffle.

The sound quality of these is incredible, she thought as the first eerie bars of O Children filled her ears. She closed her eyes and got as comfortable as possible. A small part of her was wracked with nerves; this was the first time she'd completely embraced her gift whilst alone, and she knew it was dangerous. She acknowledged her fears for a moment before putting them aside.

I'll never grow if I don't take any risks.

Courage, Noor.

She approached the Tangle carefully, with none of

her earlier recklessness or wild abandon; Miranda Salt's words had chilled her to the bone and she kept them in mind. She kept part of her focussed on the music; it would be her guide back to her body.

Strangely, Noor found it much easier to approach the Tangle now that she was calm and comfortable. A faint smile twitched her lips; if Silas was right, and it was indeed alive, it was more like a wild animal than some sort of god.

"I should make a path," she said aloud as she stood in the darkness, with the gently shimmering mass undulating softly before her. There was no gravity this time; no sense of approaching a precipice that, if crossed, would spell her doom.

"I am in complete control." Noor's voice trembled with power. "I could do anything I want here."

Start small, a little voice in her mind cautioned.

"Show me something that Elsie would want to know," she commanded, walking towards the Tangle and selecting a thread that glowed far more brightly than the rest. "Something important, something soon."

The light filled her mind, and the image of a sickly looking man, with a piece of metal in his hand and a plastic warning cone on his head appeared before her. He was drooling violently and staring at something she could not see.

"You will never be a king!" he snarled before lunging out of sight.

Noor let go of the strand with a mixture of confusion and disgust in her heart. *I'll text Elsie about lunatics wearing wet floor cones the next time I get a signal,* she thought with an uneasy chuckle.

"Maybe something more pertinent," she said quietly. She thought for just a moment, although it felt like a ponderous lifetime to her, before uttering a four word command.

"Show me Francis Marsh."

Chapter Eight – Only You

Michaela

"How many times do you need to look at that?" Ivy asked from across the room.

"As many as it takes me to be satisfied," Michaela snapped as she began to leaf through Mallory's medical report once again. She paid particular attention to his blood test results, looking for any abnormalities, no matter how minor.

"Kiki, we got it all out of him." Edgar's voice was soft; he always was the calmest of the three. "I'm sure it was just a trick of the light."

"He had eyeshine!" Michaela roared at him. Edgar cringed away from her, and Ivy frowned in displeasure.

"Eyeshine or not, you do not get to yell at him!" Ivy said sternly, snatching the report and, by extension, their shared body out of Michaela's hands. She quickly snatched it back and wobbled unsteadily; rapid switching was draining at the best of times, but in their weakened state it was downright dangerous.

"I am in control right now," Michaela said tersely, "as was agreed by both of you if Mallory showed any lingering symptoms of his Nightwalker exposure."

"Fine," Ivy snipped, "but if you so much as think about killing him-"

"I'm not going to kill him, unless he attacks me first."

"Vampires," Edgar said softly.

"Thank you for your input, Professor Wainwright."

"There's no need to be a bitch!"

"I am a bitch. One of us needs to be."

"Radio."

"What do you mean, Ed?"

"Oh yes, let's ignore the matter at hand to focus on The Word Game."

"Radio," he said more insistently.

"This is what happens when you yell at him!"

"No, this is what coddling gets you; absolutely no resilience whatsoever."

"Radio!"

"What about the fucking radio?"

"Do not yell at him!"

"Dr Livingston?" asked a voice from the doorway. Michaela spun around to see Captain Jennings peering in at her. He looked around the room, bewilderment plain on his face. "I'm sorry, I thought I heard several people arguing."

"I was talking to myself," Michaela replied carefully. Edgar waved cheerfully at the Captain, who could not see him. "Sometimes my voice can sound a bit different at times."

"Okay then." He did not sound convinced.

"He doesn't believe you," Ivy said off-handedly.

"I'm well aware," Michaela hissed quietly. She turned her attention back to Captain Jennings, who was already taking a careful step backwards. "I do apologise; my gift means that I sometimes see things from the other side, and I tend to reply to them out loud. I hope I didn't frighten you."

Michaela smiled with all the sweetness of a shark and Jennings let out a nervous chuckle.

"Radio," Edgar repeated.

"Is there anything you need from me, Captain?"

"I just wanted to let you know that I've completed

my daily examination of Miss Aoki; she seems to be healing at in incredible rate." He shook his head, almost in disbelief. "In all my time with the Bureau, I've never seen anything like it."

"What's the most unusual thing you've encountered?" Michaela asked, clearly fishing for information.

"Subtle as a brick," Ivy said scornfully. Michaela ignored her and held Jennings in her gaze. "Don't try to force him; he threw it off last time and won't take kindly to having you in his head."

"I'm not sure if this counts, but I had a pretty hairy run in with a Wendigo a few years back. It tore through most of my squad and would've killed me too, but something else in the woods scared it off.

"I'm not sure what it was, but it sure sounded big. Fifteen of us walked into those woods and I was the only one to walk out." He sighed heavily. "I sure wish I knew why, but I guess there are some things that we're just not meant to know."

"That does sound unsettling," Michaela said. Ivy made a grab for the medical report, but Michaela deftly moved it out of her way.

"Are you sure you're okay?" Jennings asked. "You seemed to twitch quite violently there."

"Spirits," Michaela said with a wave of her hand. She took a moment to glance at the report before looking back at the clean-shaven doctor. "In your travels and experience, have you ever encountered anything that could be called a vampire?"

"Vampires?" Jennings asked, almost laughing in disbelief.

"Vampires," Edgar echoed. Michaela resisted the urge to scowl at him. *He's just like a child when he gets like this.* Instead, she simply nodded at Captain Jennings.

"I'm sorry, ma'am, but I thought that vampires didn't exist." He scratched the back of his head awkwardly. "You'd think that something so culturally important would be real, but they're just a story, aren't they?"

"Technically, yes," Michaela said softly, "but we've encountered creatures before that have occupied the same ecological niche; nocturnal, haemophagic, severely allergic to certain chemicals."

"What chemicals?" Jennings took a seat, clearly interested.

"Copper, both the metal and its salts, and allyl isothiocyanate."

"Forgive me ma'am, but that sounds more like a fungal infection to me."

"It certainly was more Death Cap than undead," Michaela said with a grin. She handed him Mallory's notes. "With that in mind, what do you make of these test results?"

"I'm going to take an educated guess that Agent Marsh contracted said fungal infection at some point, yes?" Jennings asked as he carefully looked over the notes.

"Indeed. One of the telltale signs of the Nightwalker-"

"Good name," Jennings interjected.

"It is, yes. One of our number came up with it. Unfortunately, he did not survive."

"I'm sorry to hear that. I'm guessing that the most obvious sign is some kind of animal eyeshine?"

"How did you work that out?" Michaela asked, clearly impressed.

"It makes sense for nocturnal hunting, and you

looked rather pointedly at my eyes as I stepped into the darkness." He smiled at Michaela. "The accent always makes people think I'm slow, but I'm sharp as a tack. The misdirection serves me well."

"I'm sure." Michaela put a hand on her hip and took a moment to drink in the doctor's appearance. *Not too shabby,* she thought. *I've certainly had worse.*

"You have a girlfriend!" Ivy said sharply from across the room. "Try to act like it!"

Spoilsport, Michaela thought, but in her heart she knew that Ivy was right. A transatlantic tryst might be fun in the moment, but it would sour the relationship with the woman that they all loved.

"Radio!" Edgar said firmly, pointing at a small set in the corner of the room. Michaela almost growled at him, but instead strode across the room and flicked the radio on.

"There!" She hissed through her teeth at him, careful to not let Jennings hear her. "I put the fucking radio on for you!"

"...is KGCB, The Lighthouse, coming to you live on this wet and windy night."

It's not even the evening yet.

"I'm Sissy Sparrow, and I'll be your Disc Jockey through to the dawn. Let's see, what do we have here... Ooh, how about a bit of Diana Ross? This is Upside Down."

The familiar song filled the room, but there was an unusual edge to it; almost as if the sound was both stretched out and compressed all at once. It put Michaela's teeth on edge.

"Ah, I see you've found Miss Sparrow's broadcasts. She's quite the celebrity around here."

"Is that so?" Michaela asked, entirely uninterested in

his response.

"Oh yes. She's got a lovely voice." He gazed at the radio for a moment. "I wish I knew what she looked like."

"Can't you just look her up?"

"No, Ma'am."

"Why not?" Michaela asked, her curiosity piqued.

"That broadcast," he said, pointing at the radio, "comes out of the Easy."

"Radio," Edgar said again, a smug look on his face.

"I thought you said nothing comes in or out?" Michaela angrily asked Agent Salt.

"Well, Agent Marsh led me to believe that you had the full picture regarding the Easy." Miranda folded her arms and glared back at the bespectacled woman. Michaela's hand strayed to her katana, but Ivy stopped her.

"Try to calm down," she hissed, "you're in a feedback loop."

Michaela returned her hand to the table in a sulk; as much as she hated to admit it, Ivy was right. *Besides,* she thought haughtily, fully aware that the others could hear her, *a wakizashi is more suited to indoor use anyway.*

The three Ministry agents sat at a table with Agents Salt and Roebuck. The later just glared menacingly at Mallory. *Ivy,* Michaela thought, *why is he so angry with Marsh?*

Ivy crossed the room, unseen by all but Edgar and Michaela, and cocked her head to one side next to the hulking mountain of a man, listening intently. Her eyes widened in shock.

"He's angry at Mallory for trying to control his

thoughts, much like the Master could but only a fraction as powerful." Before Michaela could respond, Ivy shook her head and cut her off. "We'll talk about this later; pay attention to the briefing."

"Perhaps you'd care to take it from the top, then," Mallory said, ignoring Salt's jab, "specifically regarding this radio broadcast."

"Please," Edgar added helpfully.

"Fine," Salt said, casting one more sharp look at Michaela before continuing. "The broadcasts that come through the threshold of the Easy all originate from a single radio station that's located up in the mountains."

She pointed to a map that was almost identical to the one Mallory had shown Noor and Ivy in the Bombardier.

"We only ever receive transmissions from one woman, Cecilia 'Sissy' Sparrow, who worked there when whatever caused the Easy took place in Eighty Six. We've checked the state records office, and she is a real person; lived up in Galaxy with her husband, Patryk Nightingale, and their son, Rusty.

"Initially we believed that she was still alive inside the Exclusion Zone, but the fact that she didn't call for help or report anything wrong leads us to believe that what we're hearing is some sort of electromagnetic echo."

"Is the show always the same?" Noor asked quietly.

"No," Salt admitted after a lengthy pause. "There's always variations in the speech and music, but our scientists said that can be explained by multiverse theory or something; I'm not a physicist."

"She could still be alive, though, so there's reason to go in." Michaela kept her voice level, hoping that her building tension wouldn't betray her. *We have a chance.*

"Everyone we've ever sent in has gone dark the moment the crossed the threshold. It's like a black hole." Roebuck sighed heavily. *He's lost someone,* Michaela realised.

"Francis is still alive," Noor said quietly.

"There's no way you could know that!" Roebuck said sharply.

"Are you sure?" Salt asked, much to her colleague's annoyance. Noor nodded and Salt leant back in her chair, letting out a low whistle. She turned to face Roebuck. "This is the most solid lead we've had in over a decade; I say we let them go."

"You can't make that call, Miranda."

"I know, but I can message the Director and ask him to at least talk to Marsh and his people."

"You'd do that for me?" Mallory asked.

"I'd do that for the dozens of people we've sent over through that mirror," Salt said, the exhaustion in her voice colouring every syllable. "The fact that you're here is incidental."

"Thank you," Mallory replied, giving the Bureau Agent a warm smile.

"Don't count your chickens," she said, "I'm only asking him to talk to you. In all honesty, he'll almost certainly refuse."

"A glimmer of hope in an otherwise dark situation is still worth my gratitude," Mallory said, sighing heavily. He turned to look at his team. "Get some rest. I'll let you know as soon as I hear anything."

"I'll walk you out," Salt said as Mallory rose from his seat. Roebuck and Noor joined them, leaving Michaela alone with Edgar and Ivy in the briefing room.

“What are you thinking?” Ivy asked her inscrutable alter.

“There's another possible explanation for all of this,” Michaela said with a grin, “and if I'm right, it could afford us a golden opportunity.”

“Which is?” Ivy mused.

“A second chance for the one we love.”

She outlined her plan to both of them, who listened intently. By the time she was done talking, everyone was in agreement.

“Radio,” Edgar said excitedly.

“Yes, Edgar,” Michaela said softly, “radio indeed.”

Chapter Nine – In My Time of Need

Mallory

Mallory settled into the chair in the telecommunications room of the Forward Command Post. He checked his pocket watch; it was still set to Greenwich Mean Time, but the difference was trivial to convert.

It's almost time, he thought as he looked sadly at the watch. *I'm not leaving here without you, Francis.*

"Agent Marsh," a rich, almost growling voice said. Mallory snapped the timepiece shut and looked up at the screen. The well groomed man on the screen before him was dressed in his trademark black suit, the flame orange details shining even on the grainy image. "You look tired."

"Director Desai," Mallory said softly, "I'm sorry that-"

"No need to apologise, Mallory; I expected your mission to run into this particular roadblock."

"Then why did you-"

"He needed you to get me to the table, son." A second man's image was now on screen; he was blond, in his forties, and wore a white linen suit. "Good afternoon, Director Desai."

"And good morning to you, Director MacArthur." Desai's voice was friendly, although Mallory could detect considerable tension between the two men. "Mallory, as you have not yet been introduced, please allow me to do the honours.

"Director Crenshaw S. MacArthur, this is Lord Mallory Marsh, the Viscount Rutland, recipient of the

Eye of Empire and Inspired of the Order of the Third Eye. Agent Marsh, Director MacArthur is in charge of the Federal Bureau of the Weird and Eerie, and he and I have been opposites in our roles for well over a hundred years."

"We do look good for such old men, don't we, Mohinder?" MacArthur said with a chuckle.

"At least one of us does." Desai lit a cigar as Mallory shifted awkwardly in his seat. "No need to look so panicked, Agent Marsh; this meeting will end with the authorisation you need to go in after your brother."

"Will it now?" MacArthur asked, almost playfully.

"Come now, Crenshaw; you've been trying to figure out this little Galaxy problem for almost forty years."

"And?"

"And I know that you need help, but you'll lose face if you have to ask for it. We get our Ravenblade back and you get rid of an anomaly that's been a thorn in your side for decades." Desai grinned and a tendril of smoke escaped from the corner of his mouth. "So why don't we stop the posturing and just get on with it?"

"You're not wrong, Mohinder," MacArthur said slowly, "but there's still the matter of the Kitsune you sent on to American soil."

Desai did not respond, and Mallory sat completely still, trying not to give anything away.

"Come on, gentlemen, there's no need to be coy."

I should not be here, Mallory realised far too late. *This is not for my ears.*

"You surprise me, Crenshaw," Desai said after an uncomfortable pause. "Everyone knows that the Kitsune died out almost eighty years ago."

"All were accounted for, save for one." MacArthur

sat back in his chair. “How much do you know about the history of the Kitsune, Agent Marsh?”

“Very little,” Mallory admitted.

“Then, please, let me enlighten you.” Desai did not intercede, so MacArthur went on. “As I'm sure you already know, the Kitsune originally hail from Japan. Nobody is sure when they first appeared, but they made themselves known in the Edo Period. From the earliest Shogun, all the way through to Emperor Hirohito, the Kitsune had their claws in Japanese politics.”

“What did they do?” Mallory asked.

“What *didn't* they do?” Crenshaw replied with a chuckle. “Hell, I don't think we'll ever know just how many pies their fingers were in! The important thing is, giving them up was a key part of the unconditional surrender after the war.”

Oh god, Mallory realised as his skin prickled into goose flesh, *why on earth would we send a Kitsune here?*

“However,” he continued, “once the dust had settled and the blood had dried, of all the known Kitsune only one was unaccounted for.”

“Midori Aoki?” Mallory asked. Desai sighed heavily as MacArthur replied.

“If that's what she's calling herself now, then yes. She was the Green Fox, the Whispering Shadow; she had been a spymaster, as well as some other less than savoury occupations throughout her time at the top.” He turned to Desai, almost as if he could see him. “And now you dare to return this foul creature to our shores, Mohinder? Whatever are we to do?”

Mallory was in shock. *I knew Midori was an Kitsune, but I never realised she was a fugitive!*

“If killing her would bring you satisfaction,” the Director said, “then go ahead. I will not bargain for her freedom.”

“Oh, I'm not so wasteful as that! I'm a monster, Mohinder, and a killer, but I'm not careless with talent. No, we would offer Midori a position in the Bureau if you were to disavow her; who knows what secrets she could give me?”

Mallory thought he saw Desai smile, just a little, but the furious tone in the man's voice made him certain that he'd imagined it.

“You dare to threaten me, Crenshaw? Fine; name your price.”

“Canada.” MacArthur's response was barely out of his mouth when the reply came.

“No.” Then, a pause. “Besides, Canada is a separate entity and-”

“Cut the shit, Mohinder. Everyone knows that the Ministry has offices in every Commonwealth country around the world. You're more in control of our northern neighbour than anyone realises.”

“I won't give you Canada, Crenshaw. I'd sooner kill the Kitsune myself.”

“Well, here's my final offer...” MacArthur took a moment to gather himself. “I want a copy of the White Book.”

So it does exist! Mallory thought, his heart racing.

The White Book was the greatest treasure that the Ministry possessed; it was a list of how to kill every type of creature and Exception imaginable. It was so dangerous that the only people allowed to read it were the Director of the Ministry and the Commander of the Martinet Order.

Jess, Mallory wondered, *have you read it? Have you*

seen how to kill me?

"The White Book is not real," Desai said evenly. His cigar had long since gone out. "Rumours of its existence are pure fiction."

"That's not true, Mohinder, and I know that you've seen it." MacArthur leant forwards in his seat, his eyes dark and greedy. "If it sweetens the pot, I'll accept it with one entry removed."

"Which one?" Desai asked.

"Rakshasa, naturally."

There was a moment as Desai pondered this. Then he nodded. Mallory sighed with relief.

"Good, good." MacArthur grinned. "In which case, Agent Marsh, I will send formal permission down the wire to advance into the Exclusion Zone in the next couple of days. I trust you'll be taking Madam Aoki with you?"

"I was hoping to." Mallory was hesitant with his answer; he wasn't sure if Midori would agree to cross the veil into the Easy with the others.

"Excellent." MacArthur paused, almost as if he expected Mallory to continue. Emboldened, Mallory made a final request.

"It would be useful if we had one or two local agents to help us out when we're in the Easy; if you can spare any, that is?"

"Yes," Desai said before MacArthur could answer, "let's have this as a joint Agency venture; four of mine and four of yours."

"To rescue one of your own?" MacArthur did not sound convinced.

"And clear a blight from your landscape, not to mention save however many are inside the town," Mallory said. MacArthur and Desai both nodded, so

Mallory decided to push his luck one last time. “I don't want Agents Salt and Roebuck; I'm sure they're plenty competent, but they were openly antagonistic with my team.

“We can't afford infighting on this mission; there's too much at stake.”

“Agreed,” Desai said. “Might I request Agents Gillespie and Griswold, from the San Francisco Office? They've worked well with the Ministry before.”

“That shouldn't be a problem. I don't believe they're currently assigned a case, so I'll have them flown in tomorrow. I would also suggest Agents Skullbone and Lovage from the Seattle Office; they've both got years of mountaineering experience, along with a good grasp of the local geography. I believe each of them did a stint at the Forward Command Post.”

“That's settled then.” Desai smiled before addressing Mallory. “As for you, Agent Marsh, everything said in this conversation that was not directly related to the mission to Galaxy is to be treated with the strictest of confidence. Do I make myself clear?”

“Crystal.”

“Good. Then, gentlemen, if you will excuse me, I will let you go.”

“One more thing,” Mallory said, just as Desai was about to sign off. “I want Captain Jennings with us.”

Mallory rubbed his eyes and yawned. He glanced around the room, his eyes lingering on the darkened screens.

I can't believe they agreed to that!

He sat back in his chair and began to work out the numbers in his head. It would take two days to gather their full strength, one day to get acquainted with their gear, and one more to travel the last twenty miles to the Easy; at least half of that would have to be on foot.

"Four days," he muttered to himself. "You just have to stay alive for four more days, Francis."

The door opened behind him, and a wiry framed individual stepped into the room.

"Agent Salt," Mallory said softly, not bothering to hide his disdain, "have you been eavesdropping?"

"I'm shocked that you would accuse me of such a thing," she said, completely unfazed. "I actually wanted to see just how you managed to convince MacArthur to let you cross into the Easy."

"How do you know he did?" Mallory asked.

"The orders came down the wire about three minutes ago," she said, brandishing a small printout. "You're taking some of our best in there with you."

"I certainly hope so."

"But not me?" Salt sounded almost disappointed.

"Not you," Mallory confirmed. He considered being cruel; it would be so easy to wound her, but he chose a gentle lie instead. "There's a good chance that everyone dies on this mission, Salt; I thought you'd rather spend the last moments of your life in the warm Savannah heat instead of the bitter Oregon snow."

"I'll bet you're a hell of a poker player, Marsh, but you don't need to lie to me," Salt said heavily. "I know that I'm not a team player and that I'll just cause problems for you in there. Hell, I barely even manage with Roebuck, and we've been working together for years!"

"So you just came in here to wish me luck?" Mallory said, genuinely surprised.

"Yeah, something like that." Salt headed towards the

door once again. “Remember, Mallory, we haven't ever seen anything like this, not in forty years; when you're in there, make sure you move fast, keep your eyes open, and entertain any possibility, no matter how far fetched.”

“Thanks, Miranda. Have a safe flight back to Savannah.”

Agent Salt did not respond, instead leaving Mallory to contemplate the upcoming mission once again. A strange knot was forming in his stomach, and he spoke his fears aloud to the empty room.

“Why do I have the feeling that this is going destroy my life?”

Chapter Ten – Movers and Shakers

Noor

"A cone on his head?" Elsie's chuckle was distorted by the static, but it still brought a grin to Noor's face. "I'll have to be careful next time I'm walking past a Spoons then."

"Is it snowing there?" Noor asked.

"No, just endless rain." Her lover sighed on the other end of the line, almost five thousand miles away. "It's no fun moving house in a downpour, but at least I've got Silas to help me; many hands and all that."

"Tell me about the flat," Noor said, closing her eyes to picture the scene that Elsie was certain to paint for her.

"Honestly, it's currently just full of boxes and a bunch of part-assembled flat pack furniture. Silas and Helen are coming over tomorrow evening to help me unpack, though; is there any chance that you could dial in on a video call?" The yearning in Elsie's voice was heartbreaking. "I miss you, you know."

"I miss you too." Noor wiped a tear from her eye then grimaced as a blast of static shrieked in her ear. "Unfortunately all the interference from the anomaly means that only the most basic electronics work here; I haven't had a phone signal for days and I had to practically beg one of the tech guys to let me use the satellite phone."

"No landline?" Elsie asked.

"Not secure enough. Besides, this was only supposed to be a temporary outpost, and after almost forty years it's certainly showing its age." She squirmed a little in her bunk. "What have you been up to at work?"

"Mostly getting brought up to speed on just how far the Ministry's reach is; did you know that they have offices in every Commonwealth country on the planet?" Noor chuckled at Elsie's wonder. "Who knows where I'll end up working?"

"Make the legacy of colonialism work for you, I guess," Noor replied with a chuckle. She shivered and pulled the thin blanket on her bunk tightly around her. The vision of the future that she'd had in the Darrent hospital came back to her now. "Try and get posted somewhere warm, like Barbados or the Bahamas."

"Sounds like heaven."

"It will be." Noor paused for a moment, a wistful smile on her lips. "Have you made any friends?"

"Kind of," Elsie said, clearly avoiding the question.

"What does that mean?"

"I've not made any friends, per se, but I have met some important people."

"You have my permission to name drop them," Noor said gleefully. "Go on, dish!"

"I had lunch with the Director today, along with Kimberly Daniels."

"The Dingo herself? What's she like?"

"She's actually really nice. Everyone around here is scared of her, but if you're doing a good job, she won't bother you; she really cares about the Ministry. I'm less keen on the Director, though."

"Why?"

"He's overseen some truly awful things in the time he's been in charge, and he's very stuck in his ways." Noor could hear the disappointment in Elsie's voice. "I think he feels that he owns the Ministry and can do whatever he wants with it, including letting it become so outdated that it's practically fossilised!"

"Maybe you'll be in charge one day; he has to retire, right?"

"He's been Director for well over a century, Noor. If anything, he'll outlive me." There was a pause. "I also met Commander Holloway of the Martinet Order."

"He sounds stern!"

"She's a woman, and I think I'm going to get on well with her."

"Oh." Noor's heart fell flat, suddenly.

"Is that a note of jealousy in your voice?" Elsie asked playfully. "You needn't worry, she's not my type. She does share my thoughts about the Director, though, and thinks that there should be more accountability for the Ministry's actions, especially where the Ravenblades are concerned."

"I'm glad you're making friends, but please be careful with your policy decisions; you might accidentally make my life a living hell."

"You have my word," Elsie said. "It's getting late here, and I should let you get on."

"Heading straight to bed?"

"No, I thought I'd work on another world ending invention first!" Elsie said with a laugh.

Noor remained silent, her heart almost frozen in her chest. They were both wordless for over a minute; the only sound through the line was the gentle crackle of the anomaly's electromagnetic field.

"I guess it's still too soon to be making jokes?" Elsie asked quietly.

"You weren't there, Elsie. You didn't see the thousands of rats that came swarming out of the lake, or the monster that Pandora had become." Noor blinked away tears, snuffling slightly. “I really thought that we were going to die there.”

“I'm sorry, darling.” Noor could almost hear Elsie choosing her next words in her head. “I sometimes think there's something wrong with me, you know? I feel like my heart is closed off from the world, for the most part, and only a tiny sliver of emotion can get in at any point. Sometimes it seems like it's a blessing, but right now it feels like a curse.

“I feel like I'm all ice and clockwork, instead of flesh and blood.”

“You're as human as I am, Elsie. All you need is a little time.”

“I love you, Noor Turner.”

“I love you too, Elsie Reichardt.”

“Be safe, and come back to me soon, okay?”

“I will,” Noor said, but all she received in response was another wail of static before the connection cut out entirely.

Noor was sitting in the deserted mess hall of the Forward Command Post, just pushing the remnants of her lunch around her plate. Although she was certain that the incident with Pandora had tamped down the destructive side of Elsie's creativity, something still bothered her.

Am I jealous? She had reacted rather strongly to her girlfriend befriending other women, after all. *Maybe this is just first time jitters?*

Noor had never had a romantic relationship before, let alone one with a long distance component. She speared a rather sad looking chip on the end of her fork and stared glumly as it dangled limply above her plate.

"You'd think that Americans would at least get their fried foods right," she murmured before plonking it back down. It landed with a wet thud. She sighed heavily, hungry for her mother's cooking; familiar, tasty, and a little bit of home.

She half closed her eyes, trying to call to mind the last thing that Hasna Turner had made for her, when the door to the mess hall slammed open. Noor jumped in her seat and let out a squeal of fright.

"Sorry," said a wiry woman as she walked into the room with a large backpack in each hand. "I didn't mean to scare you!"

"Do you need a hand with those?" Noor asked, rising from her seat. The woman smiled gratefully as the Seer took one of the deceptively heavy bags. Together, they wrangled them on to a table with a heavy thump. "I'm Noor Turner, by the way; I'm with the Ministry of Supernatural Affairs."

"You're the Seer?" asked the woman, who made no attempt to hide the surprise in her voice.

"So they tell me," Noor replied with a nervous chuckle.

"You're just a fucking kid!"

"I'm more capable than I look," Noor said sharply.

"I wasn't doubting your skills," the woman said hastily, "but I am surprised that they're letting someone so young go on this mission. You do know that not one soul has ever come out of the Exclusion Zone, right?"

"I'm aware, and I'm still going."

"You've got balls, kid, I'll give you that." The woman pulled off a glove and shook Noor's hand. "Agent Verity Lovage, Seattle Office; pleased to know you."

All her fingers have been broken, Noor realised. *More than once, in fact.*

"A pleasure," Noor replied. "What's your gift?"

"I'm a Shunt," the woman said proudly. "As far as I know, I'm the only one in the whole country."

"I'm, um, a bit new to all this," Noor admitted sheepishly, "so I don't actually know what a Shunt can do. Sorry."

"No need to apologise," Verity said with a smile. She flicked her hand casually in the direction of the open doors and they slammed shut. "I'm telekinetic."

"That's fucking awesome!" Noor said, a huge grin breaking out on her face. "What's the biggest thing you've ever moved?"

"I threw a truck once, but that was with a shitload of adrenaline pouring through my system!" Verity laughed at the memory. "I can only push or throw things, unfortunately; true telekinesis is almost unheard of. I think there have been a grand total of about five Fulcrums in recorded history."

"Are there other kinds, like you?" Noor asked, her eyes wide with fascination.

"Sure," Verity said as she perched on top of the nearest table. "You've got Vortexes, Shunts, Tumblers-"

"Like Archer Treen?" Noor asked, interrupting Lovage.

"Yeah; he's one of the most skilled, if memory serves."

"But I've met him! All he does is transfer momentum."

"Affecting movement and motion through sheer force of will sounds a lot like telekinesis to me," Verity replied kindly.

"I guess it does," Noor murmured. *I wonder if he knows that.* She looked at the name tag on the bag she held. "Who's Harold Skullbone?"

"My partner," Verity said. "He'll be along in a while. He's a Squeeze, in case you were wondering."

"Which is?" Noor asked, eager to learn about the strange new world that she had been thrust into.

"He can fit through any gap, including the space between molecules in materials; in short, he can walk through walls." She smiled sadly. "It takes a hell of a toll on him, even though he won't ever admit it."

"That's amazing. How does he even find the spaces in solid objects?"

"No idea. He starts talking about inverse phase space and I just tune out."

"Is Agent Skullbone a scientist?"

"He's a Professor of Physics at Washington State University," Verity said with a smile. "He's almost seventy years old and he still insists on being a field agent. We'll be joining you on the mission into the Exclusion Zone."

"It sounds like a physicist will be useful when we head to Galaxy, and I feel better already knowing that someone with such a powerful gift will be keeping us all safe." Noor put a gentle hand on Verity's shoulder. "I'm glad you're coming with us."

They sat in silence for a few minutes, waiting for Harold Skullbone to arrive. It took a moment for Noor to realise that Verity was staring at her, a curious expression on her face.

"What?" Noor asked, removing her hand from Verity's shoulder.

"Are you really new to all this?"

"Yes. Why do you ask?"

“Something about you feels familiar, but I can't quite put my finger on it.” The American sighed heavily. “It's like I've known you my whole life, even though I could swear we only met moments ago.

“How strange is that?”

“Very,” Noor said, glad that Ivy was not there to catch her in the lie. “Maybe a past life?”

“Maybe.”

The two women resumed their silent waiting, with Verity gazing idly around the room as Noor's mind raced. She'd risked a glimpse into the Shunt's past when she touched her shoulder, flicking through her history as one might browse a stack of photographs abandoned on a bus stop bench. Much like a greasy fingerprint will mark a collection of glossy prints, Noor realised that she had left an impression on Verity's history when she delved into it.

Did I change the actual events or just her perception of them?

Noor wondered about this for a moment before deciding that it didn't matter either way; the damage had already been done. The simple act of looking had been enough to affect a change in Verity's memories, and Noor had no idea how far the ripples of her actions would go.

Edgar's words echoed through her head as she pondered the wider ramifications of what'd she'd done; one phrase, sounding over and over again.

Time travel.

Chapter Eleven – The Old Guard

Mallory

Beeeeeep!

Mallory turned around at the sound of the car horn cutting through the air, ski sticks in hand. A military vehicle that looked like a stripped down Jeep had slammed to a halt mere inches from a bespectacled older man with a ponytail of long grey hair, along with a neatly trimmed beard.

"Watch where you're going!" barked one of the vehicle's occupants.

"Will do, man," the old man replied with a smile. He pressed his palms together and smiled as he stepped aside. "Have a serene day."

"Fuck off, Griswold!" the driver yelled before the vehicle sped away through the slush.

"Alright then," Griswold said with a chuckle as he turned towards Mallory. The Ministry Agent couldn't help but return the man's cheeky grin as he strolled towards the three of them; Mallory had decided to use their time at the Forward Command Post to teach Noor and Ivy the basics of cross-country skiing.

It was not going well.

There was a faint sense of familiarity about the strange newcomer, apparently Agent Griswold, who was now followed by a short man in an electric blue snowsuit. Whilst Mallory could not pick out anything more than individual features on Griswold's face, his outfit was unmistakable; he wore a Jodhpuri suit of the purest white, with details in the pattern highlighted in vivid saffron.

I recognise that suit, Mallory realised.

He had only seen it a few times before, when he was still a child. The last had been at his Father's funeral; an awful day that Mallory did his best to keep from his mind. He was still caught in the swirl of memories when Griswold reached him and swept him up in an affectionate hug.

"It's wonderful to see you again," he said warmly. "You look so much like your grandfather, Mallory. He was a painter too."

"Likewise," Mallory replied, "although it's been almost twenty years and I don't remember you much, I'm afraid."

"No need for fear or apologies," Griswold said kindly. "I'm used to making introductions more than once in a person's lifetime."

"Are you Agent Griswold?" Noor asked.

"That I am, miss; Agent Horace Griswold, at your service, but everyone just calls me-"

"Uncle!" Mallory said with a smile as the name finally rose from the depths of his mind.

"See, you remember more than you realise," Uncle said sagely. He placed an arm around the pink cheeked young man in the snowsuit. "This young seeker is Agent Albert Gillespie, but he's Bert to me and everyone else that matters."

"A Seeker?" Noor asked, suddenly curious. "What gift does that mean you have?"

"That's not my subspecies," Bert said nervously. "It's just what Uncle calls me; it's a term for someone seeking spiritual enlightenment."

"Are you his teacher?" Ivy asked softly. Mallory could feel the tension and suspicion radiating from her.

"I'm just a lifelong pupil," Uncle said, "accompanying a young man on his first steps along a very important road."

"You're not human," Ivy said suddenly, "gifted or otherwise."

"You've a good eye," Uncle said approvingly. "What gave it away?"

"Several things, but my not being able to hear your thoughts was the main indicator."

"I like her," Uncle said to Bert, who nodded in agreement. He turned back to Ivy and gestured to her swords. "May I?"

She drew her blade and hesitated for a moment. Mallory feared that she would attack the old man, but then she nodded and proffered the hilt to him. Uncle took the blade delicately in his hands and carefully examined it.

"This is absolutely beautiful," he said softly. He ran his finger over the hamon that followed the gentle curve of the blade; the metal rang slightly at his touch. "This is imbued with black jade; did you know that?"

Ivy shook her head.

"It's a very powerful charm of protection when worn as an amulet, but in this form I think it might take on more of a destructive edge." He handed the weapon back to her, hilt first once again. "I'd wager that its companion has an equal measure of white jade in it, for serenity and tranquillity in the heat of battle."

"They were a given to me when I was just a child," Ivy said quietly. "I've had them for as long as I can remember."

"Not all things freely given are gifts, Ivy Livingston," Uncle said as she sheathed the blade. "The motives of the Kitsune are opaque to us and far reaching; to what end they armed you with the weapons of their kind, I cannot say."

"What makes them so special, Uncle?" Bert asked, his eyes still on Ivy's weapon.

"Well, this is just rumour and hearsay, but I've heard that a sword forged by a Kitsune is the only thing that can kill it."

Not the only thing, he thought, but did not want to show his hand too early.

Mallory didn't need to see Ivy's expression or the colour fade from her flushed face; the tsunami of dread that washed over him was strong enough to turn his legs to jelly. Uncle seemed to pick up on it too, and he placed a gentle hand on the Séance's shoulder.

"Don't pay too much attention to my words," he said warmly, "I'm just an old man with too much time on his hands and little else to do but think."

Ivy smiled, and Mallory felt a slight flutter of relief go through him. He fought to keep his own emotions in check and away from Ivy's receptive mind, for he knew what Agent Horace 'Uncle' Griswold was.

He's a Strix, Mallory thought, *and they are rarely, if ever, wrong.*

"A Kitsune *and* a Strix!? Nice work, Marsh." Charity said, clearly impressed at the team Mallory had managed to put together. Her voice was mingled with the crackle of atmospheric static as it interfered with the satellite phone call. "Fuck me, this is a terrible line."

"Thank you, and it's probably the anomaly's fault."

"Not entirely," Charity said, almost too quietly for Mallory to make out. "The television has been a bit glitchy here, and we've had a few internet outages too;

Tea thinks it's something to do with the solar maximum. I wouldn't be surprised if there's a big flare in the making."

"Hopefully it won't cause too much of a problem."

"Hmm." Charity did not sound convinced.

"Ever the optimist, aren't you?" Mallory said with a chuckle. "Have you heard from Thad? I know he's not supposed to break radio silence until they're ready to bring Carmichael in, but I worry about him.

"If only Ivy could tap into the ether and take a look, I wouldn't be half so anxious."

"That's the curse of being with a Tab, Marsh." Charity hesitated for a moment. "How's Ivy doing?"

"She's managing. I think the uncertainty around the origin of the anomaly has given her something to focus on, which is a relief." Mallory let out a slight sigh. "I think she, or more accurately, Michaela, is convinced that I haven't completely shed the Nightwalker contagion."

"Have you confronted her about it?" Charity's voice was flat, almost emotionless.

"No, but I've caught her looking askance at me more than once. I'm worried that she'll just threaten to shoot me again."

"I believe her exact term was 'euthanise'."

"She had a gun, Charity," Mallory said, a tired smile creeping on to his lips. "So, you think I should just talk to her about it?"

"If you're thinking about it, Marsh, then the odds are that she already knows that you suspect it too." The silence lingered between them for a few seconds. "You do suspect that she's right, don't you?"

She's as bad as Ivy sometimes.

"Marsh?"

“Yes, Charity, I have noticed some lingering signs.” Suddenly a thought flashed into his mind. “You've been watching me, haven't you?”

“It's in the best interests of everyone if I know exactly what is going on with my team, Marsh, and you bloody well know it.” Charity sighed heavily. “As for whether you're still infected, I honestly couldn't say. The eyeshine never really left you, but it's only a slight remnant. You're still keen on your red meat, but you tend to lay the mustard on thicker than most; there's nothing consistent enough for me to really be sure. ”

“Why didn't you say something beforehand?” Mallory said, a little too sharply.

“I was otherwise focussed on working out what the fuck was happening with Ivy, and I trusted you to tell me if it was becoming a problem.” Her matter-of-fact tone and complete confidence in him took Mallory aback for a moment. “So, Mal, is it becoming a problem?”

“I...” He considered lying, but thought better of it. “I honestly don't know, Charity. There are times when I'm worried that I'm going to go feral and rip someone's throat out, and others I'm completely fine.”

“But you haven't yet, so take comfort in that and use it to find strength in your weaker moments.” The line crackled once again, forcing a pause. “Is there anything else?”

“I think that a remnant of the Master's power lingers in me, Charity. I was able to control one of the Bureau Agents; it only lasted a few seconds, but it gave me an edge.”

“Use it,” Charity said without even a heartbeat's hesitation. “Use every advantage you have, however small. Hone every edge, Marsh, and you will be unstoppable. That gift is going to save your life at some point, but only if you've mastered it."

"How can you possibly know that?" Mallory asked, shocked.

"This job is dangerous; fatally so. We only beat the Hive Mother by a fraction of an inch, and that doesn't even make it into my top ten closest scrapes." She chuckled darkly. "We're all more likely to die in the line of duty than not, so you need to be better than good, Marsh; better than great, even.

"You have to be the best to get out of this alive."

"I'm not sure I'm good enough," he admitted quietly.

"Stop that," she replied, her tone harsh and angry. "You are the head of a team and you cannot afford to waver in your convictions. Things *will* go wrong, Marsh, and if you don't trust your own abilities people *will* die.

"This is your baptism of fire, Mallory, and you need to be ready for anything. You have a hell of a fucking team with you, but without clear direction and leadership all that talent will just be so much piss in the wind."

He took a deep breath to calm his racing heart before he replied.

"I will bring them back, Charity. I won't let them down."

"Damn right," she said, before adding, "and remember what I told you; use *every* edge you have."

"How-" he began.

"I'm the Head of your Division, Marsh; I made sure to find out everything about you that I could." She let her voice take on a kinder tone. "I know you don't want to, and I feel for you, but if it's that or death, choose life."

Mallory did not reply. Instead he blinked back the tears of shame and embarrassment that were collecting at the corners of his eyes. *Is nothing fucking sacred these days?*

"Marsh, are you there?"

"I'm here," he said quietly. "Does anyone else know?"

"Of course not, and I won't bring it up again."

"Thank you." Mallory wiped his eyes again. *At least I can trust her to be discreet.* "I'll bring her back to you, Charity."

"I know you will, Mal; I just wish I was going with you."

Something clicked into place in Mallory's brain just as he was about to hang up.

"Charity, the outpost here was attacked as we arrived; there was definitely a Ghost and maybe a Tracer. Do you know of any enemies that Bureau might have?"

"The Amberlight Private Detective Agency," Charity replied without hesitation. "They're more of a private military nowadays, but they started out as a Cep offshoot from the Pinkertons. They're bad news, Marsh, so try and stay out of that fight. The Ministry has a truce with them, and will occasionally use their services when we're thin on the ground, but the Bureau has been at open war with them since the fifties."

"What do I do if they attack again?" Mallory said as his blood ran cold.

"Hide or run. Do not fight them; if you kill one of their own, they will never stop hunting you." Charity made a slightly pained noise before continuing. "If you're cornered, just tell them that you work for me and they'll let you go."

"Why the fuck would they do that?" Mallory demanded. "Do you know these people?"

"We have a history," the Ghost said enigmatically.

"Trust goes both ways, Charity."

"I know," she said with some reluctance. "Fine, but it goes no further unless it's a matter of life and death, understand?"

"Of course."

"The Amberlights were founded by Ghosts originally, and all of the influential families had a stake in the agency." She sighed heavily. "The current President of the Amberlights, is my aunt, Constance Walpole; we've never been that close, but blood is blood. Association with me should be enough to keep you safe."

"Thank you for telling me," Mallory said.

"You needed to know," Charity said brusquely. "Good luck on the mission, Marsh. I hope you find your brother."

She hung up before he could respond. He stood still for a moment, just staring at the phone in his hand.

We've all got skeletons in our closets, he thought as he stowed the device in his bedside cabinet. A slight smile twitched his lips; that thought shouldn't have made him feel better, but for some reason it did.

I'll take what I can get.

Chapter Twelve – I Dream in Stereo

Ivy

Ivy Livingston's breath fogged in the frigid air and her cheeks were tinged pink with the cold as she carefully put her right hand on the hilt of her katana. Across the snow covered courtyard, Midori Aoki mirrored her motion, her jade green eyes never once shifting from Ivy's grey ones.

Michaela and Edgar sat off to her left, invisible to all but Ivy. Beside them were Mallory, Noor, and Verity Lovage; the Séance had yet to speak to the Shunt, but Noor had told her all about her, albeit a touch excitedly for her liking.

"She'll come at you fast," Michaela warned, "and she'll open with an upward cut to force you backwards; watch your footing."

Ivy nodded gently, and saw Michaela's eyes widen. All too late, Ivy returned her gaze to Midori; the Kitsune had closed the gap between them and was about to strike. *If I don't move, I'm dead.*

"Forwards!" Edgar yelled, and Ivy responded. She pivoted left as she stepped into the strike and Midori's blade flashed though the air where she'd been only a moment ago. Instead of drawing her own weapon to strike, Ivy dealt a swift punch with her left hand, connecting with her attacker's armpit.

Midori was unbalanced by the blow, and Ivy drove the hilt of her sword under the Kitsune's ribs, knocking the wind out of her lungs. *You might have taught me swordplay,* Ivy thought with a grin, *but Charity taught me how to fight dirty.*

Midori took a faltering step backwards and Ivy drew her katana in a swift horizontal arc, but hit only air. Ivy blinked in shock, startled at how fast her opponent could move, and only brought her blade up in time to block her next attack.

Midori struck again and again, raining blows down on Ivy. She blocked each one, but her wrist was beginning to ache. There was a heartbeat's pause as Midori shifted her grip and Ivy lunged blindly forwards, desperate to end their sparring match.

The Kitsune's blade came down and struck her outstretched arm. Luckily, it was the flat face of the weapon that made contact; instead of slicing her hand clean off, it broke her faltering grip and her katana dropped to the snowy ground.

Midori raised her own katana in triumph, preparing for a killing blow. Gripped by a sudden flare of anger, Ivy leapt forwards at the armed woman, driving her shoulder into Midori's chest. Ivy gripped the hilt of the Kitsune's wakizashi with one hand and pushed the scabbard back with the other.

Midori staggered backwards as Ivy pulled the blade free. She recovered and went to make her overhead strike but Ivy, wielding the wakizashi in both hands, drove it forward in a powerful thrust. The end of the weapon nicked Midori's moss green jacket as the Kitsune halted mid step. Ivy smirked at her.

“I've picked up a few new tricks since I last saw you, Mistress Midori.”

“I can see that,” Midori said. Her voice was clipped and sharp, her words clear in the freezing air. Any hint of a Japanese accent had been lost in the decades of Ministry service; Midori sounded as English as a six o'clock newsreader. She frowned at Ivy before pushing the blade away.

Ivy stood up straight and handed the weapon back to her teacher. She did not, however, notice the glimmer in the air beside her as Sora, the Kitsune's Flickerfox, flashed into existence and knocked her to the ground. It took her neck in its powerful jaws and she could feel the icy breath on her skin.

"Do you see what underhanded tricks get you, Michaela?" Midori asked sharply, gesturing to the large crystalline creature with her katana.

"My name is Ivy Livingston," she managed to croak out, desperately trying to avoid Sora's sharp teeth.

"I was informed about your fractured psyche, Michaela." Midori shook her head in disgust. "You were a prodigy with the blade! I taught you to fight, armed you with the weapons of my kin, and you throw all of your lessons in honour and discipline aside in favour of brawling like a common street rat.

"I had hoped that you had survived the fire, but now that I see you I realise that you would be better off as a memory." Midori sheathed her sword. "Sora, let her go."

The Flickerfox released Ivy and she gasped with relief. She remained sprawled in the snow as her former teacher continued to berate her.

"That was only a gentle sparring match, and yet you almost lost; if you had fought with any integrity, you would've fallen to my first strike. In a real fight, Michaela, you would die like that!" She clicked her fingers sharply, the green polish on her nails flashing in the fading daylight. "The only decent thing to do after such gross misconduct would be to crawl into a hole and die like the vermin you are. However..."

Midori sighed heavily and rolled her eyes.

"...seeing as we live in an age rife with needless decadence and rampant moral decay, I suppose I will have to settle for graciously accepting an apology for what you have become."

"A survivor?" Ivy asked defiantly, getting to her feet.

"A disappointment," Midori replied after a brief grimace at Ivy's words. Edgar and Michaela crossed the snow to join the breathless Séance, placing their hands on her shoulders and lending her their strength. The Kitsune looked at her pupil expectantly. "Well, what do you have to say regarding your behaviour?"

"I apologise for none of it," the three said in unison.

The snow fluttered down from the steely grey clouds, swirling between the two women in tight eddies and windblown flurries as they stared at each other. The others made their way back indoors, eager to be out of the freezing air. When they were gone, Midori took a step forwards and Ivy immediately reached for her weapon.

The Kitsune did not attack; she instead let out a snort of derisive laughter.

"Pathetic," Midori said contemptuously, before heading inside and leaving Ivy shamefaced and alone.

"How fucking dare she?" Ivy raged as she stalked around the plushly furnished room. Charity looked at her from her position perched on the upholstered window seat. Sunshine streamed in through the window, yet Charity did not wear her usual dark glasses.

"You humiliated her," Charity said gently. "Kitsune are haughty creatures, and Midori especially so. She'd rather die than be shown up. The fact that you were her pupil makes the wound doubly grievous."

"So that gives her the right to talk to me like that?" Ivy asked, rounding on her girlfriend.

"You bruised her ego, she hurt yours; tit for tat." Charity reached out her pale hand towards Ivy, but the other woman was not done.

"So I'm supposed to just let it go?"

"Not necessarily, but you do need to put it aside for now."

"Why?" Ivy demanded, running her fingers through her hair in frustration. "I can be angry and still focussed on the mission, Charity!"

"Because this is supposed to be our time together, and I don't want to talk about Lamplight," Charity replied quietly. She drew her knees up to her chest and wrapped her arms tightly around her legs. "I'm reminded of that nightmare every single day, and right now I just want to enjoy your company before you..."

There was a considerable pause as Ivy looked at the huddled Ghost.

"You think I'm going to die, don't you?" Ivy realised after mulling over Charity's words.

"I have a bad feeling, Ivy." Her voice was almost a whisper.

"People feel anxious all the time," Ivy replied, joining Charity at the window and putting her arms around her, "especially when they're facing a situation they can't control. I'll be fine; you'll see that soon enough."

She clearly doesn't believe me, Ivy thought when the Ghost remained tense in her arms.

"What can I do to make you feel better?" Ivy asked.

"Don't go."

"You know I can't do that, Charity."

“It's a voluntary mission; Marsh will understand.”
“I said that I would help him and I'm not going to go back on my word,” Ivy said, her irritation rising. “I don't know what's got into you today!”
“I'm just worried about you; all of you. Why don't you take a vote on it and let Michaela and Edgar have their say?” Charity stared at Ivy, her eyes gleaming with defiance.
“You can be worried about me without acting like a fussy child, Charity!” Ivy got to her feet and resumed her pacing. “Sometimes I wonder if this is a-”
Ivy paused when she realised that Charity was weeping softly, her face buried in the soft towelling of her fluffy pink bathrobe. Ivy felt the fight leave her immediately as Charity's sorrow flooded their shared headspace, and returned to her girlfriend's side.
“Charity, sweet pea, what's the matter? Has something happened?”
Charity nodded softly and let out a strained wail. Ivy contemplated probing the Ghost's mind, but thought better of it. *She'll tell me when she's ready.* Instead, she planted a gentle kiss atop her girlfriend's head and made quiet reassuring noises whilst she stroked her hair.
“I'm sorry,” Charity mumbled through her tears.
“You don't need to apologise, darling,” Ivy said. “I'm the one who snapped at you, and I'm sorry for that. Will you tell me what's happened?”
“My dad died today,” Charity said after a few seconds of mournful silence. “I was supposed to call him yesterday, but I was so wrapped up with thinking about your mission after I spoke to Mallory that I forgot.
“I called him at lunchtime today, but the phone just

rang and rang."

"I'm so sorry, Charity." She thought carefully for a moment before continuing. "Do you want me to come back?"

"No, you're right; Marsh needs you there." She sniffed and wiped her nose on her sleeve. "The funeral will be in a few weeks, though; will you come with me?"

"Of course I will. Who told you what had happened?"

"My mother; she got a call from Prudence last night, telling her to go and see him. She found him this afternoon." Her face hardened slightly. "She didn't tell me what killed him but he was old, especially for a Ghost, so it's not too much of a shock; I doubt the Ministry will push for an autopsy."

There's something you're not telling me, Charity, Ivy thought as she looked at the Ghost's tear streaked face.

"I know that look," Charity said. "I'd tell you if I could, Ivy, but I... I just can't."

"Why not?" Ivy asked, a little more sharply than she intended to.

"It's Ghost business," Charity said enigmatically. She sighed heavily and pulled Ivy into a tight hug. "I wish I could explain, but I need you to trust me on this."

"I do trust you, sweetheart." Ivy gave her a lingering kiss before turning her head slightly to look out of the window. She cocked her head to one side, listening to the world outside; there was a slight hubbub of conversation, underscored by quick footsteps and flurries of activity. "I think we're heading out."

"I hate that you have to go," Charity said quietly, "but I know that you have to. Be safe and stay alive."

"I will."

"Promise me," Charity said sternly, and her grip on Ivy's hands was suddenly tight; almost painfully so, in fact.

"You know that I can't-"

"Then lie," Charity implored, her face both pleading and panicked. "Please?"

"I promise I'll come back to you, Charity Walpole."

"Thank you." She kissed Ivy one last time. "I love you."

"I love you too," Ivy replied before opening her eyes. She sat up in her bunk and looked into the corridor as Mallory Marsh strode through the doorway. Michaela stood beside him, eyeing him up suspiciously, whilst Edgar listened to the radio in the corner. There was a heartbeat of silence before Mallory spoke.

"It's time," he said, and Ivy nodded. "We're heading in."

He reached out a hand and helped her to her feet, knowing that she would be unsteady after sharing her mind with someone so many thousands of miles away.

"Thank you," Ivy said as she took her slender cane in hand; it had once belonged to Gideon Frost, a murderous rogue Ministry Agent. *I wonder if I've killed more people than him yet?*

"Are you alright?" Mallory asked. She knew that he couldn't read her face, but the lingering traces of Charity's grief were emanating from her like radiation. Ivy took a deep breath, gathered her strength, and then nodded.

"I'll be fine. Let's go get your brother."

Chapter Thirteen – A Matter of Speculation

Noor

Noor shivered under her thermal clothes, grimacing as their vehicle hit another snow covered rock. She kept her eyes firmly on her feet as the Sno-Cat barrelled its way down another incline, gathering speed as it went.

This is insane! We are going to die before we get there!

"Yeehaw!" Uncle yelled excitedly, and Noor couldn't help but laugh a little. Midori Aoki, on the other hand, shook her head in contempt. The grey haired man ignored her and nudged Agent Gillespie, who was sat next to him, with a mad grin. "Go on, Bert, live a little!"

The snow under the vehicle's tracks cracked and gave way under the weight, sending the bright orange contraption skidding down the hill at an alarming rate. Gillespie's eyes went wide with fear for a moment and then he did something that caught Noor entirely by surprise.

He began to sing.

"It's a long way to Tipperary, it's a long way to go!" Bert sang, grinning as he did so. Noor looked at him with concern, certain that he had been driven mad with fear. "It's a long way to Tipperary, to the sweetest girl I know!"

"Goodbye Piccadilly," Uncle sang heartily as he joined in, "farewell Leicester Square!"

“What the fuck is wrong with you both!?” Noor screamed as the Sno-Cat slid to a halt at the bottom of the hill.

“Life is full of opportunities for fun, Agent Turner,” Uncle said softly, “and it is always wise to seize them with both hands.”

“Can't you taking anything seriously?” Noor demanded, glaring at Bert and Uncle in turn.

“Not if I want to get out alive,” Bert said with a grin. Noor was about to reply when the vehicle lurched into life and they got underway once more, albeit with a lot more care than earlier. Their driver, one of the National Guardsmen stationed at the Forward Command Post, mumbled an apology over his shoulder.

“So,” Ivy began as a sense of calm flooded through Noor, “do we have any theories about what's happening inside the Easy, or what caused it for that matter?”

“Nobody knows,” Uncle said with a smile. “Isn't that exciting?”

“Why would that be exciting, Griswold?” Verity said, already tired with the older man's endless sense of wonder.

“I quite agree with you, Horace,” Professor Skullbone said, smiling slightly himself. “The more we understand about the world, the more questions we seem to uncover; as a scientist, what more could one ask for?”

“I know that we don't know,” Ivy replied, her voice slightly strained, “but I'm asking for speculation. What are our options?”

That gave the older men pause, and Noor realised that Mallory was humming the tune that Bert and

Uncle had been singing moments ago. *I wish he would take them both to task a bit,* she thought, but decided against voicing her opinions when she caught Ivy shaking her head at her. Noor opened her mouth to tell Ivy to keep out of her head, but the Séance raised her eyebrows pointedly before she could say anything.

Yeah, yeah, she thought testily, *I'm just thinking loudly.*

"It could be a Scarlet Village situation," Mallory said. He continued his theory, likely explaining for her benefit. "The Scarlet Village is a building that moves around the British Isles, seemingly teleporting from place to place, sometimes with decades between appearances.

"It's a large block of flats, stylishly designed and decorated, and there are always vacancies when it appears. It draws in writers, artists, and other creatives; nobody is sure why, but the building is said to provide tremendous inspiration.

"Then, as suddenly as it came, it'll disappear again."

"What about the people that move in?" Ivy asked.

"Some of them will leave before it goes, and the others will just vanish along with it. It's been the Ministry's white whale for almost a century now." He looked wistfully into the middle distance. "I'd love to see inside; I'll bet it's absolutely beautiful."

"We'll make sure to tie a rope around your waist so we can pull you back out," Noor said with a smile. "What makes the Scarlet Village move around?"

"Nobody knows," Mallory said with a silly grin, "but some people think it's looking for a specific person or trying to deliver a message."

"What about aliens?" Bert asked. Ivy's eyes narrowed and she muttered something that sounded like 'Harlan', but Noor couldn't be sure. Bert continued. “There have always been sightings of weird lights over the Cascades, going back centuries. Given all that we know about the world, it seems kind of short-sighted to dismiss extraterrestrial life out of hand.”

“But why Galaxy?” Verity asked. “Why not New York or London or somewhere more populous?”

“I can't rightly say,” Bert said, “but it's not to avoid notice, that's for sure.”

“Is every single answer going to be some variation of 'I don't know'?” Noor asked, already exhausted by the conversation.

“I-” Mallory began, chuckling as he did so, and Noor cut across him.

“Don't, Mallory.” She groaned and leant back in her seat, staring up at the ceiling this time. *Is everyone else on this mission fucking nuts?*

“There's virtue in speculation,” Midori said, a little too sharply for Noor's liking, but she let her continue. “We must approach this phenomenon with open minds and analytical eyes; by voicing our theories, we set the wheels of deduction in motion. Whilst there is every chance that the cause of all this is something completely unforeseen, there is also a chance that one of our guesses may be correct and allows us to notice clues that we otherwise would have missed.”

“Do we really need to voice them, though?” Noor muttered.

“Absolutely!” Midori snapped, and her green eyes flashed as she glared at the Seer. Noor squirmed under the Kitsune's penetrating gaze, feeling like a pinned butterfly for a frantic moment. “Many eyes see a great many things, and each mind is different; our strength lies in our diversity."

"I... It's my first assignment; I'm still learning all of this." Noor said, her cheeks flushing with embarrassment. She blinked back nervous tears and muttered her next words. "I never wanted any of this. I just wanted to be a fashion designer."

"Inexperience is not an adequate excuse!" Midori said, her voice full of contempt.

"Cut her some fucking slack!" Ivy replied angrily. Before Midori could reply, she went on. "This isn't Lamplight or Harbin or any of the other evil shit you've been involved with over the years; this is a rescue mission and we are equals."

"How dare you!?" Midori responded, unclasping the harness that kept her in her seat with one hand and reaching for her blade with the other.

"Enough!" Mallory roared. He pointed at Midori, his face flushed with frustration. "You will speak to Noor and Ivy with respect, Agent Aoki, or I will give you over to Crenshaw when all this is done. Do I make myself clear?"

Speechless at the threat, Midori simply nodded and belted herself back in.

That told her, Noor thought smugly, but Mallory soon rounded on her.

"As for you, Agent Turner, you can either claim inexperience and stay behind, or you can prove that you are an asset to the Ministry by thinking for yourself. Which is it?"

"I'll think for myself, Mallory." Noor's voice was low and her hands trembled slightly.

"Good." He relaxed a little, but did not shift his gaze. "I have a test for you."

"I'm not so sure that's a good idea, Mallory," Ivy

said, "given what happened on the plane."

"This won't test her powers," he said with a smile, "only her deductive reasoning. Nobody else is to help her with this, understood?"

There were various nods and grunts of agreement.

"Noor, by the time we reach the edge of the Easy, I want you to tell me why Agent Gillespie started singing." She opened her mouth to protest at the absurdity of his request, but he held up a hand to silence her; he wasn't done yet. "I don't necessarily expect the right answer, but I do want you to actually think about it and give me your best theory. Does that sound fair?"

"I guess so," Noor said, who felt a little better after hearing how open-ended her test was. "What if I do get the right answer?"

"I'll be very impressed," Mallory said, settling back in his seat with a grin, "and then you can start picking lottery numbers for me."

Noor jolted awake as the Sno-Cat hit another stray rock. The daylight had faded and the snow was beginning to fall once again. *How long have I been asleep?*

"Not long," Ivy said with a kind smile. "Maybe thirty minutes or so, at the most."

"But it's getting dark already!"

"Part of it is the weather; there's a storm blowing in from the north. The other, more interesting, part of it is the disruption from the Galaxy Phenomenon," Professor Skullbone said. It was one of the few things Noor had heard him say on the entire journey. "Light is bent around the Exclusion Zone, creating a kind of holographic boundary that appears, at least to the untrained eye, to be a mirrored surface.

"It's also the reason that there's an electrical dead zone around the entire place." He smiled sheepishly. "I must confess that I've more than a passing interest when it comes to Galaxy."

"Obsession is the correct word, Harold," Verity said playfully. She winked at Noor. "You know, he's really burying the lead here. Go on, tell her why it's so important to you."

"Well, I, uh, I was the one who discovered it."

Stunned silence filled the Sno-Cat.

"You kept that one quiet, Professor!" Bert said with a nervous chuckle.

"I didn't want any of you to think that my judgment was clouded or that this was a personal matter; it isn't."

"How did you find it?" Noor asked.

"I was heading there for a job interview at Galaxy Applied Physics. I was supposed to spend the night of the Twenty Second of March at the Galaxy Motel, with my appointment at the laboratory scheduled for the next morning." His eyes glazed slightly, as if he was lost in the memory. "I phoned ahead to the motel a little after six o'clock in the evening to tell them that I would be checking in late.

"When I finally got on the road, it was already dark. I was approaching Galaxy when my car suddenly stopped. Everything electrical was dead, including my emergency torch, and the clock had stopped at ten forty seven." He sighed heavily. "It took a few minutes for my eyes to adjust to the darkness, and then I realised that up ahead the stars were in the wrong place. Instead of pressing on down a dark mountain road, I went back the way I came."

"How long did it take you to walk back?" Mallory asked.

"Not long at all; once I got ten metres or so up the road, my torch came back to life. Rather than walking, I decided to push my car back until it was operational again." Skullbone shook his head. "I know that I'm supposed to be grateful that I was running late and wasn't caught up in everything that happened, but to be honest I always felt like I'd been cheated out of the experience of a lifetime."

"The chance to glimpse beyond the veil?" Uncle asked, and Harold nodded.

"Yes. I would give anything to see what's inside."

Noor saw a row of fluorescent orange posts appear in the distance; it seemed to stretch from horizon to horizon, ringing the Easy. The overhead light in the Sno-Cat began to flicker and their radios started to hiss and pop.

We're nearing the dead zone, she realised, both excited and nervous about the mission that lay ahead.

"Well, Harold," Verity said with a sad smile, "at least you'll finally get your wish. I just hope that you live long enough to get some answers."

"A glimpse would be enough," he said softly.

"Everybody gather up your gear," Mallory said as the Sno-Cat trundled to a stop a few metres from the fluorescent markers. "We're gonna be on foot from this point."

Verity put her hand on Noor's arm and gave her an affectionate squeeze.

"Stay close to me, Noor; I'll keep you safe."

Chapter Fourteen – The Edge of Eternity

Mallory

Mallory's cheeks were flushed and stinging as the winter air chilled the exposed areas of his face. Although the group had been skiing for over an hour, they had covered very little ground. Mallory groaned in frustration as he heard someone fall over behind him.

He coasted to a gentle stop and carefully turned around to see Ivy helping Agent Gillespie to his feet. *At least it wasn't Noor again,* he thought wearily. *If I was by myself, I'd be almost halfway there by now.*

"Sorry, everyone," Bert said sheepishly. "I think I'm getting the hang of this, though."

Mallory took a deep breath, held it for a moment, and then let it out slowly, causing a swirl of fog through the air in front of his face. He let the cold wick away his anger as he reminded himself that his friends hadn't grown up skiing, like he had.

Not all gifts are supernatural, he thought.

"Does anyone want to take a break?" Mallory asked the group. Nobody spoke for a moment, but then Verity Lovage raised her hand. "Right, we'll take a moment right here. Have a snack, drink something warm, and stretch."

He walked over to Verity and helped her out of the harness that was attached to Harold's sled.

"Thanks, Mallory." She groaned in pain as she stretched.

"I'm sorry, Verity," Skullbone said sadly. "I wish I was young enough to ski again; then I wouldn't be such a burden."

"Stop apologising, Harold, or I'll throw you the rest of the way!" She helped the old man to his feet and then handed him a thermos. "Here. If you want to be helpful, you can pour me a cup of coffee."

"Do you want me to take him?" Mallory asked quietly. Verity shook her head, although she was still trying to get her breath back. "I know I might not seem like the athletic type, but I'm a lot stronger than I look."

"This isn't the time for proving your manliness, Marsh," she replied with a chuckle. She smiled at him, but her expression soon changed. "Fucking hell, you're not even tired are you?"

"I'm not," Mallory said quietly. Whilst the majority of his skills were common knowledge amongst his colleagues, his freakish endurance and stamina were a secret he kept close to his chest. *Besides,* he thought, *who knows what will happen to me if I dig too deep?*

"Not every birthright is a gift," Uncle whispered, holding his hand out for the harness. Mallory blinked in surprise; he had not even noticed the Strix's approach. "Whilst I'm sure you've the fortitude of a hundred year oak, I'm even older than that."

Mallory nodded, slightly confused by the playful smile in the man's voice and the specific metaphor he had used. *Does he know? Can he tell?*

He felt eyes boring into the back of his head, but he decided not to turn round. Instead, he thought as loudly as he could to let Ivy, or more likely, Michaela, know that he could feel her probing around his mind.

Did you find what you were looking for? Or would you like me to paint you a picture?

Although he hadn't felt the Seancé's mind approach,

he shuddered slightly when it withdrew. His shoulders sagged as he suddenly felt exhausted; not physically, but mentally. The weight of Michaela's suspicion and his fear about the Master's lingering influence had ground him down since the summer and he wanted to be rid of it, once and for all.

Enough is enough, he thought, *this ends now.*

"Livingston," he said, waving her over, "I need to have a word."

Ivy nodded and deftly made her way beside him, far more at ease in the skis than he would have believed given the scant training she'd received.

"Everything alright, Mallory?" she asked. He gestured for her to lean closer and he lowered his voice.

"Let's just clear the air about this right now, shall we?" His voice was hushed, but the air was still and Ivy could hear the sharpness in his words. "I am not a fucking Nightwalker and I am not going to go berserk and rip everyone to shreds, is that understood?"

"I didn't think-"

"Don't lie to me!" Ivy stepped back at the snarl in his voice. She hesitated for a moment before closing the gap between them once again. "I can feel your eyes on me and your mind trawling through my thoughts; you're not as subtle as you think you are."

Ivy remained silent.

"Yes, my encounter with the Master changed me, but it's no more than your encounter with Joseph changed you; we're both who we were at the start of all this, just with more awareness about what we are." He sighed heavily and placed a hand on her shoulder.

At the end of the day, trust is a decision you have to make.

Courage, Mallory.

"I'm not fully human, Ivy; not like you and Charity, at least. My father, Aubrey, was a gifted human but my mother was... something else, and her bloodline lingers in me. The Master's invasion awakened that side of me, and I'm trying to put it back to sleep but it is taking time." He smiled, in spite of the situation; speaking up about his past had certainly lessened the burden, even if it was just a little easier.

"So what are you," Ivy asked, "aside from my friend?"

He smiled gratefully.

"My mother was, or perhaps is, a Dryad. The Marsh men have always wed Dryads; it's part of our connection with the land. My ancestors have always produced male children, to continue the pact, until I was born; I'm not sure what that means for the future, but it isn't important right now.

"What you should know is that I have my mother's power in me; the bloodlust, eyeshine, and other inhuman characteristics you've seen all stem from that. My body awakened those gifts when the Nightwalker infection entered my system, and I've been waiting for it to settle back down for months now."

"Why didn't you say anything?" Ivy asked softly, placing a comforting hand on his shoulder.

"I was ashamed," he admitted. "Dryad powers only manifest in women and I-"

His voice broke a little as the hot tears stung his eyes.

"Oh, Mallory," Ivy said, pulling him into a tight embrace, "the circumstances of your birth don't make you any less of a man; not to me and not to anyone else that matters. You're the dandiest gentleman I've ever met, bar none."

"Thank you, Ivy," Mallory said with a sniffle.

"And if anyone gives you any hassle whatsoever, I'll make them do something monstrous to themselves." She let out a low chuckle.

"Ivy, you're wonderful, but you do scare the shit out of me sometimes."

"Likewise, Mallory, but I guess that's the price of being interesting."

"You're not wrong there," he said, before wiping his eyes and raising his voice to the group. "Is everyone ready to continue?"

There were murmurs of assent. He nodded and cast a worried eye at the dark clouds that were rapidly approaching. *Heavy snowfall, at the very least,* he thought. *This could turn nasty before we even get there.*

"We've got heavy snow inbound, so everyone will need to buddy up, and then we'll move out." He looked at Bert, Harold, and Noor before issuing a series of quick orders. "Griswold, you pull Harold, Midori attach yourself to Noor, and Jennings and Verity pair off. Agent Gillespie, you're with me. Ivy, can you keep track of everyone with your gift?"

"Of course."

"Then you'll ski in the middle, but maintain visual contact with at least one of us." He turned to Bert, who was nervously fumbling with a karabiner at his waist. "You ready for this, Gillespie?"

"No," he said in a shaky voice, tinged with optimism, "but Uncle says that no-one is truly ready for anything. We'll be fine."

I hope you're right.

"Okay, folks," Mallory said as the first flakes began

to fall, “let's get moving!”

The wind howled around the rescue team as they skied ever closer to the Easy. Snow buffeted and battered them, reducing their visibility to only a dozen metres or so; this close to the phenomenon, not even their compasses were working, so Ivy was guiding the group.

“I can't see a damn thing!” Agent Gillespie yelled to Mallory, who grunted in agreement. “Are you sure Agent Livingston knows how far away we are?”

“We don't really have any other options,” Mallory replied, but whether the wind whipped away his words or Bert simply had no better ideas, his ski buddy did not respond. Mallory squinted his eyes and stared through his tinted ski goggles at the snow muddled horizon.

We could walk right into it without even realising it.

There was a rush of movement beside him, and he turned to face Uncle.

The Strix was doing better than any of them, handling both the wind and cold without any apparent issue. *Maybe his great grandmother was a snowy owl,* Mallory thought and Ivy's snort of laughter was audible even with the stormy conditions.

“The Professor wants to talk to you,” Uncle said, his voice carrying as easily as if it were a calm clear day. Mallory gave him a thumbs up and leant down to hear Harold Skullbone's words.

“Professor?”

“Agent Marsh. I wanted to warn you that we won't easily be able to perceive the edge of the Exclusion Zone.” Mallory nodded, and Harold went on. “However, it does swirl gently, like the tidal edge of a black hole; the rotation will be against the wind, which will give us something to look out for."

"Thank you, Professor; I'll keep my eyes peeled." Mallory stood up just in time to see someone attach a safety line to Uncle's backpack; it took him a moment to recognise the snowsuit. "Noor, what are you doing?"

"I'm attaching Midori and me to Agent Griswold," she yelled over the storm.

"Why?" Mallory asked, confused.

"I don't know, but I have to!" she replied, and he could do little else but shrug.

Seers, he thought, *are useful when they want to be, but downright maddening when they-*

His mental train was derailed as he felt the safety line at his waist tug and he whirled around to see that Agent Gillespie had carried on for another few metres. He was about to yell at him when his eyes focussed on the snow just behind Bert.

It's moving the wrong way.

Bert took another step towards it.

We're already here!

There was a strange snapping sound, followed by and immense force pulling Mallory forwards as Bert crossed the event horizon. The two collided in a clatter of skis, poles, and military equipment as they hit the ground with a thud.

"For fuck's sake, Gillespie!" Mallory roared as he shoved the younger man off of him. Bert groaned and rolled on to the mossy ground, crumpling a nearby fern. It took Mallory's mind a moment to register the lack of snow, but when his brain caught up to his eyes, he let out a strangled cry.

"Where's the snow?" Bert asked.

Mallory did not respond; he was staring into the cloudless night sky. Above them, the moon and stars glowed gently through the trees and a light mist was rolling through the chilly air. What had caught the Artist's eye, however, was another addition to the celestial theatre.

"Is that-" Bert began, following Mallory's gaze.

"Halley's Comet," Mallory confirmed.

"But that's due in like fifty years!" Bert said. "We can't have jumped that far into the future!"

"We haven't." Mallory's mind was running wild as he looked around for his friends. "We're alone."

"Where do you think they are?" Bert asked nervously as something moved in the forest nearby.

"I have no idea."

"Well, where are we?" He grabbed the sleeve of Mallory's snowsuit nervously. The Artist continued to scan the horizon until he found what he was looking for.

"We're on the outskirts of Galaxy, Oregon," he said, pointing at the radio mast, "and I'd wager that it is the Twenty Second of March, Nineteen Eighty Six."

Interlude One – A Night Like Any Other

"Patryk?"

The woman gasped as she woke up, unsure of where she was. It took a few moments for her heartbeat to settle into a steady rhythm as the flash of panic and uncertainty faded. She looked over to the other side of the bed, where the covers lay slightly crumpled but otherwise unused.

Patryk must be out walking again; he so rarely comes to bed with me any more.

Sissy's eyes adjusted to the gloom fast and the details of the room swam into view. The door was slightly ajar and the curtains were open, just as she left them. She rubbed her arms as she sat up in bed; her skin was prickled into goose flesh and a shudder ran through her back. She let out a little cry of surprise and pulled the covers tight about her. Everything was as it should be, so why did she feel so damn spooked?

The faint starlight was enough to read the clock by her bed. Sissy groaned and leant over, turning the alarm off just as it began to chime. *I could let it ring if I wanted to,* she thought, *but I can't bear the sound of it.* Rusty slept like the dead and Patryk was... wherever, so she didn't need to worry about making too much noise. A grin spread over her face. *I have the run of the house and I can do as I please!*

Her smile faltered a little.

If I'm home alone, why do I feel so watched?

Sissy's heart started to race again and she reached over to flip on the lamp. The warm light bathed the room and it was exactly the same as it had ever been. The hair on the back of her neck stood up a little as she stared at the inky blackness of the window.

"Hello?" Sissy asked in a trembling voice.

She knew that she should stop looking at her reflection in the glass, but she couldn't seem to tear her eyes away. She could see her lip trembling slightly as the tears threaten to burst forth. The darkness felt like it was pressing against the window, heavy and opaque.

What would happen if the glass broke and it came rushing in?

There's no moon tonight, she realised, *and no street lights to push back the night; just me and my little lamp.*

What if there's nobody else out there?

Maybe the dark had swallowed the world and everybody in it; it certainly felt that way to her. What if Sissy Sparrow was the last person left alive and her bedside lamp was the last light in the universe?

The floodgates failed and the tears came spilling out as she sat, transfixed by the night. With the tears came the scream, full-throated and terrified, at the prospect of being swallowed up by the dark; of flickering out like a candle.

There's no one to hear you, no one to help you. You're all alone.

"Patryk!" She screamed his name over and over again through the sobs. "Patryk, oh please, help me!"

Her breath came in ragged gasps between choked screams and desperate pleading. Sissy closed her eyes and curled up into a ball atop the bedclothes, still wailing in terror.

She heard his firm stride in the hallway, the creak of the door as it was flung open, and the swoosh of the curtains being drawn against the dark. She felt his weight settle on to the bed behind her and his strong arms gathered her up against his chest; he held her tight and safe. He ran his fingers through her hair as the tears slowly started to subside.

"Thank you, Pat," Sissy murmured into his shirt. "I felt so alone."

He held her wordlessly until she began to feel better.

She flipped on the kitchen light and quickly pulled the curtains closed; she already felt guilty enough about spending so long with them open in the bedroom. She gently swirled the coffee in the pot, drinking in the aroma. *Buying one with a timer was the best idea I ever had, second only to marrying Pat.*

Getting ready used to take her forever when she had to drag herself out of bed before she could even think about making a cup of coffee. Add to that measuring it out, waiting for it to brew, and then allowing it to cool enough to drink; her life was a waking nightmare. Even after all that sleepy effort, it would still taste like shit.

Let's face it, she thought, *I'm no good to anyone until I've had my first cup of joe.* She poured a generous mug and took a long sip.

"Fuuuuuuuck, that's good," she groaned. "I never could get my head around why you hated coffee, Pat."

He simply stared at her from across the room, smiling softly. He pushed up his wire-rimmed glasses and blew his sandy brown hair out of his eyes. She grinned at him and he folded his arms in mock seriousness. His sleeves were rolled up just past his elbows; it was a look that always made her weak at the knees.

"You're too damn handsome for your own good, Dr

Nightingale." Sissy leant back against the counter, the warmth of the mug seeping through her sweater. "There ought to be some sort of law against it."

She tore her eyes away from her husband to glance at the clock, and swore under her breath; it was ten past eleven already. She had spent far too long dallying and needed to be out the door in fifteen minutes. She downed the rest of her coffee, winked playfully at Pat, and poured the rest of the pot into her flask. It all went into her backpack along with her sandwiches, a bar of chocolate, and her editing folder.

She laced up her boots and put her jacket on; even though winter was over it still got chilly fast in Galaxy overnight. She went to slip her backpack on when a sudden thought hit her; she needed spare batteries! Sissy shook her head and laughed a little.

I can be such a forgetful ditz at times.

She rattled around the kitchen for a few minutes, humming to herself. It was always easier for her to find something if she was making noise whilst she looked; her mother was the same. She would make soft trumpeting noises as she pottered around the house doing her little tasks.

Her home felt so quiet after she died. After everyone left the wake, Sissy just stood there in the eerie silence, listening to the house creak and settle. It was one of the worst nights of her life, up to that point. *Life always has a way of making things worse, though, doesn't it?*

She found the batteries and slipped a handful into her bag; some for her Walkman and others for the flash-light. She stopped dead in her tracks, looking at Pat. He was stood exactly where he was earlier, just watching her with those soft grey eyes that she always found so enchanting.

"Thank you for earlier, Patryk. I was so scared."

"I'll always be here for you, Sissy."

"Promise?"

"Promise." They stared at each other for a moment. "Have a good show tonight, sweetheart."

"I will. I'll miss you as soon as I'm out the door."

"I know you will."

"I... I miss you already." She blinked back the tears that were forming. "I miss you so much, Patryk."

She wiped her eyes and looked away. *Get yourself together, Sissy.* She closed her eyes and took a deep breath, centring herself. Once she opened her eyes, Patryk was gone. She rubbed her face with her sleeve and with a final sniffle, she walked out of the door and into the night.

Part Two: Dead Air

Chapter Fifteen – Three People, All Alone

Michaela

Michaela saw Bert Gillespie and Mallory disappear a fraction of a second before Ivy did, but it was enough time for her to take control of their shared body. The rotating snow that marked the edge of the Exclusion Zone juddered as the two men passed through it and vanished.

Michaela's mouth was opening to call out a warning when the event horizon expanded outward, catching them all by surprise. Before she could make a sound, Michaela hit the rough bark of a tree with enough force to knock the wind out of her.

"That's a Lodgepole Pine," Edgar said cheerfully as he ran his hand over the orangey-brown bark. Michaela fell backwards on to the soft earth and looked up at him in a state of shock.

"No snow." Ivy's words mirrored Michaela's thoughts as she stepped out from behind the pine Edgar was inspecting. "Ed, stop molesting the tree and keep a lookout."

"Something went wrong," Michaela said with a groan as she reached down to unclasp her skis. "Where are the others?"

"Fucked if I know," Edgar said, now excitedly peering into the darkness.

"They're all scattered throughout Galaxy, as best I can tell," Ivy said after a moment. "Getting a fine bead on them is difficult, though; there's definitely something weird going on here."

"Weird," Edgar echoed happily.

"Weird indeed." Michaela removed their shared backpack and began to rummage through it. After a moment she found what she was looking for and yelled out in triumph. "Gotcha!"

She pulled a pair of reliable hiking boots from the depths of the bag and immediately started to remove her cumbersome ski shoes. *I am so glad I packed these.* She grinned madly as she laced her new, far more suitable, footwear up.

"It's chilly, but not cold," Ivy said, "so I'd keep the snowsuit for now just to keep some warmth in. Leave the skis behind, though; they're not much use to us now."

"Any guesses to what's going on here?" Michaela asked, looking pointedly at Edgar, who was always a source of *unburdened* insight.

"Time loop, perhaps, or a localised black hole. Possibly a cursed radio broadcast. Too early to tell at this point."

"What makes you think this is a time loop?" Michaela asked, now getting to her feet.

"The comet," Edgar said, "and the radio tower is set up for FM broadcasts but it looks like it's using an earlier dipole transmitter, specifically one set up for HF signals."

"Which means what?" Ivy asked.

"It was designed for use in the mountains," Edgar replied helpfully.

"Thank you, Edgar, you are such a wealth of useless trivia sometimes," Michaela said drily.

"It also hasn't been overhauled since the mid-eighties," he said pointedly.

"Oh my god," Ivy said as the ball dropped. Edgar's image flickered for a moment in Michaela's vision before refocussing with an entirely different outfit. Gone were the flight coat and pineapple patterned shirt, replaced with a ruffled shirt and an antique military tunic.

"Why are you dressed like Adam Ant?" Michaela asked, practically trembling with exasperation.

"Avoiding anachronisms," Edgar responded. "Comet, radio mast, outfit; all congruent for Nineteen Eighty Six."

"Well, that might at least explain why no-one ever came back out of here," Michaela said as she checked her weapons. Her swords were unscathed, and the two Taylor & Bullock Giantslayers in her pack had passed through the event horizon of the Easy without getting damaged. "It seems that our minds and gear aren't affected by the time discrepancy; small mercies, at least."

"They aren't affected *yet*," Edgar said excitedly.

"You sound entirely too pleased about that," Ivy remarked as she peered out into the dark forest. "I wish we'd packed the sniper rifle; it had a night vision scope in with it."

"Technology is a crutch," Michaela said sharply. "Don't you remember anything Mistress Midori taught us?"

"Why would I want to remember anything from that point in our lives? I'm having a hard enough time holding myself together as it is; opening up old wounds isn't going to help with that."

"If this is true time travel," Edgar continued, seemingly oblivious to the tension between the two women, "Project Lamplight hasn't happened yet."

"So we go with my plan?" Michaela asked warily.

"Yes. We can get to the radio tower and broadcast a

warning!" He beamed at his other selves gleefully.
"Isn't that a paradox?" Ivy said after taking a moment to think the proposal through.
"Yes." He gave her a thumbs up for emphasis.
"And what happens then?" Ivy's voice wavered as she spoke, and she took a faltering step back towards Michaela.
"No idea, but it would be fun to find out!"
And she'll be safe.
"What's out there?" Michaela asked softly, moving beside Ivy. She quietly clicked the safety off on one of the revolvers. "What did you see?"
"I'm not sure, but whatever it was, it wasn't alone."
"Monsters!" Edgar said in a hushed tone, joining the other two. "Definitely not ghosts, though."
"Is that so?" Michaela carefully turned her gaze from the dark treeline to face him. "You can't feel any?"
"Oh, there are hundreds, but they aren't sleeping."
"Maybe they don't know that they're dead," Ivy suggested.
That's not particularly comforting, Michaela thought, *although it does lend credence to the time loop theory.* She caught sight of movement in the corner of her eye, and looked at Ivy once again.
"You're sure our friends aren't nearby?"
"Positive."
"Right, I'm going to need a clear field of vision; would the two of you be kind enough to step back, as it were?" As soon as the words were out of her mouth, Ivy and Edgar had vanished. Despite the danger of the situation, she couldn't help but chuckle. "We're like some perverse nesting doll."
She looked into the darkness again, and frowned. As

much as it pained her to admit it, Ivy was right about the night vision scope.

Why wasn't I born a Tracer instead?

She shuddered, even in the relative warmth of her snowsuit, and peered into the gloom. She couldn't be certain, but she thought that she saw something vaguely humanoid step into the shadow of a nearby tree.

I wish I wasn't alone, she thought. *I wish Charity was here.*

Michaela tried not to stare, but she couldn't help it.

The pretty blonde girl, part of the Green Group, was sitting with her best friend beneath the tree on the other side of the courtyard. He was singing softly, his voice carrying with supernatural clarity to where Michaela stood, alone and friendless.

She gets more pretty every day, she thought. Although she didn't fully understand why Hillgreen's skin and hair grew more bleached as the Project went on, Michaela Inglewood could tell that it was something to do with the training that they were undergoing; she shuddered at the thought of what might be happening to her.

Hillgreen's gaze, hidden behind dark glasses, immediately focussed on Michaela.

Oh no! I let my thoughts slip out again!

Michaela tried to covertly exit the courtyard, but a shrill whistle stopped her in her tracks. She glanced over her shoulder just as the freakishly nimble Hillgreen kicked her to the ground. She gathered up a handful of Michaela's hair and ground her face into the dirt.

"Why do you keep staring at me, Blackcat?"

"I'm sorry, I won't look any more," Michaela muttered, before she began to sob softly.

"Answer her!" The Welsh boy's voice was painfully loud and Michaela tried to clap her hands over her ears, but Hillgreen pinned them with her knees. "Do you want me to pop your head like a balloon, Blackcat?"

"Please just leave me alone," Michaela begged.

"But you are alone," Hillgreen said viciously. "You're a friendless little freak and you don't even deserve to be here."

"I have friends!" Michaela lied through her tears. "They just aren't here!"

"Then what are their names?" Hillgreen hissed, a snide smile on her face.

"Their names?" Michaela asked, panicked. She thought for a frenzied moment. "There's Ivy, who's really pretty and clever and a doctor, and Edgar who takes me to the pictures and buys me popcorn and-"

Her words were cut short as the boy kicked her in the face.

"Joseph!" Hillgreen said, shocked. "That's too far!"

"We could kill her and nobody would miss her," he said, his eyes wide with maniacal glee.

"Please, don't," Michaela said thickly, her mouth full of blood.

"Let her go, Hillgreen." Another boy, slightly older than all three of them, had wandered over. His voice was flat and dispassionate, which matched his appearance; grey hair, grey skin, and grey eyes.

"Stay out of this, Vis!" Joseph took a deep breath and stared down the newcomer, who simply removed his grey gloves in response. His fingers were freakishly long and twitched in a way that filled the other boy's eyes with fear.

"Please don't start anything, Florence," Vis said quietly, addressing Joseph. Hillgreen went to lunge at the grey youth, but he turned sharply and seized her head in his freakish hands.

"Joseph, help me!" Hillgreen screamed. All the Welsh boy could do was look on in horror. Michaela rolled over to get a better view of what was happening.

"Now, Hillgreen," Vis said patiently, "you can either stop picking on people or you can forget what colour your eyes used to be. It's up to you."

"I'll stop, I'll stop!" Hillgreen said through the tears that were now flowing freely.

"Good." Vis let her go, and she scrambled away from him and Michaela. Joseph helped her to her feet and the two of them returned to their favourite spot beneath the tree. Vis reached down to help Michaela, but she recoiled from his terrifying hands. "Oh, I'm sorry."

He deftly donned his gloves and this time she took his hand in hers and allowed him to haul her upright. He tutted softly as he inspected her bloody face.

"Is it bad?" she asked with a wince.

"It could've been a lot worse. You need to learn to stick up for yourself, Michaela."

"We're not allowed to use our real names!" Michaela said with a shocked gasp.

"I don't care about that." He sighed and looked around at the armed guards who had not dared intervene in Michaela's beating. "This place is evil, and it's all going to go to hell one day. We should at least know the names of our friends before it all falls apart."

"I don't have any friends."
"Sure you do. I'm your friend." He held out one gloved hand. "I'm Oliver, Oliver Wainwright. It's lovely to meet you."
She shook his hand with a laugh; it made her face hurt, but she didn't care.
"It's lovely to meet you too."
The two were still laughing when the sound of a gunshot rang out over Betony Island. Everyone in the courtyard, guards and children alike, turned in the direction of the noise. The air was still, thick with tension.
Then somebody screamed and all hell broke loose.
Michaela opened her eyes, banishing the memory to a distant place in her mind. Even then, the smell of smoke and the agony of being burned alive clung to her for a few seconds before finally receding and leaving her alone in the darkness of the mountain forest.
"I may be alone," she whispered as she placed a hand on her katana, "but I am no longer helpless. This forest may be full of monsters, but I am an apex predator."
She turned her gaze to the distant radio tower.
"Nothing is going to stand in my way." She looked back at the shifting shapes that moved in the darkness and drew her blade. "My name is Michaela Inglewood and I am a survivor of Project Lamplight. I am not afraid any more.
"Death before dishonour," she said firmly, before striding into the night.

Chapter Sixteen – Fate Revealed

Noor

"Are you sure we're not dead?" Noor asked as she leant against the gnarled trunk of a tree.

"Not yet," Midori replied, her green eyes flashing in the darkness. She had drawn one of her swords and was slowly circling the small clearing they'd paused to rest in, guarding the perimeter. Agents Griswold and Skullbone were talking in low voices a few metres away.

"What are you two whispering about?" Noor asked as she gingerly removed her ski boots. The going had been hard on her and she'd fallen several times due to both the darkness and her cumbersome footwear. "If you've got any bright ideas, let's fucking hear them!"

"We were discussing the possible causes of what's happening here," Harold said cautiously, "and my best guess is that there was an accident at the Galaxy Applied Physics facility. The time differential and lack of escaping signals all point to a black hole or something like that."

"Do you agree?" Noor asked Uncle.

"I can't say either way, not with any certainty." He thought for a moment, then continued. "What I will say, however, is that this doesn't feel like an industrial accident."

"What the fuck is that supposed to mean?" Noor demanded as she rubbed her sore feet.

"I've seen enough disasters in my time to know what to look for; there are certain hallmarks, certain signs that manifest time and time again. This place has none of them."

"But the time dilation, Horace!" Harold protested.

"Yes, yes," Uncle said, a trace of irritation creeping into his usually calm demeanour, "that is important but I feel that by focussing on that, we won't see the wood for the trees, as it were."

"Well then, what do you suggest?" Professor Skullbone sounded more tired than usual, and Noor's frustration cooled slightly as she realised just how frail he was.

"This might sound strange, but can you remember how we got here? In detail, I mean?"

"The boundary transition at the event horizon was rather chaotic, so no, Horace, I cannot."

"How about the beginning of this conversation?"

"I..." Harold began, but then faltered.

"Noor, how about you?" Uncle asked.

"I'm not sure," she replied, "but I'm sure I could if I tapped into the Tangle."

"Is that so?" Uncle said quietly.

"Why wouldn't it be?"

"I think I see what you're getting at, Horace," Harold said after a moment. "Noor, have you ever used your power whilst asleep?"

"I don't think so, but I've only had it a month or so."

"Only a month!?" Midori said, whirling round from the darkness to face her. "How can that be?"

"I told you it was only my first assignment!" Noor yelled, far louder than she meant to.

"Your gift manifested unusually late," Midori replied. "In Seers, this is unheard of!"

"She's not a Seer," Uncle said. All three of them turned to look at him. "What? We're in the thick of it now, so this is the time for total and absolute honesty.

Noor, I'm sorry to tell you this, but you aren't a Seer."

"I am!" Noor felt the panic rising in her chest. *He's wrong, he has to be!* Her heartbeat thundered in her ears. *He doesn't know me!*

I can't go back to being ordinary!

"No, you aren't." He walked over to her and placed a hand on her shoulder. "Seers get flashes of the future or glimpses of the past, but the most important thing is that they cannot control those visions; you can."

"Then what am I?"

"You can select individual strings from the Tangle, can't you?" Noor nodded and he continued. "I'd be willing to bet that with a little practice, you could not only see the possibilities laid out before you but select the one you want."

I can already do that, to a certain extent, she thought, but said nothing.

"Who knows what you could achieve by looking backwards into someone's life?" He smiled at her. "Seers can't manipulate the Tangle, Noor, but you can."

"You aren't possibly suggesting that she could-" Midori began, her voice dripping with scorn, but he silenced her with a look.

"I am, Mistress Aoki." His voice was kind, but firm. "I know that your people are both wise and long-lived, but I have been alive since antiquity and I have seen more variety and strangeness than you could imagine."

"But what am I, if not a Seer?" Noor asked, almost pleading with desperation.

"You're one of the rarest Exceptions of them all, Noor, the likes of which hasn't been seen for millennia." Uncle helped her to her feet and smiled at her proudly. "Noor Turner, you are a Fate."

"They don't exist!" Midori protested after almost thirty minutes of silent walking. "It's preposterous!"

"There are plenty of things that we assume aren't real purely on the basis that we haven't seen them," Uncle said as he helped Noor hobble along in her cumbersome footwear. "I'd wager that Noor didn't know anything about our world before her gifts were awakened a few weeks ago. Am I right?"

Noor nodded in agreement, her mind still reeling from what Agent Griswold had told her.

"You see, we're all lifelong students, no matter how long we live. Remember, it was only in the last few decades that the existence of Peepers was finally confirmed, and they infest entire buildings!"

"What are Peepers?" Noor asked.

"Pests," Midori responded and Uncle sighed.

"Not everything that inconveniences you is a pest, Mistress Aoki." He gestured to the forest around them. "This whole ecosystem is alive with cryptozoological marvels and sentient creatures aplenty; Pixies, Dryads, Fauns, Imps, and so many more have lived beside the ordinary humans for countless generations.

"Just because you can't see them, doesn't mean they're not there." He smiled broadly. "I was in Prague a few years back with young Bert on the trail of the Marrovikt family; old Scandinavian blood, from deep in the arctic circle. The name is a bastardisation of Marrow Wight, I think and-"

There was a scream from behind them, and they turned just in time to see Harold Skullbone fall to the ground, one hand clutched to a bloody wound on his chest. The nearby foliage rustled as his attacker disappeared into the dark undergrowth.

"Professor, are you alright?" Noor said as she clumsily made her way to his side. She pulled a small penlight from her pocket and shone the beam on his chest. After gingerly moving his hand out of the way, she sighed with relief. "It's not deep, but we'll still need to bandage this up. I need you to keep pressure on this for a few minutes. What did this to you?"

"It looked like a nightmare," Skullbone said, grimacing with pain.

"That isn't helpful!" Midori hissed. She held a blade in each hand and had adopted a defensive stance.

"We need more details, Professor." Noor searched through her pack as she spoke, desperate for a first aid kit. What she found instead surprised her.

"Boots?" Harold said with a pained chuckle as Noor pulled them out of her bag. "You might've put them on earlier, you know."

"I didn't know they were in there," Noor said quietly. "Truth be told, I didn't even pack my own bag; Ivy did it for me."

"At least part of her Lamplight training stuck, it seems." Midori sheathed her weapons and snatched the pack up. After a few moments of rummaging she pulled out a nondescript grey pouch and a red first aid bag. "Excellent."

"What's that?" Uncle asked as he helped Noor into her more suitable footwear.

"A field surgery kit," she said, and showed them the bureau logo emblazoned on the waterproof material. "If it isn't standard issue, I'm assuming she stole it from the Forward Command Post."

"Trust a Kitsune to train a thief," Harold hissed.

"I can either stitch you up or finish the job,

Skullbone," Midori said sharply. "Which would you rather?"

Oh god, we're going to fucking kill each other out here! Her heart began to race once again. *I need something to restrain Midori!*

Uncle seemed to have the same thought, but unlike Noor instead of panicking, he simply started talking.

"Are you folks familiar with the legend of Orpheus?" His eyes twinkled in the moonlight as he spoke.

"The Ancient Greek myth?"

"We can start there," Uncle said, finishing up with Noor's laces. "I assume you know the basic outline; singer's love dies, he travels to the underworld and bargains for her life, then he sings her to the border of the underworld but loses her when he gives into doubt."

"Is this important?" Midori asked impatiently.

"We can't go anywhere until Harold is stitched and bandaged, so it'll help pass the time and keep the nightmares at bay."

"How do you reason that?" Harold said as Midori set about patching him up.

"Just trust me," Uncle said, and he gave Noor a wink. "Now, the Orpheus of myth is exactly that; a pure fiction conjured up to entertain and teach a morality tale. The Orpheus of legend, however, was a real man.

"We are going back a long time, so my memory gets a little bit fuzzy, but the important details are still clear as day. Orpheus was a man, but not an ordinary one; he was an Exception just like people can be today. Can you guess his gift?"

"Are you saying that *The* Orpheus was a Shriek?"

Harold asked, his tone both pained and intrigued.

"That I am. Noor, do you know what a Shriek is?"

"No, but I'm guessing it has something to do with your voice."

"That's right. A Shriek can yell or scream loud enough to shatter a person into pieces or vibrate their brain into jelly; it's a ghoulish power that comes entirely from their superhuman hearing. Orpheus could do this, but he chose a different path.

"Instead of using his voice to kill, which he would've been very capable of, he instead taught himself to cure people with it. He could whistle a cut closed, hum a broken bone back together, and-"

"Sing the dead back to life?" Noor asked, and Uncle nodded. "He really brought someone back from the dead?"

"Yes. He only managed it once, and the person hadn't been dead for very long." He smiled at the memory. "Still, bringing someone back to true life was a power unheard of, and soon word of his skills spread across the land. Shrieks came from all over to beg Orpheus to teach them his ways."

"Did he?" Midori asked.

"He offered each of them an ultimatum; he would teach them how to heal, but only if they truly swore never to kill again. Every single Shriek promised to give up violence, but he refused to train any of them." Uncle chuckled softly. "In learning the intricate songs and sounds of the body, he had learned exactly what a lie sounded like. Not one of his would-be pupils were honest with him."

"So what happened?" Noor asked, almost transfixed by the tale.

"Most that he refused begged and pleaded, but to no

avail. Some threatened him, but he knew that if they killed him, the secret would be lost forever. Finally, one day a woman he refused killed him."

"What a waste of potential," Midori scoffed as she finished closing up Harold. "If Orpheus was as skilled as you say, then he was a fool."

"Perhaps, but I admire the strength of his convictions." Uncle looked past Midori and into the moonlit forest. "It seems that our shadowy assailants have moved on for now."

"Do you think we'll ever see another like him?" Harold asked.

"Oh, I'm certain we will. All it requires is the right person at the right time. Someone of tremendous talent raised with unconditional love and total compassion; someone who would never dream of using their power to harm."

"So not in our lifetimes then," Noor said with an uneasy smile as she saw something lurking in the distance. "Although I have a feeling that none of us are going to be around much longer."

Chapter Seventeen – The Bert Game

Mallory

"What's the first thing you're gonna do once we reach town?" Agent Gillespie asked gleefully as they trudged through the dark woods towards the radio mast.

"I'm going to find some fucking shoes that are made for this terrain, even if I have to mug someone to get them." Mallory looked at Bert as he answered, astounded by the young man's seemingly boundless optimism. "*If* we make it, that is. What about you?"

"I'm gonna walk right into the drug store and I'm gonna order myself a chocolate phosphate."

"You do realise that it isn't *Eighteen* Eighty Six, right?" Mallory said, but a small smile still crept on to his lips. "That's an interesting gift you have, Agent Gillespie; is there a Weasel somewhere in your bloodline?"

"Yup. Mama was a Weasel and Pa was a Porcupine."

"What's a Porcupine?" Mallory asked.

"One of those!" Bert said excitedly as a quilled rodent grunted through the undergrowth a few metres ahead of them. Mallory shook his head and chuckled.

I walked right into that one.

"In all seriousness, my grandmother was a Weasel. Other than that, I come from a long line of Sleuths and Tracers, which makes sense in a weird sort of way." He smiled at Mallory. "I used to wish that I was like them, but I just don't have the temperament for all the serious gumshoe work."

Bert sighed heavily and stretched his fingertips up

towards the moonlit sky.
"I always knew that I would die somewhere like this."
"You're not going to die here, Agent Gillespie; not whilst I have anything to say about it!" Mallory put a hand on the young Bureau Agent's shoulder. "You don't get to give up yet, not when my brother is still missing.
"Now are you gonna pull yourself together, or do I need to hit you?"
"No, you don't need to throw hands with me, Agent Marsh."
"Good." Mallory let go of Bert's jacket and took a deep breath. "So, how does it work?"
"How does what work?" Gillespie asked, but the playful tone in his voice was enough to raise Mallory's eyebrows. "Oh, you mean the Bert Game?"
"The Bert Game?"
"That's what Uncle calls it." Agent Gillespie took a moment to check that his service weapon was loaded. "I'll show you mine, if you show me yours."
"My gift only works in specific places; I can only tap into the Knots in the Tangle that are left in the wake of violent acts. It's kind of like automatic writing, only with a much stronger visual component. It's not pretty, but I'm sure you'll see it yourself before too long."
"Is that all?" Bert asked after a lengthy pause.
That's all you're going to get for now, Mallory thought before nodding distractedly.
"Well, I guess you could call me a bit of a joker," Bert said with a sly smile. "As long as I don't take anything seriously, it can't hurt me."
"That's what I'd guessed," Mallory said, nodding

along. “I'm assuming that the protection extents to anyone that's caught up in your antics?”

“Bingo,” Bert said with a smile. “What tipped you off?”

“The singing.” Mallory grinned. “My mentor, Elspeth Whist, had a similar gift; it wasn't quite the same level of protection, but you couldn't lie to her after she sang to you. Agent Griswold is a good teacher for you.”

“He really is, but in a lot of ways we're like chalk and cheese. I'm quite a fearful person at heart; when you get to know me, you'll realise that it's all bluster and bravado.” He smiled sadly at Mallory. “I never wanted to be part of the Bureau.”

Francis never wanted to be a Ministry Agent, but here you both are, Mallory thought, but he left this unsaid. Instead, he just waited for Bert to continue. The young man sighed once again and sat on a hickory stump, his eyes glazed and unfocussed.

“You see, Uncle experiences things differently; he doesn't feel the same fear that would take the heart of ordinary men, like us.” Agent Gillespie paused for a moment, staring slyly at Mallory. “Then again, Marsh, you aren't like me, are you?”

“I don't know what you mean, Bert,” Mallory lied. He gently moved his hand to the butt of his revolver. “Why are you here, Gillespie?”

“I was ordered to come here, Marsh.”

“I only wanted volunteers!” Marsh shook his head in a panic. “I never expected them to send someone so young!”

“I'm old enough to serve, Mallory,” Bert said quietly. “Old enough to die.”

“Bert, I-” Mallory began, but the Bureau Agent

pointed his service weapon at Mallory. The Artist jumped as Gillespie pulled the trigger, firing the weapon several times in quick succession. The rounds whistled past Mallory's shoulder and hissed through the darkness where they found their target.

A blue clad police officer toppled back into the undergrowth as Bert took aim at a second figure charging at them through the brush. Mallory whipped his Jack around, the under-over revolver kicking hard in his hand.

“Did that police officer...” Mallory's voice trailed off as the second officer fell lifelessly backwards into the bushes.

“He didn't have a face,” Bert confirmed, his voice entirely too calm for Mallory's liking. “Nothing but smooth, pale skin.”

“What the fuck is going on out here?”

“Hold the light steady,” Bert insisted, as he hauled the corpse bodily into the trembling torch beam. Mallory tried to avert his gaze, but to no avail. Bert looked on with amazement, whistling through his teeth as he wiped his hands on his trousers.

“What the fuck is that thing?” Mallory asked.

“No idea, but I don't think it's fully human; maybe a kind of simulacrum instead, or-”

“A nightmare?” Mallory suggested.

“Yeah, that would make a lot of sense.”

“I can't really remember how we got into this forest,” Mallory admitted after a moment. “I'm not sure if we've been here hours or days.”

“Did we have anyone else with us?” Bert frowned as he searched his memory. “I remember there being others, but I can't recall any details.”

"If there were others," Mallory said, looking at the mast on the horizon, "that's where they'll be heading. Why can't we remember?"

"Maybe whatever is causing all this doesn't want to know that the world has moved on?" Bert grunted and shook his head. "That isn't important right now, however; what we need to focus on is working out exactly what we're up against."

"I don't even know where to start," Mallory said as his stomach rolled over once again. Even glancing at the smooth, featureless face made him feel trapped and suffocated, like a careless child caught in a plastic bag. "How can something like this even be alive?"

"There are different shades of life, Agent Marsh," Bert said darkly. "I don't think this is one of the more palatable kinds."

"What the fuck are you talking about?"

"Some creatures are complete life forms, with souls and dreams and all the rest. This thing," he said, gesturing at the police officer, "is not the full package; it's a half-remembered dream, just a stray quirk of motion that gives the impression of life."

"You sound almost envious," Mallory muttered.

"Take its shoes," Bert said, distractedly. "We're no good to anyone thumping around in ski boots; the least we can do is be ready to run at a moment's notice."

"Good idea," Mallory replied as he unlaced the sturdy hiking boots and yanked them from the pale creature's feet. "Do you think that they were once like us?"

"What do you mean?"

"Agent Salt said that over a hundred Bureau Agents have been sent into Galaxy over the past forty years or so; something had to have happened to them, right?"

"Let's find out," Bert said as he slipped a small knife from a pouch on his belt. He deftly sliced open a gash where the creature's mouth should be and pried the jawbones apart, speaking as he worked. "Every Bureau Field Agent is given a tracker in their top left molar when they first join up with their respective field office; if this is indeed one of our people, they'll have a false tooth with a beacon inside it it."

There was the sharp sound of cracking bone, followed by a wet squelch as Agent Gillespie extracted the ersatz tooth and dropped it into Mallory's palm.

"So this confirms that it's one of your people?" the English Artist asked, and Bert nodded. "Who is he?"

Bert examined the minute engraving on the surface of the molar.

"He is a she, and her name is Linda Collins; she went missing almost twenty five years ago." Bert shook his head anxiously. "This is bad, Mallory; this is really bad. Something is changing these people, remaking them into these... Faceless creatures."

"How long do you think we have?" Mallory asked. *Francis has been lost in here for months.*

"I don't know, but let's assume that whatever is causing this is spread by touch and- oh shit!" Bert leapt backwards as the Faceless Officer suddenly twitched and trembled on the damp moonlit ground. Its mouth, freshly opened, now yawned wide and emitted a deafening shriek; the undulating sound tore through the still night air, piercing as an air raid siren.

Other voices responded, growing closer by the moment. Mallory swiftly laced up his new boots as Bert emptied his service weapon into what remained of Agent Collins. His blood ran cold when he saw just how little damage the rounds did.

We are not equipped for this.

"Marsh, where the fuck do we go!?" Bert cried out as he shoved Collins away. Two more of the Faceless police officers burst into the clearing, their voices undulating and whooping in the chilly night air.

"We need to get into town!" Mallory replied. He brought his Jack round to aim at the nearest of the Faceless, but at the last moment dropped his aim down to blow out its kneecaps. The creature howled as it toppled to the floor.

Who knows how long that will keep it down for? Mallory grabbed Agent Gillespie by the shoulders and hauled him in the direction of town, crashing through the undergrowth as they went.

"This would be a really good time to play the Bert Game!" Mallory yelled as they mantled over a fallen tree. The wailing sirens had been joined by flashing lights in the hills above them, and the Faceless were gaining ground with each passing moment.

One of the uniformed officers leapt from the treeline ahead of them, and Bert immediately closed the gap between them, seizing the hands of the Faceless as he did so.

"May I have this dance?" he yelled madly, and Mallory felt something stir in the air between them; Bert's spell of protection had settled on them, but who knew for how long?

"We need to get to town or the radio station," Mallory called out, his voice caught in a jaunty tune that he did not recognise. "Can we dance all the way there?"

"We can try."

Bert did not sound optimistic, however, and his voice was already strained.

We aren't going to make it, Mallory realised, *not unless I do something drastic.*

Mallory pulled his hair out of the messy bun underneath his hat and shook it out so that it fell in loose tresses behind his head. *We'll get as far as we can,* he thought with trepidation, *and then it's time for me to claim my inheritance at last.*

"Don't worry, Bert," Mallory said softly, "I won't let anything bad happen to you."

I am the Viscount Rutland, he thought proudly, *and there is just as much sap as blood in my veins. As long as I stand amongst the trees, I am invincible.*

Chapter Eighteen – Blades of Water

Michaela

"Are those sirens?" Ivy asked, looking through the darkness beside Michaela.

"Sirens," Edgar confirmed. "Our friends are in danger."

"We have to get to the radio station," Michaela said firmly. "That's where we agreed to met up. There are too many opportunities for ambushes in the wilderness."

"God damn you, Michaela, are you really just going to leave them to fucking die?" Ivy roared as she grabbed the mycologist's shoulder, whirling her around on the spot. Michaela immediately stepped forward, pressing the blade of her katana into Ivy's neck.

"We are being tracked," Michaela hissed through gritted teeth, barely loud enough for Ivy to hear. "We need to be a united front, now more than ever, or we will never leave this fucking forest alive!"

Their shared heart thundered in their ears, and the two women regarded each other with wild eyes and ragged breaths. Ivy was about to speak when a glimmer of dark movement caught Michaela's gaze.

She turned on her heel, smartly drawing her katana diagonally down across her body before sharply thrusting up with the leading edge of the blade. The Kitsune-forged steel easily split the flesh of her featureless assailant, leaving a fine mist of blood hanging in the air in its wake. Michaela neatly cleaned the gore from her blade with a sharp twist of the weapon; her heartbeat had barely quickened in the time it had taken her to efficiently dismember her opponent.

My skills might have gathered dust over the years, but now I stand, illuminated, in the Lamplight once again.

"No face," Edgar remarked as he peered at the uniformed corpse at their feet. "No distinguishing features whatsoever; most unusual."

"Interrogate him," Michaela instructed, gesturing with her katana at the dead police officer. "I want to know everything about him; who he is, how he came to be here, and what happened to him."

"Can't." Edgar shook his head for emphasis.

"Why not?" Michaela angrily swept a stray strand of hair from her face. "Edgar, we are under a fucking time limit!"

"He isn't dead," Ivy said after cocking her head to one side and listening to the motionless corpse. "Perhaps in a kind of stasis, at least for now, but this one absolutely isn't dead."

"Not even sure if we can die here," Edgar murmured, looking nervously at the sky.

"Something in the trees?" Michaela asked.

"There's a storm coming," he replied, wrapping his coat tightly about his arms. "Bad weather and worse luck."

"Maybe we can turn the inclement weather to our advantage," Ivy suggested. Michaela was about to respond when the wounded creature at her feet suddenly thrashed in her direction. Startled by the violent motion, Michaela brought the katana down on the Faceless time and time again; her strikes were entirely without grace and finesse, just a panicked frenzy of motion.

That was... inelegant, she thought afterwards, as her cheeks flushed with shame.

"Like a lumberjack chopping down a tree," Edgar agreed, a little too gleefully for her liking. "Look, it's already healing!"

Michaela could see that he was correct; the wounds were already knitting back together, with almost no scar tissue left in the wake of the horrific injuries she had done. *This is not good at all. How the fuck do we fight something that we can't kill!?*

"The wakizashi!" Edgar cried as another of the Faceless crashed into the clearing. "Wield both blades together, white jade for balance and black jade to unmake these monsters!"

Michaela had no time to reply; instead she drew the shorter blade with her left hand and dropped into a fighting stance. In the sky above her, thunder rumbled and lightning flashed as the heavens opened.

Here comes the rain.

"I can't do it!"

"Can't or won't?" Midori said archly. Michaela Inglewood squirmed under the Kitsune's gaze. "There is no difference in the outcome, regardless of motive; either you are capable of the feats I expect of you or you have no purpose on this island."

"But Mistress Aoki, I-"

"If you tell me that you can't do as I have asked one more time, I will have Sora rip you limb from limb." The Kitsune lowered her voice and leant in close to the child's face. "I will offer you a way out of this torment, if you are strong enough to take it."

Midori produced a razor sharp needle of black metal

and held it mere millimetres from Michaela's unblinking eye. The Kitsune smiled evilly before offering Michaela a final exit from the waking nightmare of Project Lamplight.

"I hold before you the dokubari. It is a poisoned needle, the most deadly on earth. In three dozen heartbeats from now, I will strike; if you are truly incapable of the path laid out before you, I will kill you.

"Remember, even the faintest scratch is fatal, and I will not miss; it would be wise to accept your fate."

Michaela let her teacher's words wash over her as she counted down the heartbeats.

Seven.

"One single touch is fatal."

Three.

"Choose your fate, child."

One.

Michaela turned on her heel, dropping to her knees as the dokubari flashed through the air where her face had been but an instant before. The young Séance moved entirely on instinct, letting her opponent's mind and spirit betray her intentions; whilst her advantage was not true precognition, it was as close to it as she would ever get.

I can't best her, Michaela soon realised. Even with her superior empathetic predictions, Michaela was losing ground; a fraction of a second here, half a heartbeat there. *Soon I will make a mistake, and she will take my life from me.*

Michaela realised that she had no more time left, and emptied her heart of any fear, trepidation, and doubt that still lingered there. She stepped forwards into Midori's next blow, and hissed with pain as she felt the dokubari pierce the flesh of her left hand.

She looked away from Midori's eyes; away from the woman's pained gaze towards the palm of her hand that was held tightly in Michaela's fingers. The dokubari pierced both women's hands, binding them together in death.

"What have you done?" Midori asked breathlessly.

"I couldn't win," Michaela whispered, "but I refused to lose."

"But you will die!"

"Death before dishonour, Mistress Aoki." Michaela smiled slightly as she felt her body weaken. The two women dropped to the ground and the Séance closed her eyes, satisfied with the outcome of their conflict.

Then Michaela felt a few drops of cold liquid on her lips, and life surged through her once again. She opened her eyes with a gasp and stared at Midori Aoki, who was administering the antidote to herself with only seconds to spare.

"Why?" Michaela demanded, sitting up unsteadily as she did so. "You promised that this would be the end!"

"I never expected you to so willingly accept your own mortality," Midori whispered softly, "and I much less expected you to sacrifice yourself in order to best me. You showed true spirit today, Michaela; something that I did not believe could be found in your people."

"So I get to live?" Michaela asked bitterly.

"Yes."

"Even if I don't want it?"

"*Because* you don't want it, Michaela. You showed that you are capable of looking past your own selfish desires and acting in the service of something greater than you; I am proud of you, Michaela." Midori gestured to the pair of swords at her waist. "Tomorrow I shall forge you your own set of swords; they will serve as a reminder of the lesson that you have learned here, today."

"Which is?"

"Life is only truly lived by those willing to risk it."

Here comes the rain.

The first icy drop hit Michaela's face as the closest of the Faceless burst into the clearing. Michaela turned sharply, bringing both of her blades round in a vicious arc, leaving a bloody vapour trail lingering in the air behind her stroke.

The first of the Faceless fell as she guarded her body with the wakizashi and struck at her targets with the katana. Each blow was a little faster than the previous, each strike more savage. Soon, Michaela was moving as fast as the rain than poured around her; a perfect torrent of violence and deadly precision.

The ringing of blades began to fill the air as the tidal wave of bloodshed soaked her to the very bone. Her hands were slick with gore and her hair was matted with coppery, salty blood. Still, it was only after a solid minute of stillness that she finally allowed herself to relax out of her combat stance.

Michaela's breath came to her in ragged gasps as the exhaustion finally hit her. Even though she'd only been fighting for less than ten minutes, she had felled almost sixty of the Faceless. Her jade-imbued steel hadn't simply slain her opponents; it had completely obliterated them.

Michaela waited for the sirens to resume, or for the fallen enemies to rise up once again, but the bodies remained where they had come to rest; for better or worse, they were truly dead now.

The icy rain continued to fall, refreshing Michaela's worn out body, but not cleansing the gore from her filthy clothes.

"That was impressive," Edgar said after a few minutes.

Michaela did not reply, but she did give him a grateful smile.

"You need to move," Ivy said, placing a gentle hand on her shoulder as she did so. "There are going to be more of those things coming this way soon enough."

"I know, I know," Michaela said with a groan, getting to her feet. She turned to look at Edgar. "Do you really think it's Nineteen Eighty Six, Ed?"

"That's definitely the comet," he replied, pointing at the cloudy sky.

"Then we need to get to the radio," Michaela said.

"Of course we do," Ivy replied, "the plan is to warn Charity's parents, after all."

"Yes, it is, but I want to try something else." Michaela felt her heart race in her chest slightly. "I want to broadcast a public warning about Project Lamplight over the radio; if we have gone back in time, we might be able to stop all those people dying."

"But then won't we cease to exist?" Ivy asked, suddenly nervous.

This conversation feels familiar, she mused, but pushed the thought aside.

"Yes," Michaela said sadly, "but we have to try to save as many as we can."

"I'm with you, Kiki," Edgar said. "Ivy, are you in?"

"I don't think it's going to work like that," Ivy said softly, "but I'd kick myself if I didn't try it. Fuck it, what's the worst that can happen?"

"At least we'll be together," Michaela said with a sombre smile. "I can't think of anyone else I'd rather face my fate with."

"I can think of one," Ivy muttered.

"That's true," Michaela admitted, "but think of the horror that we can spare her, if we manage to do this."

"This might be the last thing we ever do," Edgar said sadly.

"It's a hell of a swan song, if that's what this turns out to be," Michaela said, fixing her gaze on the blinking red lights of the radio broadcast tower. "It has been a pleasure to fight alongside you both."

"Likewise," Ivy said.

"Nobody I'd rather share a mind with," Edgar said quietly, and the two women echoed his words before striding off into the darkness.

Chapter Nineteen – Song of Solomon

Mallory

"Come on, Bert!" Mallory yelled as he led the young Bureau Agent through the dark streets at the edge of the town. The dim glow of a traffic signal illuminated the nearby junction; it was lit up like a beacon in the night.

They'd given the Faceless the slip in the tangled trees on the way into town, but Mallory was certain they'd be back soon enough.

If we can just make it to the radio station, Mallory thought as his heart thundered in his chest, *we can get some of the others to help us.*

"I would give anything to have Thaddeus here right now," he muttered.

Bert went to respond, but his words were silenced when a police car screeched on to the road ahead of them. The words 'Galaxy Sheriff's Department' were emblazoned on the side, and no sooner than the vehicle had come to a halt did a gigantic Faceless burst out through the driver's side door.

He was over eight feet tall, a colossal bear of a man, and he bellowed and roared like a maddened animal as he he charged towards the two men. More Faceless poured through the streets, seemingly materialising out of thin air.

This just keeps getting worse, Mallory thought as he dragged Bert towards a gap between two dilapidated bungalows. He took careful aim with his double barrelled revolver, making sure to make each and every shot count; even with his steady trigger discipline, he knew that they were desperately outnumbered.

"There's too many of them!" Mallory yelled as his Jack clicked empty once again. He fumbled in his pocket for a reload, the fingers of his left hand rapidly counting how many more rounds he had left.

Two speed loaders, he thought with a panic. *That's just twenty eight shots.*

He watched in horror as Agent Gillespie emptied an entire clip at one of the Faceless; fifteen shots and it just kept on coming. Bert's grin faltered and the Faceless lashed out at him with a grasping hand.

Mallory snapped the break closed on his weapon and aimed at the creature's blank face. The Giantslayer kicked in his hand as he scored a head shot on the Faceless. Blood, bone, and brain splattered over Bert's face and panic took him. He dropped to the ground and scrambled backwards, away from the smooth skinned policemen that were swarming into the alley around them.

"I can't do it, Mallory!" he yelled, his voice wild and shrill. "I can't stay calm enough!"

"Of all the times to not have Teaser around," Mallory muttered as he frantically looked for an exit. His eyes widened slightly as a few nearby trees swayed slightly in the breeze. *We're only a couple of streets away,* he realised.

We can make it.

"Get up, Bert!" Mallory yelled. Bert still whimpered on the ground.

"I can't do it, Mal. They're gonna get me!"

"On your feet, Gillespie!" Mallory's voice deepened and a shade of the Master's power coloured his words; Bert was powerless to resist and clambered awkwardly to his feet.

That's twice, Mallory thought, both worried and strangely detached at the same time; he would process that later, when they weren't at the risk of being overrun.

"Mallory, what are we going to do?" Bert said, his voice trembling with terror as he fired blindly; he no longer cared whether his shots found their targets at all. "Mallory?!"

"Head for the treeline, Bert," Mallory said forcefully, as his blood ran cold in his veins. "Run, now, as fast as you can. I can't promise that I can protect you when it begins."

Both men ran as hard as they could, with the clamouring horde hot on their heels. As soon as they were in the shade of the canopy, Mallory called out to his companion.

"When it takes you, don't fight it; just let it happen."

"What?!" Bert looked at Mallory as if he had lost his mind. "Mallory, what the fuck are you talking about?"

"I am not human, Agent Gillespie." Mallory's words creaked with the voices of a thousand trees and a darkness settled in his eyes. "I just need you trust me."

"But, Mallory-"

"Everything happens for a reason, Bert." Mallory allowed a small smile to creep on to his lips. "This is why I am trans; it saves my life in this moment."

The nearest Faceless, the hulking Sheriff, was almost upon them.

"Run, Agent Gillespie," Mallory said, suffusing both the Master's power and his mother's magic into his words. "Run for your life."

The Sheriff swung at Mallory as he unleashed the Dryad birthright that lurked within the very fabric of his flesh.

I will always be my father's son, Mallory thought proudly, *but in this moment I am my mother's daughter.*

Then the smile faded as the music began.

The pain was greater than anything he'd ever experienced. He screamed in agony, but his vocalisations were lost in the cacophony of eldritch singing and inhuman harmonies that poured from his lips like a bloody flood.

His arms twisted and bent, bones snapping and shattering as the power pulsed through him, burning him up like a wildfire. *I am incandescent with suffering,* Mallory thought, barely cognisant of his own passion, *but I am also transfixed by ecstasy.*

He was the most alive that he had ever been, and all other sensation would surely feel like the creeping chill of the grave by comparison. *Francis always said that Father had described Mother as the most vital creature to have ever have lived,* Mallory thought hazily, *and if this is how she felt, then he did not do her justice.*

Mallory sighed as he felt his hair curl and twist about his face, caressing his olive skin like the most delicate of lovers. His clothing, sensible winter gear and tactical camouflage, began to rot and fray, splitting apart at the seams; even his beloved hat was destroyed. The pilfered police boots collapsed into nothingness, allowing his bare, elegant toes to wriggle and nestle in the rich mountain soil.

He was dimly aware of the Faceless as they were flung back and forth by his Dryad's song, their bodies shattered against trees and dashed against the dimly lit bungalows at the edge of town.

I hope Bert's gift keeps him safe.

Soon his attention was drawn back to the agony that burned in his flesh, however. He clasped his hands to the surgery scars on his chest; wounds that were being healed back to their previous state and undoing all the hard work that he'd put in during his transition.

I'm going to need another mastectomy, he realised with horror, before slapping his hands to his face. The flesh there had also been robbed of any of testosterone's influence; when he finished dancing, it would be as if the past five years had not even happened. *It will be worth it, to survive,* he thought, lying to himself.

He continued to dance, now nude as the day he was born, and the ground around his feet came alive with English Bluebells, Early Purple Orchids, and Cowslips. The heady scent of rich earth and spicy floral notes filled Mallory's nostrils, carrying his mind along in the turbulent tides of the Dryad's pungent psychoactive perfume.

One of the Faceless reached out for his naked form, but Mallory turned away, spurning his featureless admirer. He felt the creature die of grief at his rejection, and only then did he truly understand the power that he had walked away from all those years ago.

I wonder if anyone would even recognise me?

Mallory looked at the woody knots that decorated his newly dendrified skin.

Would I even know my own face?

“What if she never comes, Mallory?” Francis asked on a balmy September evening, sitting on the veranda of Rutland Manor. He clinked the ice cubes idly in his glass; it had held freshly squeezed lemonade only a few moments ago.

"She will," Mallory replied, not even looking up from his canvas. This was not the first time he'd had this particular conversation with his brother, and he knew that it wouldn't be the last. "There are only Marsh men living here, and we still care for the wood, so nothing has changed."

"I always thought that she would appear before I turned thirty." The ice cubes tinkled once again, grating on Mallory's nerves. "What if I can't have children, Mal?"

"You're the Lord Marsh," Mallory said, carefully applying pigment with his brush. "That means that you have to, whether you want to or not."

Mallory painted in silence for a few more minutes, before voicing the question that he knew Francis needed to ask.

"For over two thousand years, the wood has always provided, Francis. Why would things change now?"

"Well, you know..." Francis said awkwardly, looking off into the middle distance.

"If we're going to talk about this, you're going to need to say it out loud."

"You know that I don't see you as anything as my brother, Mallory-"

"But?"

"But there's never been a man quite like you, Mallory." Francis sighed heavily. "It's not clear what that means for the agreement between us and the Dryads."

"They said that our bloodline would continue for as long as we continued to have sons, Francis. We've kept up our end of the bargain." He paused, hesitating before finishing his thought. "Maybe you're just not here often enough, Francis; it was only when Father stepped away from his Ministry role to focus on his theological research that he met Mother. Perhaps that's all you need."

"A break from work?" Francis asked, incredulously. "I'm a Ravenblade, Mallory; you know that the Ministry would never allow it."

"You're a Marsh, first and foremost." Mallory spoke softly, almost too quietly for his brother to hear. "Father understood that."

"Father put too much stock in old stories and legends."

"Perhaps you put too little faith in them," Mallory replied testily. "I can't recall our mother's face, but the way father spoke about her... His words are burned into my brain; I only hope that I ever love someone that much, even if it is just for a little while."

The memory of her has faded, he thought, *just as summer fades to autumn in one last beautiful gasp.*

There was silence for a moment, and then Francis spoke, his voice barely audible.

"Did you really believe all the things he said about her?"

"Absolutely."

"You don't think it was all talk?"

Mallory did not reply, but he shook his head sadly as his father's breathless words of adoration filled his mind and crossed his lips.

"My beloved is to me a sachet of myrrh that lies between my breasts. My beloved is to me a cluster of henna blossoms in the vineyards of Engedi." He looked tearfully at Francis. "I hope you understand one day, Francis. I really do."

Chapter Twenty – The Night Creatures

Noor

"What do you think is out there?" Noor asked nervously as the nearby clatter of gunfire filled the air.

"I'm not sure," Uncle replied quietly, before giving Noor's hand a reassuring squeeze. "What I do know, however, is that young Bert will be keeping Mallory quite safe; that much I'm certain of."

I wish Elsie was here, Noor thought sadly. *She'd invent something to get us out of this.*

"Who are you thinking about?" Harold asked softly. "You've got that look of wistful longing that's either reserved for an absent lover or a particularly noteworthy cheeseburger."

Noor chuckled, even in spite of her melancholy mood.

"Laughter is good medicine," Uncle said, his tone encouraging.

"It's also a good way to get caught," Midori said, her words sharp and chastising. "We need to move quietly, now; soft and swift as shadows through the town."

"I think I'm going to knock on the first illuminated house we see," Uncle said. Before Midori could reply, he continued. "They've been stuck in this mess for almost forty years, Mistress Aoki; there's a chance that they might actually know what is going on."

"Life is rarely so simple," she said moodily.

"But sometimes it is," Harold said, nodding in agreement. "I agree with Horace; we could use as much local knowledge as possible."

"We should still proceed in silence!" the Kitsune

hissed.

"I disagree," Noor said after a minute or two to consider her words. "Something is wrong with this place; something is sapping our strength and making the shadows deeper and more dangerous than they've any right to be. That's why you told us the story of Orpheus, isn't it, Uncle?"

"Yes, it most certainly is," he said with a chuckle. "You'd give Bert a run for his money; maybe I should take you on as a Seeker instead of him."

"Will you tell us another story to keep our spirits up as we walk?" Harold asked.

Uncle nodded, but Noor wasn't looking at the Strix; instead she was staring at Midori, who had frozen completely still. *Something is very wrong,* she realised. Uncle followed her gaze and immediately picked up on the Kitsune's discomfort.

"What's wrong?" he whispered. She did not speak a reply, but instead inclined her head at a nearby tangle of bushes as she slowly, deliberately drew the longer of her two swords. Horace's fingers twitched and large talons sprouted from where his nails had been mere seconds before. Harold raised an ageing pistol in one shaking hand.

"Who's there?" Noor called out, and the night exploded in response.

The grizzly bear tore through the bushes and straight towards Harold Skullbone. The old man moved more swiftly than Noor could ever have imagined, his thin angular body crushing and stretching to fit through the most infinitesimal spaces between both bear and trees.

Noor shuddered and Harold moved like some gargantuan mechanical spider, clattering and chittering as he scuttled over the inky black fur of the nightmarish grizzly bear. *That is gonna haunt my dreams tonight,* she thought as he drove a sharp stiletto knife into the bear's chest again and again, seemingly to no avail.

As soon as he was clear, Midori stepped forward to deliver a powerful crossways cut that went all the way down to the bone. Still, the bear kept coming, almost four hundred kilos of bloodstained fur and rippling muscle unleashed and driving headlong.

The Kitsune reached into her jacket and produced a thin metal spike, which she stabbed sharply into the bear's neck. It seemed to have no effect.

"What sorcery is this?" Midori yelled, her voice panicked as she struck again and again with her sword. The bear roared in anger and slammed her in the side of the head with one massive paw. It flung her to one side, like a rag doll, where she landed limply with a grunt. The colossal predator turned to face Noor and bellowed at her, its foetid breath making her eyes water.

Uncle attacked just as the bear leapt at Noor, sinking his talons deep into its flesh. He groaned with exertion as he dragged the apex predator away from the cowering Fate, doing far more damage than Midori could ever hope to with such an elegant weapon.

The bear threw its massive bulk to one side, breaking free from Uncle's grip. Professor Skullbone wrapped his unnaturally limber form around the bear's torso, coiling tightly like some pale, bony constrictor. The monster howled with rage and thrashed from side to side. The Professor struggled to maintain his grip, and could not react fast enough when the shaggy, matted form of the bear slammed him into a nearby aspen.

The trunk splintered with a mighty crack, and the Squeeze's elongated form fell limp. Uncle regained his feet just in time to see Harold fall, and he let out a blood curdling scream. He took three swooping steps forward and placed his taloned hands on the bear; one on its throat and the other covering its eyes.

He let out another piercing scream before he began to mutter in a low, Slavic language. The bear struggled in his grip, but the Strix would not let go. After a few seconds of whispered words, the first moth forced its way out of the bear's bloody jaws. It was joined by another, then another, and soon an unrelenting tide was flooding through the bear's maw and ragged eye sockets.

Noor closed her eyes until it was over.

"How did you do that?" she murmured as Uncle let the corpse of the bear drop to the ground.

"It's old magic," he said, his voice still thickly accented, "from a much older place."

He slumped back against the nearest tree and looked at the shattered corpse of Professor Harold Skullbone, and then to Noor once again.

"I'm weakened, Noor; I need to feed." He smiled at her sadly. "I'm sorry that you have to see this."

He dragged his wiry frame, which now sprouted tufts of grey feathers, over to Harold's body. He deftly ripped the man's torso open with his razor sharp talons and began to cram handfuls of meat into his mouth.

"Don't!" said a weak voice.

Horace Griswold turned to face Midori, his luminous disc-like eyes glowing faintly in the darkness. The Kitsune pointed a trembling finger at the razor sharp needle that had been embedded in the neck of the bear; the needle that had scratched Harold Skullbone when the bear had slammed into him one final time.

Uncle ignored Midori's warning and resumed eating.

"No!" She got shakily to her feet, balancing awkwardly on her sword. "The dokubari! You must not!"

"Let me feed, vixen." Uncle's voice resonated with power; ancient and strong.

"It is poison! You will die!"

"I will not be slain by some witch's trick; who do you think first taught humans how to make such venoms?" He laughed darkly, his mouth dripping with blood. "Hecate taught her favourite children, the Hydras and the Striges, how to bottle her essence.

"I will not be harmed by my Mother's milk."

This is too fucking much for me, Noor thought as she curled up in the roots of a nearby tree. *I can't watch Uncle eat the Professor.*

She pulled the hood of her jacket over her eyes, and stuffed her hands over her ears. She felt someone approach, and peeked through a hole in her hood. Midori Aoki stood over her, her blade held in a guarding stance.

"Try to get some sleep," she said softly, barely loud enough to be heard over the disgusting sounds of Uncle feasting. "I'll keep you safe; you need to rest."

Noor was about to thank her, but she fell asleep before she could respond.

"Are you still alive?" Edgar asked, offering her a cup of tea.

Noor looked around, startled. *When did I get here?*

"Just now," Edgar said with a smile. "I thought you'd

appreciate a cup of tea."

"Thank you." She took a deep sip; it was Marsala Chai, sweet and warming. "This is perfect; just what I needed. Are you three holding up okay?"

"Michaela is getting us through the worst of it; she's a fighter, that one. Ivy is doing her best to reach out to the others; she had a bead on Mallory and Bert for a while, but she lost them a short time ago."

"I'm sure they're alright, Edgar."

"I'd know if they weren't," he replied darkly. He sat back in his chair, his fingertips steepled. "You've lost Harold, haven't you?"

"Just now. He was taken by the biggest bear that I've ever seen."

"It wasn't a bear," Edgar said sharply, "it only looked like one."

"Does that make a difference?"

"It means everything!" He got abruptly to his feet and began to pace back and forth across the tiled floor. "Things in this place are not what they seem; everything is scarier and more dangerous than it should be."

"But why?"

He avoided the question, instead refilling her tea cup.

"Edgar, what do you know?"

"Tell me about where you grew up, Noor." He pressed the cup into her hands and peered over his sunglasses at her. "Tell me everything you can."

"Is this a test?" she asked warily.

"Of sorts," he responded kindly, "though not of you. I have developed a working hypothesis about this place, and I need to run it by someone who isn't in my head; at least not so intimately as Ivy and Michaela."

"Okay then. I'm from Dartford. I grew up at number eleven, Norman Road; that house is destroyed now, however."

"Yes, the infamous Reichardt Drop; I heard about that one."

"I lived there with my..." She paused, suddenly struggling to remember her family. "Edgar, I can't remember; why can't I remember?"

"Try a different language," he suggested. "One that isn't linked to here."

"Can you still understand me?" Noor asked, switching effortlessly to Urdu.

"I can," Edgar replied. "This is my mind, after all; the rules work however I want them to."

"Why can I think of my family more easily if I'm not speaking English?" Noor asked him, a perplexed look on her face.

"Because Urdu has no connection to Galaxy; that part of your identity is uncorrupted." He took her hand in his. "This incarnation of Galaxy, filled with gigantic bears and faceless policemen, isn't real. We're in someone's idealised version of the town, and eventually their truth will overwrite us."

"What can we do?" Noor asked. She gulped nervously. "Do we have to kill them?"

"No, we don't have to kill them." He squeezed her fingers tightly in his. "I would never ask you to do such a thing. All we have to do for now is find them; once we know how they are maintaining the illusion, we can work out how to release everyone from it, safely."

"We don't have long, do we?"

"Less than two and a half days," he said softly.

Noor nodded for a moment, and then drained her

cup. She looked at Edgar, her eyes burning with resolve.

"What must I do?"

Chapter Twenty One – On the Fence

Ivy

"At least the sun is rising," Ivy muttered as she staggered along the mountain trail towards KGCB; the Galaxy Community Broadcast station. She heard the soft patter of feet running behind her.

"Here we go again," she said wearily as she turned and dropped, crossing her swords in one fluid motion. The Faceless's momentum carried it through her strike, separating the severed limbs and bisected torso, which clattered to the ground either side of her.

A second attacker was hot on the heels of the first, and she stepped into its attack, slicing vertically this time. Her motions were mechanical, yet still efficient and deadly. *I need to rest,* she thought as she wiped the crimson, sunrise tinged blood from the steel on to her trousers. *I'm going to die of exhaustion, otherwise.*

"Edgar," she said into the still morning air, "is there any chance that you could take over, please?"

"I'm the better fighter," Michaela said, stepping out from behind a nearby tree. "I'll take the wheel for a while."

"You're more fucking tired than I am!" Ivy said incredulously. "We both need to rest, and Edgar can keep us alive, at least for a few hours."

"I can fight!" Michaela said angrily, losing her footing slightly as she leant forward. Her hair fell in dirty tangles around her face, making the black bags beneath her eyes look even deeper than they were.

"You're about ready to fall over, you stubborn bitch!" Ivy said, even as a hint of a smile crossed her face.

"What are you grinning at?"

"Defiant, even until the end."

"Well, someone has to be!" Michaela replied haughtily. She sighed heavily. "I don't even know where Edgar has got to, let alone if he's capable of fighting off those things!"

"I was busy," Edgar said, suddenly standing between the two women. "Noor and I were doing detective work."

"Noor?" Michaela replied, smiling slightly. "She's alive?"

"Yes. As far as I know, of our original contingent, the only fatality so far has been Professor Harold Skullbone." Edgar looked past his two alters and into the forest. "He was killed by a bear; an unnaturally big one."

"Did you learn anything useful?" Ivy asked, leaning heavily on her katana.

"You'll break that if you treat it like that!" Michaela snapped. Ivy ignored her, and looked pointedly at Edgar, awaiting his response. "I mean it, Ivy, if you break my sword I'm going to shove it up your-"

"We're dreaming," Edgar said loudly, putting a restraining hand on Michaela's shoulder. "Or at the very least, we're inside someone's idealised version of this town."

"Ideal?" Ivy asked incredulously. "There are Faceless flesh horrors running all over the place! Who the fuck dreams up something this awful?"

"Someone for whom the alternative is far worse," Michaela said softly. "If the choice was to stay here or go back to Betony, I know which way I'd cast my vote."

"Noor is going to investigate the town to try and work out who is causing all this," Edgar went on, "and she'll check in with me periodically. I'll keep her updated on our location so she can eventually rendezvous with us."

"Good work, Ed," Ivy said. "What do we do when we find the person or people behind this?"

"Kill them?" Michaela suggested.

"Kiki," Ivy said as she rolled her eyes, "have you ever considered, maybe just once, not being your usual murderous self?"

"Yes; exactly twice, now that you mention it," Michaela replied sarcastically. "Besides, I was just being pragmatic."

"Not sure it will work like that," Edgar said. "The illusion has calcified; hardened, fossilised, even. We might have to convince them to let go of it voluntarily, rather than forcing them out of it."

"So killing them might just trap us here forever?" Michaela said, her shoulders sagging, and Edgar nodded sadly. "Well, that's me all out of ideas; I guess we're fucked then."

"If only we had a qualified therapist with us," Ivy said testily.

"I think we're a bit beyond the pale for you, Ivy." Michaela yawned. "Although, by all means, please give it a go; we've got nothing but time, after all."

"We actually have around sixty hours," Edgar said quietly, "although it might be a bit less."

"How do you reckon that?" Michaela asked, sounding genuinely frightened for the first time.

"We've been in here somewhere between twelve and eighteen hours," Edgar said, "although if we split the difference we can call it fifteen. All of the things we're doing in here stand a good chance of being entirely imaginary. Eating, drinking, and sleeping all serve to maintain the illusion of being alive, but there's a very strong possibility that our minds are being blinded to the simple fact that we are slowly dying."

"Dehydration, exhaustion, starvation," Ivy murmured, feeling the fight leave her entirely. "What can we do?"

"We have only one option," Edgar said, striding towards the radio station and the rising sun. "We have to wake up."

"So you think all of the Police Officers we've killed so far were already dead?" Ivy asked. Edgar nodded. "It's strange to think that this place had such a numerous law enforcement agency."

"Oh, they aren't part of the Galaxy Police Force," Edgar said off-handedly.

"They aren't?"

"No; they've lost who they once were and have been consumed by this place. That's what will happen to us if we stay here too long."

"Jesus fucking Christ," Michaela whispered. "That's horrifying."

"It's important," Ivy said as they neared the outer fence. "It gives us yet more information about how all this works. Midori was right; there's virtue in speculation, no matter how nebulous."

A shriek caught Ivy's attention; another of the Faceless was charging along the forest path towards her. She sighed heavily and hefted the swords. *I can barely stand,* she realised, blades trembling violently in her grip.

"Let me," Edgar said, and Ivy felt the familiar

stomach churning sensation of being body swapped as the bespectacled man took over their shared form. She staggered slightly, suddenly lighter than air and thrice as nimble.

Edgar took a few swift steps backwards, closing the distance to the radio station fence. He gently tossed the blades aside and adopted a fighting stance; where Ivy normally preferred firearms and Michaela was wedded to the Kitsune swords, Ed relied solely on the speed and strength of their body.

Ivy couldn't help but smile as he reached up and behind to firmly clasp the upright support pole of the fence in his hands. As the Faceless approached him, he hauled himself out of the range of its swiping fingers.

He took to pole dancing like a duck to water, Ivy thought, awed. She'd dabbled for fun, but Edgar had developed the skill to an extent that was downright freakish. He dropped on top of the Faceless, wrapping his legs over its shoulders and delivering punch after punch as he ploughed it into the ground.

He disengaged as soon as they hit the dirt, rolling back towards the fence as his assailant lay stunned on the floor. He scrambled back up the vertical pole, breaking several key structural supports as he climbed to the very top edge of the fence.

The Faceless was beginning to get to its feet as Edgar perched, agile as a cat, atop the fence. He leant forwards, shaking the frame hard as he did so. The remaining anchor points failed, sending the taut metal wire mesh crashing to the ground, accelerated by the addition of Edgar's body weight.

It hit the Faceless as it turned its featureless mask of skin to look at the approaching fence; the force of the impact allowed the metal wire to slice clean through it, separating the dismembered horror into neat cubes of meat as a now blood soaked Edgar landed artfully on the path.

"A sword is more efficient, you know," Michaela said softly, although she was clearly impressed. Edgar did not reply; instead he and Ivy both turned in the direction of the radio station as they heard a door open.

"Oh my god!" The woman who had just exited into the morning sunlight clapped a hand to her mouth when she saw the slick of gore between her and Edgar. "What the hell happened out here?"

"Skill issue," Edgar said casually, looking at the cubed viscera.

"What?" The woman, clearly exhausted and very confused, looked at him with puzzlement in her eyes.

"Hmm," Ed muttered, "people time."

Ivy nearly vomited as Edgar switched her back into their body; the salty, coppery scent of blood was almost overwhelming and her limbs trembled, both from exertion and the adrenaline comedown.

You have got to give me more warning!

"One of those police officers attacked us," Ivy said, picking up and sheathing the swords with shaking hands. "We had no choice. We aren't going to hurt you."

"Us?" the woman asked, looking past Ivy into the forest. "Are there more of you?"

Shit.

"There are about eight or so of us, but we got separated," Ivy replied, not being entirely untruthful.

"She probably doesn't know that she's dreaming," Michaela hissed, as if the woman would overhear her. "Make sure that you proceed with care!"

“My name is Ivy Livingston; I'm a psychiatric doctor working as part of a joint British and American taskforce. We're looking for several of our colleagues that have gone missing in this area over the past...” She paused for a moment, working out what she should say. “They went missing a little while ago. Have you heard about anyone from out of town passing through recently?”

“Only one that I can think of,” the woman said after a few seconds of contemplation. “Yeah, just the Scaredy Man; that's it.”

“Scaredy Man?” Ivy asked, raising an eyebrow in confusion. “That's an odd name.”

“He's an odd fella. Last I heard he was still down by the stream, in the old hunter's hide. He's English, too, if that's any help at all?”

“That sounds like it could be our man,” Ivy said, a small smile crossing her lips. *Some fucking luck at last.* “Is there somewhere safe we can go to regroup and wait for the rest of my team?”

“Sure, you can come to my place. There's a whole bunch of pens and poster board in the station if you wanna leave a sign for your friends.”

“Thank you,” Ivy said gratefully. “You're an absolute lifesaver.”

“Being kind doesn't cost a thing,” she said cheerfully.

“By the way, I didn't catch your name,” Ivy said, knowing full well what it would be.

“I'm Cecilia Sparrow, Sissy to my friends. I'm the night DJ here at the station.” She grinned at Ivy. “It's nice to see a new face; there have been some mighty weird things happening around here lately.”

“I'll bet,” Ivy muttered. She strode over the bloodied

fence, towards the station. “Is there somewhere inside that I can get cleaned up?”

“There's a little staff wash room; you should be able to get the worst off in there.” Sissy looked Ivy up and down as she walked past her. “It sure seems like you've had a hell of a night.”

“Sissy, you have no idea just how right you are.” She chuckled at the madness of it all. “Have you lived in Galaxy long?”

“All my life,” Sissy said with a smile. “I met my husband, Patryk, when he came to work at the Observatory, and my son was born in the town. My mother used to say that Galaxy had its own gravity; once you get here, you're here for good!

“She said that to Rusty when he was barely three hours old,” she said, her eyes misty with memory. “I remember her exact words, even now; *you'll never leave this place alive.* Such a morbid thing to say to a baby, but that was my mother for ya... Look at me, talking your ear off! Let's get you cleaned up.”

“We're going to die here, aren't we?” Michaela asked softly.

It's starting to look that way, Ivy thought, and Michaela burst into tears.

Chapter Twenty Two – Good For Nothing

Noor

"Dreams?" Midori scoffed once Noor had finished passing on Edgar's plan to her allies. "Is that the best she can come up with?"

"I must confess," Uncle said sombrely, "that as tempting an explanation as that is, I agree with Mistress Aoki. I do think some sort of experiment gone awry is what has caused all this chaos."

"I think Edgar is right," Noor said quietly. "It just feels correct."

"I think we should change direction," Midori said, pointing with her sword, "and head into the centre of town instead of towards the radio station. From there we can re-equip and rearm ourselves, commandeer a vehicle, and then strike out for the Applied Physics building."

"The plan was to meet at the radio station if we got separated!" Noor said angrily. "It was agreed upon before we even decided to bring you!"

"You are a junior operative, and we are hundreds of years your senior," the Kitsune said haughtily. "You will do as you are told, or we will leave you behind; is that understood?"

"We need to meet up with the others," Noor said, almost pleading. "They could need our help!"

"They're almost certainly dead already," Uncle whispered, staring into the middle distance. "We're all that's left, Noor."

"That isn't true! Edgar told me that everyone else is

still alive!"

"You had a dream," Midori replied nastily, "and we are not throwing away our lives on the wish fulfilment of some silly little girl. You will either follow us, Agent Turner, or we will leave you to die."

"I am not as worthless as you think I am!" Noor turned to Uncle, her face flushed. "Tell her!"

"You're talented, that much is certain," Uncle said, "but you're still just a human. There will be other Fates, one day."

This is all wrong, Noor realised as the Strix gave her a tearful look. *Something is happening here; something strange.* Her brain flashed back to her conversation with Edgar and the way that her mind had started to dwell on her darker, more disturbing thoughts and desires.

"Stop it, both of you!" Noor snapped, sending both of her companions staggering back a step or two. "This place is changing us, but only if we let it! Horace, you're turning into a fatalistic old man; that isn't who you are and you fucking know it! You would never consider letting Midori abandon me, nor would you discard Edgar's theory so quickly.

"As for giving up on Bert, well, I think you'd rather die than let your young Seeker down."

"But-" Midori began, but Noor rounded on her, eyes blazing with righteous fury.

"No." The Fate's voice resonated with power, more felt than heard, and the Kitsune froze in place. "You have forgotten why you're here, Midori. The threat of this place is insidious; it has robbed you of your goodness and left only a violent caricature in its place. You are a shadow of your former self."

Midori growled angrily and drew the longer of her

two swords. She stepped forward, slashing through the air at Noor. The blade hissed through the space between them, the lethal edge closing in, hurtling towards the young woman's face.

Noor did not even blink.

The katana halted, trembling slightly, millimetres from Noor's skin. Midori's eyes twitched and convulsed as her entire body was locked rigidly in place. The Fate's left hand was resting gently on the exposed skin of the Kitsune's neck.

Noor's pupils jiggled slightly as she rifled through Midori's memories, tossing the irrelevant ones aside with all the care of a burglar who would become an arsonist soon enough. She continued to search, not caring if the Kitsune was re-exposed to some of her most nightmarish experiences as she did so, until she found what she was looking for. She took the memory of a smiling younger man, dressed in a stylish suit with a Ministry issue revolver dangling lazily from his hand, and flooded Midori's mind with it.

The man's face filled every nook and cranny of the Kitsune's brain, leaving her with absolutely nowhere to hide.

"This is why you are here!" Noor's voice thundered through the still morning air. "This is who you have come to save! What is his name, Midori?"

"I... I don't remember," moaned the Kitsune, dropping the sword to the ground and falling to her knees. She clutched her hands to her head in agony. "I don't remember!"

"That's not good enough," Noor said sharply. She found yet more memories and continued her mental onslaught.

"Please," Midori begged tearfully, "please stop!"

"You will remember why you are here," she said in a threatening monotone, "or I will burn your brain out of your fucking head."

"It hurts!" Midori screamed, as beads of blood began to well up in the corners of her eyes.

"It stops when you remember, or when you die. You are free to choose."

"I can't!"

"What is his name?" Noor's hand tightened around Midori's throat as the Kitsune started to go limp. *I should stop before I kill her,* Noor thought dimly, but she was swept up in the unrelenting, intoxicating tide of her own power.

"I... I can't..." Midori mumbled as her face slackened and saliva dribbled out of her mouth.

"TELL ME HIS NAME!" Noor screamed. The images that flashed through Midori's mind became an incomprehensible strobe of one man's face over the years. "TELL ME!"

"I... urgh... Fra..." She tried to get the words out of her quivering lips. "Francis! Francis Marsh, FRANCIS MARSH!"

Noor blinked slightly, suddenly struck by the urge to just kill the vile woman before her once and for all, but Uncle's voice pulled her back to herself.

"For heaven's sake, Noor, let her go!"

She shook her head, as if waking from a nightmare, and released Midori. The Kitsune fell backwards into a sobbing heap and crawled away from the Fate as quickly as she could. Noor reached out to help her to her feet, but Midori slashed at her with vicious claws and growled savagely.

"Don't you ever touch me again, you fucking monster!"

Before Noor could respond, there was a crashing sound in the trees nearby. She turned around in time to see Agent Gillespie, battered, bruised, and exhausted, stagger out of the undergrowth, followed by an impossibly beautiful woman, with olive skin and long tresses of dark hair, fully nude except for an ornate hawthorn necklace.

There's something strangely familiar about her, Noor thought, but Bert, looking at the three of them in bewilderment, got his words out first.

"What the fuck is going on here?"

"It's good to see you, young Bert," Uncle said after a few heartbeats of silence. He looked at the woman, his face a mixture of sympathy and concern. "Thank you for saving my Seeker, Agent Marsh; I know this can't have been easy for you."

"Mallory!?" Noor asked, her jaw dropping as she realised the woman was her fellow Ministry Agent. "What happened to you?"

The words were barely out of her mouth as Mallory crossed the clearing, snatching a handgun from Bert's belt and pressing it hard underneath her chin. Instead of fear, however, Noor felt a strange glittery sense of calm descend upon her; all she could think about was how appealing and beautiful Mallory was.

"Noor, if you bring up how I look again, I'm going to blow your fucking head off!" His voice was strangely musical, but he still growled out the words. Noor, completely besotted at this point and captivated by the all-consuming scent of bluebells and ancient woodland, reached up to take the gun out of his hand.

"It's okay, Mallory," she murmured dreamily as she fumbled for the weapon, "I'll do it myself if you want.

You don't need to shoot me, I'd be glad to do it for you."

"Mind your glamour, son," Uncle said firmly as he pulled Mallory away from Noor. It took a few moments for her head to clear, but when it did she looked at him with unrestrained terror. Uncle placed a comforting hand on her shoulder and explained. "Agent Marsh comes from a very old bloodline of Dryads; he's clearly tapped into that to survive what he and Bert encountered out there, much as we did with the bear."

He looked at her pointedly before flicking his gaze to the still unsteady Midori for a fraction of a second.

"We all have hidden depths, Noor; that's what makes us special, and also dangerous." He let go of her shoulder and his tone grew a little firmer. "Sometimes the courteous thing to do is not mention the things we do to survive. Do you follow me?"

"I understand," Noor said, grateful for his silence. She turned to Mallory and slipped off her jacket, before handing it to him. "Take this, you must be chilly."

"Thank you," Mallory said quietly, slipping the garment on. "I'm sorry I threatened you; this has been a pretty awful day for me."

"I can't even imagine. For what it's worth, I'm glad that you're alive, though." She looked at the treeline; only a few hundred metres away was the ravaged corpse of Professor Skullbone. "We lost Harold last night. A bear took him."

"Have you seen any of the Police Officers?" Bert asked.

"No," Uncle replied. "Not helpful to the cause?"

"They don't have faces," Mallory said with a

shudder. “Just smooth, featureless skin and the only sound they make is this godawful siren shriek; this whole place is like a-”

“A nightmare?” Noor asked.

“What do you know?” Mallory responded, immediately rounding on her. His eyes were deeply distracting and Noor found that she had to look over his shoulder to even formulate a reply.

“Edgar has a theory that this is someone's dream of Galaxy, instead of the town itself,” Noor said after a moment to gather her thoughts. “He thinks that someone in the town is the *dreamer* or whatever, and we need to find that person to undo all of this.”

“Ed's alive?” Mallory said with a smile, and Noor nodded. “Where is he?”

“He was last heading towards the radio station with Ivy and Michaela, but he said not to follow him there; he'll let me know where to meet him and-” Noor stopped in the middle of her sentence, suddenly lost in the complex web of the Tangle.

“Noor?” Mallory asked. “Are you alright?”

“We have to follow the evening songbird,” Noor murmured, barely aware of what she was saying. “If we follow it home, it will lead us out of the birdcage.”

“That sounds like fucking gibberish to me,” Bert said with a nervous laugh, “so it's probably the most important thing I'm ever gonna hear, right, Uncle?”

“Spoken with true wisdom, Bert.” Uncle grinned broadly at him, before turning back to Noor. “Are you okay?”

“Yes,” she said after a moment of hesitation, “I think I will be.”

“Do you have any idea where we can find this evening songbird?” Mallory asked.

"I'm afraid not," Noor said, "but I got the feeling that it will find us rather than the other way around."

"Should we just wait here?" Midori asked. Her voice was small, uncertain, and she watched Noor with intensely suspicious eyes.

"No. Edgar said that we have to find the dreamer; we should head for the town and start interviewing people."

"That's where we've just come from," Mallory said. "The town is crawling with the Faceless cops."

"That's where we need to go," Noor said, sighing heavily. "Edgar said that we don't have much time to wake up, or we're going to die here."

"But those police officers are inhuman!" Bert said nervously.

"They might be monsters," Noor said as she helped a cautious Midori to her feet, "but so are we."

Chapter Twenty Three – The Woman on the Radio

Ivy

"I feel so much better now that I'm not covered in blood," Ivy said as she stepped out of the small bathroom.

"Blood?" Sissy said, raising her eyebrow in confusion. "That time of the month, huh?"

Well, that's concerning. She looked Sissy in the eye, but the radio presenter's face was completely serious.

"It isn't unexpected, though. Something must be maintaining the illusion, or else they'd have seen through the inconsistencies by now." Edgar spoke calmly as he leant against the wall of the sound booth; he'd waited outside whilst Ivy had cleaned herself up, but Michaela had given her no such privacy.

"Do you remember what we talked about before I popped into the bathroom?" Ivy asked cautiously, expecting Sissy to have absolutely no memory of what they'd agreed on.

"Of course I do, silly! I was gonna take you down to meet the Scaredy Man; if he's still down by the stream, that is." She walked over to a locked cabinet and fumbled for a moment with a small set of keys before taking out a Winchester Model 1886 lever action rifle. "I know you Brits can get a bit funny about guns, but this is bear country and I'd rather have it and not need it, than need it and get torn to pieces because I didn't have it."

"I'd personally go with the Marlin 1895 SBL..." Ivy

began before trailing off into awkward silence. *That gun hasn't been invented yet,* she realised. “Ignore me, I'm getting confused with something a friend must've told me years ago.”

“Well, just as long as you're not gonna be jumpy if I have to use this thing,” Sissy said with a laugh. “Those are mighty fine swords you've got there; did your father serve in the Pacific?”

“I don't know my father,” Ivy replied quietly. “These were given to me by a... a friend. She trained me in their use and, even if I say so myself, I'm quite good with them.”

“Then I guess we'll make quite a team!” Sissy said with a grin. “My Daddy taught me to shoot when I was just a girl. He said it was important that I knew how to look out for myself. I'm sure he's just itching to teach Rusty, my son, any day now.”

“I learned to shoot when I was young too,” Ivy said as they started to walk back towards the front door of the station.

“Too young,” Michaela said darkly, looking back at the radio booth. “Are we going to do this or not?”

Ivy froze in place, torn between the desire to change the past, however fruitless that might turn out to be, and to rescue her friends. She looked at Edgar, who just shook his head solemnly.

“It's been almost forty years, Ivy,” he said sadly. “None of this is real; changing things in a dream won't do a thing to help anyone on Betony Island.”

“But-” she started to say quietly.

“No!” Edgar said sharply. “Put it out of your mind, right now. This place is affected by the ghosts we bring with us; do not pull Lamplight into this town.”

“He's right,” Michaela said with a defeated sigh.

"We've got enough on our plate without dragging up the nightmares of the past. It was never more than a fool's hope, but it sustained us when we needed it. Let's just leave it at that."

"Dr Livingston, are you alright?" Sissy asked, peering closely at Ivy's face.

"Yes, sorry." Ivy tried to give her a reassuring smile. "I was just wool gathering for a moment."

"You, uh, you're crying," Sissy said before carefully wiping the tears from Ivy's cheeks. "Are you certain that you're doing okay?"

"I promise, I'm fine. I was just making my peace with something that happened a while ago." Ivy deftly tucked her pistols into her belt at the small of her back as Sissy dried her tears. *No sense making things even weirder for her.* "Is it far to the hunter's hide?"

"About two hours' worth of hiking, if you're feeling fit, but mostly downhill though, which is a blessing." She chuckled as she opened the main door of the radio station. "Coming back, however, not so much."

Ivy braced herself for the carnage that awaited them outside, but when she stepped into the morning sunlight, nothing could have prepared her for what she saw.

"What the fuck?" she said with a gasp.

"What's wrong, Ivy?" Sissy asked, but the Ministry Agent was too stunned to reply.

The fence was standing once again and the shredded corpse was nowhere to be found.

"Keep an eye on her," Michaela said, and Edgar nodded in agreement. Ivy turned to face the cheerful disc jockey, who was already gesturing towards the path through the woods.

"Come on, Doc," she said as she started walking,

“we've got a way to go and the going is always easier before noon.”

“Yes, of course. I'm coming.” Ivy trotted to catch up and Sissy chuckled once again. “What's so funny?”

“You are! You're a strange one, Ivy Livingston, and I've seen my fair share of them throughout the years.” She nudged Ivy playfully in the ribs. “Honestly, the look on your face! Anyone would think that you'd seen a ghost!”

“So,” Ivy said after half an hour of walking, “tell me about life here in Galaxy.”

“What do you want to know about it?” Sissy said after taking a swig from a wide mouthed canteen. She offered it to Ivy, who gratefully took a gulp.

“That's not actually hydrating you,” Edgar muttered, but she did her best to ignore him.

“It's a small town up in the mountains; what do people actually do up here?”

“Well, a fair few people work at the various shops and whatnot in the town. My mother used to work at Galaxy Hospital, although it's more of an old maids' ward than anything else.” She smiled at the thought. “It's relaxing up here, so people come here to heal. I like to think that it helps them, but at least the ones that don't make it die somewhere peaceful. Is that a wicked thing to say?”

“I don't think so. I've seen plenty of people die badly over the years; a clean, dignified death is sometimes the only positive thing a person has left.”

“Ain't that the truth.” Sissy took a moment to breathe in the mountain air. “There used to be a mine, but that was before my time. Then the government or whoever came in and built the Galaxy Applied Physics laboratory on top of the old shaft; they say that there's a maze of tunnels and rooms spread out throughout the mountains, full of god knows what.

"Then there's the Observatory, where my Patryk works. He's an astrophysicist." She smiled proudly. "We're a certified Dark Sky Site, so we get some of the best astronomers this side of Hawaii passing through. I think that about sums it up, really, although it does give us one of the highest densities of scientists per capita in the entire country, if not the world.

"It isn't much, but it's a claim to fame." She winked at Ivy. "The Observatory is mostly manned by night owls, like myself, so I've always got plenty of listeners for my overnight show."

"It sounds idyllic," Ivy said, and she meant it.

"It really is." She peered up at the cloudless sky. "Sometimes I wish I could just enjoy these sunny mornings forever."

Be careful what you wish for.

"I've known a few physicists in my time," Ivy said, trying her best to be conversational instead of interrogative, "and I can't think of anything that they'd need an old mine for. What sort of things do they get up to at the lab?"

"Beats me," Sissy said with a shrug, "but I've heard all kinds of rumours over the years."

"Do tell."

"Well, Patryk could probably explain some of these better than me," she said, smiling as she held court, "but the one that always stuck out to me was that they were trying to build a portal to another dimension."

"Like a gateway between universes?" Ivy asked, intrigued. Sissy nodded.

"There was no False Cardinal or any other sign of a

thin place on the map," Edgar said.

"What else?" Ivy prompted.

"Pat told me something about neutrino research, but it went over my head. Apparently you'd need something deep for that."

"You would," Ivy replied. "Project Poltergeist took place in the twenties and thirties, and that was really deep underground."

"I thought you were a medical doctor?" Sissy asked, clearly impressed.

"I'm a generalist," Ivy said with deliberate vagueness, and Michaela snickered slightly. "I think the rocks around here are too volcanic for a neutrino detector, though."

"Hell, maybe you should be the one telling me what's what!" She stretched her arms and slowed down slightly. "I did hear from one of the wives of one of the scientists that they were trying to build some sort of time machine from an artificial black hole; they sent a letter to the radio station and everything."

Now that is more promising. Michaela nodded; a black hole's time dilation would certainly explain the bizarre things they were experiencing. Edgar, however, remained unconvinced.

"I still think that you're looking for too literal an explanation for what's happening here," he chastised. "This *is* a dream, after all; things don't have to make sense in the same way."

"Sissy," Ivy said after a moment of contemplation, "I have a bit of a weird question for you."

"I'm a night DJ," she said, "I guarantee it won't be the weirdest I've ever had."

"Have you ever noticed anyone in Galaxy that was a

bit strange?"

"Strange how?"

"Did you ever hear about anyone that..." Ivy took a deep breath, "that had special powers?"

"Such as?" Sissy asked, not unkindly.

In for a penny, in for a pound.

"I know someone who can turn invisible," Ivy said softly. "Another one of my friends can see things before they happen, and I can sometimes read people's thoughts, although it isn't as easy as it sounds. Have you ever encountered anyone like that?"

Sissy stopped walking, the dappled sunlight playing on her face in a delicate pattern as the morning breeze stirred the branches of the trees. She seemed deep in thought, and Ivy wondered if she had pushed the woman too far and too fast.

"You're being serious, aren't you?"

"I am."

"I can't say that I've ever seen anything myself," Sissy said, "but I've heard too many stories from too many people in my time to doubt you."

"You really believe me?" Ivy asked, shocked.

"I do."

I'm going to tell her, Ivy decided.

"Don't!" Edgar said, but before the Séance could reveal the situation in Galaxy to the kindly disc jockey, there was the sound of movement from the treeline. Ivy and Sissy both turned sharply to see a man skulking in the bushes.

He wore a tattered ghillie suit, patched with local flora and debris, and his grey hair was matted and tangled. His lined face was gaunt and his mouth was hidden by an equally grey and shaggy beard. He twitched fearfully and cowered as the two women looked on, but when Ivy caught sight of his eyes, bright and youthful in a sunken, elderly face, there was no doubting who he was.

"Francis Marsh?" Ivy asked, and the Scaredy Man nodded hesitantly. "My name is Ivy Livingston; I'm from the Ministry and I came here with your brother."

"Mallory?" he croaked, his voice hoarse from disuse.

"Yes." Ivy smiled warmly at him. "We've come to rescue you."

"He's here? In Galaxy?"

"He is."

Francis shook his head sadly as he began to weep. "Then he is doomed as well."

Chapter Twenty Four – Better Off Dead

Mallory

"I can't believe we're heading back to town," Bert muttered as they trudged through the darkening forest. "We barely even got out alive last time!"

"We've got reinforcements now," Mallory said, shivering slightly. He pulled the borrowed jacket and makeshift kilt tight around him. "I'm more concerned about dying of exposure before we get a chance to find any real clothes."

"Do you think Noor really is communicating with Dr Livingston?" Bert whispered, clearly afraid that Agent Turner would hear him.

"She's talking to Edgar," Mallory corrected, "and yes, I think she is. He's one of the most capable agents I've ever had the privilege to work with, and he's also one of my closest friends. If Ed is on to something, then we're in luck."

"It must be nice to have such faith in your friends."

"Don't you trust Horace?" Mallory asked, carefully picking his way through a particularly thorny patch of undergrowth. *I would kill for a decent pair of shoes.*

"I trust him, and he's taught me so much, but I wouldn't exactly call us friends." There was a pause that tugged at Mallory's heartstrings. "I don't really have any friends, to tell the truth; I've always been a bit of a loner. I guess it comes with the territory."

"It doesn't have to," Mallory said quietly. He reached out and took Agent Gillespie's hand in his. "I'd call you my friend, Bert, if you'll have me?"

"It would be an honour, Mallory." He squeezed the

other man's hand affectionately. “What are we gonna do if we run into more of the Faceless? Are you gonna hit them with your dryad spell again?”

“No,” Mallory said. “I don't think I've got any more in me. In fact, I'm amazed that I survived the last time. We'll put Horace and Midori up front; they're both highly capable fighters and they should keep us safe.

“I'm kind of hoping that Noor will see any trouble coming from a mile away and that her songbird will find us sooner rather than later. Sound like a plan?”

“It sure does.” There was a lengthy time of walking in silence before Bert spoke up once again. “Thank you, by the way, for saving me.”

“It's what anyone would've done,” Mallory said, flushing a little. “Keeping people alive when you can isn't a noble thing, Bert; it's the bare fucking minimum.”

“Still, I've met too many people in my time who wouldn't have given me a second thought. You're a good man, Mallory.” He stumbled over a root and swore loudly. “Why is it so fucking dark out here?”

“It's a designated Dark Sky Site,” Mallory said, thinking back to the map. “I don't think there are any street lights for almost twenty five miles in any direction, and the mountains block out any residual light pollution from further away.

“It's a beautiful place to live.”

“Yeah, but it's a shitty place to die,” Bert muttered.

“I doubt that many people do.”

“You'd be surprised,” Bert said softly. Mallory raised an eyebrow in the gloom, and he went on. “Galaxy Community Hospital was originally for the locals and people convalescing from illnesses such as tuberculosis, but in the ten years or so before the Easy appeared, the whole thing changed. Sure, it still served the locals as and when they needed it, but it became more of a hospice than a hospital."

"I didn't know that," Mallory said softly. "It sounds like this place is steeped in death."

"It sure is." Bert looked at him, his eyes wide. "Can't you feel it in the air?"

"Death?"

"Grief. The whole forest is fucking rank with it." He shuddered. "Not the healthy kind, either, but the kind of stifled, choked grief that kills you in your bed in the early hours of the morning."

"It seems almost cruel to condemn somewhere so beautiful to become a living mausoleum." Mallory said. He realised that he was still holding Bert's hand, but he did not let go.

"That's mountain country for you," Bert said, "especially the old mining towns. Accidents, recessions, dried up veins; so many things can kill a community stone dead. The West is built on the bones of the desperate and the hopeful alike."

"Do you write, Bert?" Mallory asked.

"Poetry," Agent Gillespie confirmed. "I wish that I could have made a living out of it, but I have a powerful need to eat every so often. I hear that you're a painter."

"I am."

"You've got artistic talent, and you come from old money; why did you join up with the Ministry?"

"When it comes to the Ministry, you're either policing others or getting policed yourself; I saw what they did to my brother and decided that I'd rather be the one kicking in the door. I wish it wasn't that way, but they don't give you any choice."

"It's that bad?"

"They will never stop hunting you," Mallory said sadly.

"Have you ever thought about running away?" Bert asked.

"I can't," Mallory said. "I'm too tied to the land, both literally and figuratively." *But you have, haven't you?* "I've got someone close to me on the inside, though. She's a good person and I think she's going to change things for the better."

"Faith in your friends, once again," Bert said with a smile.

"I've got faith in you, too." Mallory was about to continue when Midori spoke up.

"We're nearing the outskirts of town," she said sharply. "We should examine our weapons and redistribute what we have."

"I'm hoping we won't have to fight," Mallory said.

"You are free to hope for the best," Midori said softly, "but I will plan for the worst."

"Here," Bert said as he handed Mallory his service weapon. "You'll need this."

"You're a better shot than I am, Bert, and..." Mallory trailed off as he looked at Agent Gillespie. Although the totality of his face was impenetrable to him, his body language was not. "Bert, what's wrong?"

"I, uh, I don't think I should have this any longer." He pushed Mallory's fingers closed around the gun before taking a step back. "I've been feeling a bit off for a while; I was hoping that it would pass, but it's only got worse."

"What are you talking about?" Midori said sharply as Noor and Uncle joined them. "We're wasting precious time!"

"It's taking you, isn't it?" Mallory asked, and Bert nodded solemnly.

"Tell us everything you can!" Uncle said forcefully. "We need all the information we can get!"

"I have to tell her," Bert said quietly. "I don't know who or what, but I know I need to. It's like a splinter in my mind, digging deeper and deeper, getting louder and more forceful with every passing second."

He dropped to his knees, trembling softly.

"I'm forgetting who I am. I can't remember my family; their names, their faces, they're all gone." He let out a shuddering sob. "I'm nobody; just an empty shell of a person."

He sobbed again and this time his voice was tinged with the faintest shriek of a police siren.

"You must tell us more!" Uncle demanded. He grabbed Bert's shoulders and shook him violently. "Focus! Our lives depend on it!"

"Who am I?" Bert sobbed, pawing at his face. His features were beginning to fade, and even though Mallory couldn't see it happening, the young man's actions were evidence enough. He opened his mouth and the undulating wail of a siren was unmistakable. "I don't want to go!"

"Your name is Albert Gillespie, but you're Bert to everyone that matters," Mallory said as he took the terrified man's hands in his. "You wanted a chocolate phosphate at the drug store, and you're not cut out for all this gumshoe work!"

Bert continued to twitch and moan. Uncle tried to push Mallory aside to continue his interrogation, but the Artist turned to him and unleashed the full force of the Master's power on him.

"Get away from him."

Mallory's words struck everyone around him like a tidal wave, forcing them all to stagger backwards. In any normal moment, he would have been terrified of his own power, but instead he turned his attention back to Agent Gillespie.

"I'm sorry, Bert," he said tenderly as he took the man in his arms. "I promised I would protect you, but I failed."

"Thank... Thank you, Mallory," Bert managed to croak, through his agony.

"But I didn't save you!" Mallory yelled tearfully.

"Th-thank you for being my friend." Bert took Mallory's hand tightly in his. "Let me go."

Mallory didn't say anything in response. Instead, he let out a shuddering sob before he shot Bert. He felt the young Bureau Agent go limp in his arms, but he still held him, frozen in place with sorrow.

"Why did you do that?" Uncle roared. "We could have used him to learn more about-"

His words were cut short as Mallory shot him in the mouth.

Silence hung in the air as day faded into night.

Midori and Noor hung back as Mallory set about burying Bert and burning Uncle's body. He took the clothes from the latter, pleased to be warm once again. He silently handed both his Jack and Bert's service weapon to Midori.

"What am I supposed to do with these?" she asked.

"You wanted to take an inventory of our armaments, so do so." Mallory's voice was flat and his spirit was broken. "We still have to find my brother, and that means going into town."

"But there's only three of us!" Noor said nervously.

“What if we get separated or one of us gets hurt?”

“Then we die.” Mallory's words were matter-of-fact. “If we go into town, there's a chance that we get out of this. If we stay here, we definitely die.”

“Or we turn into one of those things,” Midori muttered. Mallory nodded. “It's your mission, Agent Marsh; if you say we're heading into Galaxy, then that's where I'll go.”

“Noor?” Mallory asked, looking over at her with his face illuminated by the firelight. “Are you in, or are we leaving you behind?”

“I'm coming,” she said after a moment of hesitation. “I do have a question, though.”

“Ask away.”

“How did you know how to kill him?” Noor asked, gesturing at Uncle's blazing remains.

“I had a case in the summer that dealt with creatures called Nightwalkers; they were vampires, for all intents and purposes.” He frowned at the memory. “I nearly died, and nearly got my team killed. We had some downtime afterwards, so I started researching into everything vampire adjacent that I could.

“Striges were part of that research.” He chuckled darkly. “Their power lies in their words, so if you shoot or stab them in the mouth mid-sentence it kills them outright. It is best to burn the body, though, just to make sure.”

“But his powers-” Midori began, but Mallory cut her off.

“They don't work on me.” He stared at her. *I wonder if she looks shocked?* “Their magic comes from their gaze; if you look upon their face, they have power over you.”

“It's almost as if you were uniquely set up to kill

him," Midori said, mulling it over. "I'd be willing to wager that Desai requested his presence on this mission."

"You'd win that bet," Mallory said, getting to his feet. "I'd wondered about that myself. Do you think he's making a play for the Bureau?"

"I would," Midori said, handing the pistols back to Mallory, "but I'm a Kitsune; treachery is what I do."

"Then I'm glad you're on our side," Mallory said with a playful grin.

"For now," she responded, her voice equal parts mirth and threat. Mallory extended a hand to Noor.

"Are you ready?" he asked. She nodded and took his hand. "Then let's head into town and find out what the fuck is happening here."

Chapter Twenty Five – The Old Maids' Ward

Noor

"It's so dark," Noor murmured as they finally reached the outskirts of the town. "Not one street light."

"You can see the comet so clearly!" Mallory whispered, pointing at the celestial traveller. "Even with everything that's happened, I'm still glad that I got to see it."

"I've never seen so many stars in my life," Noor said, craning her neck back to look at the sky above them.

"Keep your eyes on the streets," Midori hissed, her clawed hands resting on the handles of her swords. "If we run into any resistance, we hide, flee, and then fight, in that order."

"Are we really that low on ammunition?" Mallory asked, and she nodded curtly.

Hide, Noor thought, *I can do that.*

She took a deep breath.

If I could survive the Piper and her rats, I can survive this.

"Are you sure that you don't want a weapon?" Mallory asked softly as he moved next to her.

"I don't know how to use one," she admitted, "and I'm not sure I'd have the stomach for it even if I did."

Midori muttered something in response, but Noor didn't hear her. She was about to ask her to repeat herself when something at the edge of her hearing caught her attention.

"Stop!" she hissed. Mallory and Midori froze in place, hugging the left side of the narrow avenue. Noor strained her ears, and the sound came again.

Footsteps.

Running footsteps; dozens of them. She opened her mouth to alert her friends when the sirens began, pouring through the air from all around them. *There must be loads of them!*

The first Faceless police officer rounded the street less than ten seconds later, running at full pelt towards the three Ministry Agents. Mallory and Midori both bolted down a nearby alley, but Noor froze in place, paralysed by fear.

"Noor, come on!" Mallory called, but he did not wait for her.

Oh fuck, she thought, her mind flooded with panic, *I'm going to die.*

The first police officer was joined by dozens more as they flowed around the corner like a pale, featureless flood of flesh. Her heart thundered in her ears as she looked around frantically for somewhere to hide. The leading Faceless was almost upon her, and a scream was forcing its way up her throat as her hands trembled uselessly by her sides.

Its blank face was inches from her when she blurted out the words that saved her life.

"I live here!" Her voice was nervous and shrill, but the Faceless froze in place. "I've always lived here, you can just ignore me!"

Her gift gave power to her lie, and she felt herself subconsciously write herself into the history of both the Faceless police officer and the town itself. The horrific thing stood before her for a few seconds before politely tipping its hat and taking off down the alley in pursuit of Mallory and Midori.

How the fuck did I just do that? Noor wondered as the other Faceless parted around her like a river around a rock. She closed her eyes and tried to let the torrent of nightmarish creatures pass her by like a half-remembered dream.

"I hope Mallory and Midori make it," she said once she was alone in the street once again. She took a deep breath and looked towards the heart of Galaxy. A few windows glowed gently as light escaped around the edges of the blackout curtains the residents used.

All the curtains were issued by the Observatory, Noor thought, suddenly certain that she was right even though she had no way of knowing that information. *This is a strange gift, indeed.*

"There's so much town to search through," she said as she began to walk down the deserted road, "how will I even know where to start?"

She felt the distant, wild mass of the Tangle stirring as she spoke, and a small smile crossed her face. *I don't need to know,* she realised, *because the universe is going to show me.*

The air was surprisingly warm for such a high altitude and the weather was unseasonably clear for a March night. Noor was beginning to enjoy the solitude of the town; the endless echoing of her footsteps the only sound for miles, save the distant gentle creak of the trees.

I think I finally understand why people go for nighttime drives, she thought with a smile. *Something stylish, ideally with the top down, with the wind in my hair and good music on the radio; maybe one of*

Patryk's tapes, so Rusty can fall asleep.

She stopped dead in her tracks.

"Who the fuck is Patryk?" she asked the empty street. A shiver ran down her spine as she spoke and she realised that whatever it was she'd tapped into, it was important. Noor took a moment to mentally file away the thoughts she'd been having before looking more closely at where she was.

"Galaxy Community Hospital," she said. "Maybe I had that thought here for a reason."

She tried the front door and was surprised to find it unlocked.

"Hello?" Noor called as she carefully made her way into the dimly lit foyer. "Is anyone here?"

There was no response.

The reception desk was unmanned, and a single green shaded lamp twinkled in the gloom, illuminating the stack of patient files that teetered unsteadily beneath it. As Noor moved forward, a glimmer to her right caught her attention; the reflection of the lamp on the glass of a picture frame.

Interesting, she thought as she peered at it. *These must be the staff.*

She muttered the names of the doctors and nurses that were scribbled in untidy handwriting at the bottom of the image, almost without thinking, until one made her stop short.

"Kayleigh Sparrow, Head Nurse," she said. "Sparrow; why is that name familiar?"

She shook her head to clear it, hoping that the Tangle would provide more details, but no elucidation came. She sighed heavily and let it go, continuing down the list of names. She only got through four more staff members before a second name caused everything to click into place.

"Cecilia 'Sissy' Sparrow, Candy Striper," she exclaimed. The woman in the striped outfit was clearly the daughter of the head nurse; perhaps she had volunteered at her mother's insistence? "Sissy Sparrow... wait, you're the woman on the radio! I guess you didn't have your mother's calling..."

Noor was about to continue reading off names when a white light burned into life on a board behind the reception desk and the gentle ding of a bell filled the air. She peered across the dingy space, straining her eyes to read the words alongside the light as the bell rang once more.

"Palliative Care," she murmured. She walked over towards the stairs and studied the map on the wall. "Third floor, through the Women's Long Stay Ward."

I could take the lift, she thought, but the occasional flicker of the electric lamp made her decide against it. *I don't want to get stuck, especially not here.*

She took a deep breath and started up the stairs. As she climbed step after step, floor after floor, a question began to form in the back of her mind.

What the fuck am I going to find up there?

The door to the Women's Long Stay Ward was closed when she reached it. The visiting hours were stencilled on to the frosted glass, but were far too faded to read. In her entire journey through the hospital, Noor had not seen another soul.

"Where the fuck is everyone?" she wondered aloud. "Have they all been turned into those Faceless Police Officers?"

She hesitated for a moment, her hand trembling fearfully in front of the door; what if she stepped into this room and couldn't get out?

Maybe I should just go and find the others, she thought as she took a tentative step backwards. *After all, Edgar told me to canvas the residents of the town, not go poking around an abandoned hospital; isn't that what I should be doing?*

She was halfway back to the stairs when the call bell dinged once again, this time more urgently. The sound stopped her mid stride, trapping her halfway between fear and conscience.

What if someone needs help?

She took a shuddering breath, only now realising just how terrified she really was.

Am I the sort of person to just leave someone in need?

Paralysed by indecision, she wondered aloud at what her friends would do.

"Elsie would leave," she said as she took a step forwards, but her stomach sank at her next words. "Shy would've already been through the door, though, and I know he would never forgive me for walking away."

Elsie came for you when Finley's men kidnapped you, said a little voice in the back of her head. *She's a better person than you give her credit for; maybe because it makes you feel lesser?*

"I am a good person," Noor said, her voice cracking with emotion. "I help people!"

Then prove it.

She turned on her heel and strode towards the Long Stay Ward, shoving the door open as she reached it. The heavy wood and frosted glass clanged against a trolley as she entered the room, making her jump.

It took her eyes a moment to adjust to the soft amber

glow that suffused the ward, but she was soon able to make out the thin, frail forms that huddled in the beds, their bodies swamped by blankets and bedclothes. The patients were old and fragile, and Noor moved forwards quietly; a part of her was afraid that the slightest noise would cause the delicate women to shatter.

Heart monitors beeped and ventilators pumped as the residents of the ward slept, their chests rising and falling, almost imperceptibly so. In fact, if it had not been for the machines keeping track of their vitals, Noor would've assumed that the patients were all dead.

The call bell rang out and a light blinked on, bright as a lighthouse, above a door at the end of the ward. Noor didn't need to read the words on the whitewashed wood to know what lingered behind it; Palliative Care, the realm of those already doomed.

I wonder if everyone in here will be moved into there soon enough? She shuddered slightly. *This entire town is drowning in death.*

Noor turned the handle as soon as she reached the pale door, but it didn't budge. The bell dinged again, sharper and more insistent as she threw her weight against the wood; the locked door did not so much as rattle.

"Why is it locked?" she muttered, looking down at the keyhole. She bent down to peer through it, but it was blocked with something. She scrabbled for a moment before her fingernails caught on a sliver of fabric. She pulled it out, her blood running cold as she did so.

The call light flashed once again, illuminating the pink and white of a candy striper's uniform. Noor stepped back from the pale door as a heavy thud reverberated through the air, followed by another and another; something was pounding on the wood, desperate to be let out.

She turned to flee, but froze when she noticed that an extra hospital bed, empty but neatly made, stood in the centre of the room. She took a tentative step towards it, and picked up the patient chart attached to it, hoping that it would give her some clue to the identity of the dreamer at the centre of all this.

"Patient name; Noor Turner," she whispered as a chill ran up her spine, "Place of Birth; Galaxy, Oregon."

The chart trembled in her hands.

"What have I done?" She looked back at the bed; where the covers had previously been neatly drawn, they were now pulled back invitingly, as if welcoming her home. She dropped the chart in shock, and her eyes grew wide when she caught sight of her hands.

They were withered, old, and studded with liver spots. She reached up to touch her face and felt the lines of age that had marked and weathered her once youthful skin.

I'm old, she realised, horror filling her heart. *I don't want to die here!*

Noor screamed in terror and ran for her life.

<u>**Chapter Twenty Six** – Seeing the Wood for the Trees</u>

Mallory

Why is nothing ever easy?

Mallory panted as he and Midori left Noor standing, still as a statue, on the main street of the town. He hoped that she would be alright, but he was in far too much peril to give her more than a passing thought.

The Kitsune was slightly faster than he was, even with his Dryad heritage, and her senses were keener too; it made sense to let her lead the way. He clicked the safety off both the pistols he carried, preparing to make a last stand if the situation called for it.

There's no way that Francis is still alive, he realised sadly as they continued to run. He could feel the despair building in his heart, but he refused to give in to its siren song. *I might have one last dance in me,* he thought, *maybe just enough to allow Midori to escape.*

He was about to voice his desperate plan when they rounded a corner and found themselves in a dead end; stark brickwork, without windows or doors, hemmed them in on all sides. Mallory aimed his guns at the onrushing tide of Faceless, but never got to pull the triggers.

Instead, a green haze rushed around both Ministry Agents, obscuring and disguising them from their pursuers. The Faceless rushed towards them and Mallory almost cried out, but Midori put one arm around his neck and a clawed finger to his lips.

They can't see us, he realised, *but they might be able*

to hear us.

Mallory held his breath and hoped that the thundering of his heartbeat was localised only to his ears. He felt his panic rising, so he closed his eyes and thought of those that he loved. Thaddeus's smiling face, the softness of Jess's skin, and the cloying smell of liquorice that accompanied Teaser Malarkey wherever she went; the signs and signifiers of his family.

I am chosen by many, he thought, growing calmer by the second, *and today I choose to live.*

He opened his eyes to find that most of the Faceless had departed; only the lumbering giant with the Sheriff's badge remained. Mallory watched him for a minute or two; he moved differently from the others, with more purpose and less frantic flailing.

He's more of a person, he realised, *more of his old self, perhaps?*

And then it hit him and he gasped at the obviousness of it all.

The Sheriff's featureless face snapped round to look in their direction, and he began to stride towards them. At the same time, Midori's grip around his throat tightened, preventing Mallory from making any further noise.

She stepped to the left, dragging Mallory with her, their footsteps muffled but not silent. Luckily, the heavy footfalls of the Sheriff's work boots drowned out theirs and they were able to slip away as he searched for them. Midori pushed the Artist against one of the walls and covered his mouth with her hand.

"If you make so much as a whimper," she whispered, her voice soft as a falling leaf, "I will leave you to your fate."

Mallory didn't respond; he figured that silence was by far the best option.

The Sheriff continued to search for what felt like hours, but was most likely only ten minutes or so. Mallory's stomach turned over with fear at more than one occasion; he hadn't felt so afraid since he'd first encountered the Master and his Nightwalkers in their lair within the bowels of the Warneford Hospital.

There was a moment where he had to fight to swallow a scream when the Sheriff was almost right on top of them, but he knew that Midori would be true to her word and would leave him in a heartbeat. Instead, he closed his eyes tight, and lost himself in memory.

"The key to putting it all together," Teaser said as she hunched over her tray of photographic developer, "is noticing the important things first."

"That's obvious, Tea," Mallory said around a mouth of bagel. "That's what literally everyone does whenever they look at anything."

"I do wish you wouldn't eat so much mustard," she said, wrinkling her nose, "and it isn't what everyone does; they find the edges and put the important bits in last. They miss things, which for the average person is fine, but if I miss something, I'm likely to end up inside a fucking wall, or worse."

"I'm a painter, Tea! I notice things; it's what I do!"

"What's across the street?" she asked without hesitation.

"What?"

"If you step out of the front door of the Folly, what's across the street from you?"

"It's just houses," he said, suddenly uncertain. "Isn't

it?"

"Nope," she said and he could hear the grin in her voice. "It's a church."

"Is it?" he asked, sure that he couldn't have missed something so obvious.

"It is, and a very distinctive one at that; it has a Venetian bell tower and everything." She turned to look at him. "Go and check, if you don't believe me."

It can't be, he thought as he put his half eaten bagel down and headed into the stairwell. He trotted down the stairs, two at a time, until he reached the front door. He took a deep breath before stepping on to Canal Street and was dumbstruck by what he saw.

Teaser was right; there was a church right there. Mallory crossed the street and read the little plaque that adorned the distinctive building's wall.

"St Barnabus's," he muttered, "also affectionately known as the Jericho Basilica, was consecrated in Eighteen Sixty Nine."

Mallory sighed heavily, then began to chuckle at the absurdity of it all. *She's going to be fucking insufferable for the rest of the day,* he thought. *I should put more mustard on my bagel; that'll show her.*

He returned back to Teaser's makeshift dark room, still laughing softly as he went. The Tracer was waiting for him, leaning against her chemical bench.

"Did you find it?" she asked playfully.

"I can't believe I fucking missed it!" he said, throwing his hands up in mock despair. "I should hand in my gun and my badge."

"We don't have badges," Teaser replied, "but I'm sure they'd take your hat in lieu of one."

"Hey now, let's not take things too far!" He placed a

protective hand on his yachting cap. "I really thought I was paying attention, though, Tea. I make sure to look all around me, wherever I go!"

"That's the difference between you and me, Mal," Teaser said, with just a hint of smugness in her voice. "You look, but I see."

He opened his eyes, and the Sheriff had finally moved on. Midori waited for a few more minutes before releasing him from her grip. He opened his mouth to tell her what he'd realised, but she stunned him with a slap that sent his vision flashing white.

"What is wrong with you?" she hissed. "You nearly got us both killed!"

"There's no need to hit me," Mallory said sullenly, rubbing his jaw.

"Stupidity must be punished," she said curtly.

No wonder Ivy dislikes you so much, he thought, but he decided to move their conversation in a more constructive direction.

"I know where we need to go," he said softly. "I gasped when I figured it out because it's so bloody obvious."

"Well, where is it?"

"The Police Station," he replied. He wasn't sure what to expect in response from her, but the second slap caught him entirely off guard. "What the fuck was that for?"

"Stupidity. Must. Be. Punished." Her words were clipped and razor sharp. "Going to the Police Station is folly!"

"We're being hunted by police officers," Mallory said quietly, "and when this place takes people, it uses them to replenish its ranks; there must be something important at the Police Station."

She went to slap him a third time but he pressed the muzzle of his Jack underneath her chin before the blow could land.

"That won't kill me," she said firmly.

"I know," Mallory replied, "but it will fucking hurt."

The two stared at each other for a moment, until the scales fell from Mallory's eyes. He grinned and lowered the pistol.

"What are you smiling for?" Midori demanded.

"You know I'm right, but you're afraid, aren't you?" He holstered his weapon and began to walk towards the main streets of Galaxy once again. "My Father always said that Kitsune were cowards; far better suited to backroom politicking than the stresses of fieldwork.

"I can see now that he was correct."

Midori said nothing, but hung her head in shame.

"We don't have long left to get out of here," Mallory said, "and I would rather not die in Oregon, of all places, so we need to face up to our fear and cut right to the heart of this."

"But the Faceless-" Midori began, but Mallory cut her off.

"Something's changed," he said, realising that the oppressive mood that hung over the town had shifted, becoming less violent and more mournful. "I don't think they'll bother us any longer."

"That's a small comfort," she said, sighing in relief.

I don't think we're out of danger yet, he thought, but said nothing. Instead, he just continued to walk steadily, certain that she would follow him.

"Where is everyone?" Midori hissed as they hurried

through the dark streets towards the Police Station.

"You don't need to whisper," Mallory said. He could already feel the tide of grief that was seeping into the town affecting him, but he took comfort in knowing that they were approaching the end of their ordeal. "There's nothing else out there now, except us and whatever is causing this."

"How can that be?"

"I don't know," he said, a little exasperated, "but if I had to guess, I'd say that one of our group has managed to reach the dreamer and has begun the process of waking them up."

"Then we don't need to do anything," Midori said, slowing down, "and we can just retreat back to the edge of town and wait this out."

"They might not have all the information they need," Mallory said, "and we stand a better chance if we're all together. Besides, we still haven't found my brother, and that's the entire reason we're here."

There was only silence from the Kitsune, but Mallory took it as acquiescence. He scanned the nearby buildings and smiled in triumph when he saw the white stone facade of the Galaxy Police Station.

"We're here," he said, drawing his revolver and flicking off the safety.

"I thought you said that the Faceless were gone?" Midori asked, worriedly drawing her swords.

"I think they are," Mallory said evenly, moving ahead slowly, "but I've been wrong before."

The station was deserted and in complete darkness, save for the single blinking red light on the radio receiver in the corner of the main room. Mallory approached it, warily checking around him as he went.

I'm not getting caught by some kind of nightmarish

angler fish, he thought, *not after all I've been through.*

He reached the radio unmolested and gently placed a finger on the button that would allow the transmissions to come through. There was a brief hiss, followed by a crackle of static, then five faint words drifted across the airwaves.

"Ten Fifty," the distant voice said. "Ten One Hundred."

Mallory waited for more, but after almost five minutes of dead air he gave up. He rummaged around the desk, smiling in triumph when he managed to click on a small lamp. Now that he could see, he quickly located what he was actually looking for; a list of police communication codes.

He scanned down the list, raising his eyebrow as he did so.

"Have you found something?" Midori asked quietly.

"Yes," he replied, "I think I have."

Finally, this is all starting to make sense.

Chapter Twenty Seven – Breaking the Spell

Ivy

"What's wrong, Francis?" Ivy asked as the Ravenblade continued to cower in the treeline as she and Sissy tried to coax him along the path. "Why won't you come with us back to Sissy's place?"

"It isn't safe," he muttered, clinging to a tree and looking fearfully at the darkening sky.

"I won't let anything happen to you," Ivy insisted, patting the handles of her swords for emphasis. "And Sissy's house is far enough out of town that not a soul is going to come looking for you there."

It isn't safe," he repeated, digging his nails so deep into the bark that it made Ivy wince. Beside her, Michaela sighed heavily and Edgar peered at Francis over the top of his sunglasses in bafflement.

"What isn't safe, Francis?" Sissy asked gently.

"All of it," he said, on the verge of tears. "We're too open, too exposed; too outside. Don't you feel vulnerable?"

"Is it because of the Police Officers?" Ivy asked quietly, and he shook his head.

"No," he said, continuing to peer upwards, "it's the sky."

"The sky?" Ivy said, moving next to him and placing a reassuring arm around his shoulders. "Why is the sky dangerous?"

"It all is," he said, burying his face in his arm as he wept. "I can't do anything about it and I feel so powerless."

"Do you want me to put the whammy on him?" Michaela asked coldly. "I'm sure I could get him moving with the right mental push."

Don't you dare, Ivy thought, loud enough for her alter to hear and roll her eyes dismissively in response. *I think I know what this is.*

"Francis," she began gently, "what does your gift do?"

"I..." he said hesitantly, "I'm an Architect. I can reshape and control physical space, but only in artificial environments; I have no control over the natural world."

"I see," Ivy said, vaguely remembering Mallory explaining something to her about this some months ago. "Does your gift come with any drawbacks?"

He nodded.

"Can you tell me what they are, please?" she asked politely.

"When I manipulate space," he said, "I inadvertently alter time too; they're linked. I get older or younger, but it's very difficult to predict or control."

"Is that all?" Ivy said, probing his mind with her own.

"I think so." He peeked out from his sleeve at her. "Why?"

"Does the lack of control you have when you're in a wild environment make you feel nervous, Francis?"

"Yes."

"Unsafe?"

"Very."

Gotcha.

"Has anyone ever talked to you about agoraphobia before?" He shook his head. "No? That's okay. It's a form of anxiety disorder that is triggered by certain environments, often unfamiliar ones. I think you've been out here and running for so long that it's done a bit of a number on you."

"That sounds bad," he said sadly. "Will they lock me up?"

"No, of course not. The clinical outcomes for agoraphobia are mostly positive, actually, with the most important thing being that you have support from people you trust." She took his filthy hand in hers and let her emotions flow into him, filling him with a sense of calmness and safety. "Sissy and I are here with you, but you need to come with us.

"I promise that you'll feel better when you're inside a building, and Sissy will make you the best cup of coffee this side of Portland, won't you?"

"I sure will," the DJ said with a kind smile. "If it makes you feel better, I'll also talk the whole way back. Would that help?"

"Yes," Francis said, finally letting go of the tree, "I think it would."

He took a few tentative steps on to the path, and Sissy took his other hand in hers. He smiled gratefully, but still avoided walking underneath the open sky. They had a few false starts, but they eventually fell into a reliable rhythm as they trekked along the mountain path towards Sissy's house in the forest.

"What would you like me to talk about?" Sissy asked when they were under way.

"Why don't you tell us about yourself?" Ivy asked, and Edgar nodded approvingly. "I'm sure you've led a storied life."

"Well," Sissy said with a warm laugh as the first stars started to appear, "where do I even start?"

Ivy half listened to Sissy as she chattered on, but the bulk of her attention was on the treeline and the deepening gloom beyond; once or twice she was sure that she saw movement and humanoid shapes.

"Time is running wrong," Michaela said after a while. "It shouldn't be this dark already."

"Agreed," Edgar said. "By all rights, it should still be afternoon."

"It could be Francis affecting the flow," Michaela suggested, but she didn't sound convinced.

"There's something moving up ahead," Edgar said, peering through the twilight. "I have a theory that I want you to test, Ivy."

Just tell me what to do.

"I want you to tell her that there's something wrong with Galaxy. Avoid specifics, especially the time loop, but I do want you to tell her explicitly about the Faceless Police Officers."

Are you sure? Ivy thought, suddenly worried.

"I am," Edgar said.

"Try and throw some suspicion on the Applied Physics facility," Michaela said. "If this is a dream, we'll need a focal point to end it."

"Capital idea, Michaela," Edgar said, and she bowed gracefully. "Yes, you should definitely do that."

But-

"Quickly," Edgar said, as something dashed through the trees to their left, "do it now!"

"Sissy," Ivy blurted out, trying to control her own panic as she caught a glimpse of a Faceless Officer less than ten metres away. "Sissy, I need to tell you why I'm here."

"You're looking for your friends," she said, sounding

very confused.
"I am, but we're part of a task force that was sent here to investigate an incident at the Applied Physics building; something terrible is happening in this town."
"Oh my god," she said, looking at Ivy with wide eyes, "are we safe?"
Edgar nodded.
"Yes, we are, but some people weren't. There's something in the air that has been changing people; mutating them into strange monsters. This is going to sound bizarre but they were becoming-"
"Police Officers?" Sissy asked, interrupting Ivy, who nodded. "They didn't have any faces, did they?"
"That's right," Ivy said, "and they were chasing people."
"They wanted to tell them a secret," Sissy said reflexively, "but if you heard it you would die."
"That's right," Ivy replied, trying to hide her shock. *This is getting interesting.* "But that's stopped now, hasn't it?"
"It has?" Sissy asked, her face flushed with relief. "Are you sure?"
"I am. Whatever was making the Police Officers has stopped and they're all gone now. They can't hurt us any more."
"I'm so glad to hear that," Sissy said. "I'm not surprised about the Physics building, though. I always knew that it was evil. My mother worked there for a while, you know."
"She did?" Ivy asked. A quick glance confirmed that the Faceless Officer had vanished and Edgar gave her a thumbs up.
"Yes. She was Head Nurse at the Community

Hospital for ages, but she moved to the Applied Physics lab to get better pay." Sissy smiled at the thought. "I used to be a Candy Striper at the Hospital, at my mother's urging, but I couldn't stick it out."

"Why not?" Francis asked, his earlier fear seemingly forgotten.

"I just felt like everyone there was just waiting to die," she replied sheepishly. "It seemed like I was drowning in death; swamped and smothered by it. Hell, I couldn't even go and see my mother when she was in the Palliative Care Unit just before she died.

"I just couldn't face it." Sissy sighed heavily, wiping tears from her eyes. "I've always been squeamish around death; I'd much prefer a comforting lie to a harsh truth. I know that makes me a coward, but it also makes me an excellent radio host."

"How did your mother die?" Ivy asked, keeping her tone firm, but tender.

"She got cancer from working at the Physics lab. I told her not to work there, that it was an evil, wicked place, but she wouldn't listen to me." She halted for a moment, her lower lip quivering. "They killed her, and they never had to face any consequences.

"They killed this whole damn town," she said sharply, grief and anger twisting her face into a mask of pure hate. "They turned this entire place into a fucking graveyard and nobody knows what they did."

"You know," Ivy said, putting her hand on Sissy's shoulder. "And now we know, too."

"Will you help me put it all right?" Sissy asked, her voice desperate.

"I will," Ivy said, "but let's get Francis inside first, okay?"

"Of course," Sissy said, and she started walking

again. “We're almost there.”

“Glad to hear it,” Francis said, giving her a strained smile.

“You'll get to meet my husband, Patryk, and my son, Rusty.”

“If they're even half as kind as you, I'm sure they're wonderful people,” Ivy said.

“Thank you,” Sissy said, looking Ivy in the eye. “It's rare to find a person so willing to help a stranger, even less so in this day and age.”

“You're welcome,” Ivy said, giving her a smile. “Besides, you helped me first; what sort of person would I be to refuse someone so kind?”

They continued to walk on in silence, and soon the faint porch light of the Sparrow house came into view. Ivy looked at Edgar, who nodded; he'd reached the same conclusion that she had.

“We're in the dead centre of the Exclusion Zone, for sure,” he said, staring first at the house, and then at Sissy. “It's her, isn't it?”

It must be, Ivy thought, but a lingering shadow of doubt hovered in her mind. *I'm sure we're right,* she thought as they entered the house, *but I can't help but feel we've missed something vital.*

“I wish the others were here,” Michaela said quietly.

“They might not have any more information,” Edgar replied.

“I know,” Michaela whispered tearfully, “but that doesn't mean that I don't miss them.”

Interlude Two – Music Playing in the Darkness

Patryk drummed his fingers on the wheel of his aging Lincoln Continental as he cruised through the deserted streets of Galaxy. Rusty, his son, was asleep in the back seat.

Works like a charm, every single time, Patryk thought with a smile. Both his and Sissy's unconventional schedules tended to play havoc with their boy's sleep pattern, but a night time drive with his father always allowed Rusty Sparrow to drift off into a restful, dreamless slumber.

Patryk was a night owl, like his parents before him, and their parents before that; the Nightingale family had always shared a love of the quiet stillness that came with a clear country night. He had one arm resting on the open window; his rolled up shirt sleeve allowed the cool spring air to flow over his exposed skin.

"It's a nice night," he muttered to himself, "maybe I'll put the top down and enjoy the sky."

He thought about it for a moment, before deciding against it; the commotion would definitely wake Rusty. *I'll pop some music on instead.* He smiled and fished a tape out of the little pile on the dashboard before slotting it into the player.

He grinned and began to sing along when the voice of Freddie Mercury filled the car, and he turned up the volume as loud as he dared.

"We'll be waiting for the moonlight," he sang gently as he turned on to the main street, preparing to take his usual route through the mountain forest. Tonight, however, he stepped hard on the brake pedal, bringing the Lincoln to a halt as a terrified Asian woman ran up the street towards him, frantically waving her arms.

In the back seat, his son did not stir.

"Thank you so much for stopping," the woman said breathlessly as she climbed into the passenger seat. He was surprised to hear her pronounced English accent. "I'm so glad to see another person; a real one, that is."

"Miss, are you alright?" Patryk asked her, his eyes flicking towards Rusty once again. "Do you need to go to the hospital or-"

"No!" she said, her eyes wide with fear. "I promise I'm not on drugs or anything; I've just had a really scary evening."

"I believe you. Are you all alone out here?" he asked, starting up the car once again. "I've not seen you around town before."

"I'm here with a few colleagues," she said sadly, "but we got separated."

"This is gonna sound weird," Patryk said with a slight smile, "but my wife brought home two English folks this evening who had nowhere to go. One of them was an odd fella with a beard, and the other was some kind of doctor; she had clearly been in a terrible accident at some point, or a fire."

"The doctor; was her name Ivy Livingston?" the woman asked excitedly.

"Yes, ma'am," Patryk said. "Is she one of your colleagues?"

The woman nodded and wiped tears of relief from the corner of her eyes.

"Would you like me to take you to her?"

"Yes, please," she said, "that would mean the world

to me. I'm Noor, by the way. Noor Turner."

"A pleasure to meet you, Noor," he said warmly. "I'm Patryk, with a 'y' if that matters to you at all. I'm an astronomer."

He gestured to his Galaxy Observatory ID and Noor let out a small gasp. He glanced at her for a few seconds before returning his eyes to the road.

"What's up?"

"You're Patryk *Nightingale*?" she asked, placing a curious amount of emphasis on his last name.

"All my life."

"Of course you are," she said with a chuckle. "Tell me, Patryk with a 'y', do you believe in coincidences?"

"No, ma'am," he said.

"Me neither, Patryk," she said softly as the music continued to play. "Me neither."

Part Three: Extinction Burst

Chapter Twenty Eight – Brothers in Arms

Mallory

The trek along the mountain road was hard going; even the gentle incline was punishing after a while. Midori groaned and grumbled as they went.

"Are you sure this is the right way?" the Kitsune asked, huffing a little as she did so.

"Yes," Mallory said tersely, tired of having to answer the same question for the umpteenth time. "The codes that came over the radio were for a vehicular accident and a fatality. The centre of the phenomenon sits on a mountain road, so it makes sense that the whole thing hinges on a fatal car crash right in the centre of the Easy."

"But-"

"For fuck's sake, Midori!" Mallory yelled, whirling around angrily to face her. "How many times do I have to explain this to you? I'm sure that if I was Francis you'd take his word for it on the first go, wouldn't you?"

"But he is a Ravenblade, though-" she began, but he was having absolutely none of it.

"I don't care if he's the Queen of fucking Sheba," Mallory roared, "he still got stuck here, didn't he? He couldn't figure out how to get out of here, so I had to come and rescue him."

"We're still here too," Midori said quietly, and Mallory drew himself up to his full height to continue to yell at her. He leaned in close enough to fleck her face with spittle.

"We have been here two fucking days, and we're

already far closer to ending this thing than he ever was!" His hands trembled with fury. "So, please, just listen to me for once, you narcissistic, cowardly, condescending bitch!"

She growled at him and reflexively placed her hand on the handle of her katana. As she did this, however, Mallory utilised one of the lessons Charity had taught him to both shove her away from him and snatch the pearl from her necklace at the same time.

She responded with a slash that would've cut him in half had he not leapt backwards. Before she could strike again, he held up the pearl to show it to her. He couldn't see her expression, but her howl of rage and indignation confirmed what he had suspected.

"How dare you!" she yelled, quivering with fury.

"What's wrong?" he asked slyly, a quiet grin creeping on to his face. "Is this important?"

"I will cut you down where you stand!"

"And then I'll drop it," he said softly. "It might bounce off down the road or it might hit the ground hard enough to break, and wouldn't that be a shame?"

"You wouldn't-" she began, but shrieked in horror and lurched forward slightly as Mallory gently tossed the pearl into the air before deftly catching it again.

"Sorry, I missed that," he said with a smile before carefully stowing the pearl in his pocket. He patted it for emphasis. "You can have this back when we're done here, *if* you start acting as more of a team player. Deal?"

"You insolent little shit!" She spat at him, and he sighed heavily.

"Look, we're running out of time and I just want to get out of here alive, ideally with as many members of my team with me as possible; why can't you just work with me here?" She was silent at his words. "If it's rules and regs that are getting you down, then please remember that I am your commanding officer for this expedition and you are the insubordinate one in this particular exchange."

"Mohinder Desai-" Midori began, but he spoke across her yet again, his frustration finally getting the best of him.

"Desai offered you to the Yanks, Midori. You're expendable to him; just a curio to be bought, traded, or disposed of as necessary." He wished that he could have seen the look on her face, but her silence said it all. "I spoke up for you, you know, and I asked for you to come with us, rather than be left languishing in some Bureau black site."

"You did?" she finally said, her voice small and uncertain.

"Yes," he replied, suddenly weary, "and you don't need to thank me; you just need to stop slowing me down."

"Did he tell you about the pearl?" Midori asked. Mallory shook his head. "Then who did?"

"It doesn't matter," he said. "All that's important now is getting this done. Then, if we're both still alive, you can have it back. Do we have an agreement?"

"How do I know that I can trust you?" she asked warily.

"I'm a man of my word," he said, "and, right now, you don't have any other choice."

"Fine. We have a deal." She was about to say something else when the sound of an approaching car drew their attention. They both looked down the mountain road at the vehicle that was closing in on them; a white Lincoln Continental. A person with long dark hair leant out of the passenger side and waved excitedly at them.

"Mallory! Midori! I can't believe you're still alive!"

It took him a moment to recognise her voice, but it clicked as the car slowed to a halt beside them.

"Noor?"

"And this is home," Patryk said as he slowed to a halt outside an impressive house, surrounded by fir trees and lodgepole pines. There was a spacious deck that extended from the first floor and large picture windows facing out across the valley.

I'd love to spend a few months here, Mallory thought wistfully, *just drinking in the atmosphere and painting everything in sight.*

The front door opened and a twitchy, ragged man with a shaggy beard peered nervously out into the darkness. Mallory waved awkwardly; Noor had mentioned that Ivy was holed up at the Sparrow house, but had neglected to mention this strange other.

He can't be Harold Skullbone, Mallory thought, *so maybe he's one of the other Bureau Agents?*

"Mallory?" the man said shakily, and the Artist's eyes widened and he began to run towards the bearded man.

"Francis!?" he cried as he leapt into his brother's trembling arms. "Francis, what the fuck have you done to yourself?"

"I could ask you the same thing," Francis said, a little of the fear leaving his voice.

"I was just doing what I needed to survive," Mallory replied, his face flushing with shame.

"Me too, little brother," he said, lowering his voice. "I could feel myself physically fading, so I used my gift to alter my own wristwatch time, as it were. It's kept my body alive, but I fear it's done a number on my mind.

"Luckily enough, I happened to run into a head doctor whilst hiding out in the forest."

"You've met Ivy, then?" Francis nodded and Mallory grinned. "She's the one that worked out how to remove my... uh, fungal infection, as it were."

"Oh, right!" Francis said as he led Mallory inside. He glanced around before whispering conspiratorially. "She's the one that's shacked up with Charity Walpole, isn't she?"

"That's right," Mallory said a touch awkwardly, "but I prefer not to gossip about my colleagues."

"Of course, of course," Francis said, almost gleefully, "but you have to admit that it is a strange pairing, isn't it?"

"Francis," Mallory said, exasperation and exhaustion making his voice waver slightly, "can we please not do this now? You have no idea just how shattered I am."

"Mal!"

Mallory turned at the sound of Ivy's voice, but the swift fist bump, high five, and simultaneous click that comprised their secret handshake confirmed that it was, in fact, Edgar in the driving seat.

"It's good to see you, Ed," he said, relieved that the Séance had survived the horrors that Galaxy had thrown at them. "Noor said that you were coordinating things."

"Herding cats," Ed said with a chuckle. "I do my best."

"Still, I'm glad that someone sensible is in charge," Mallory said, taking Ed's hand in his and palming the pearl to him. He lowered his voice to the barest whisper. "Hold on to this for me, will you?"

"Hold on to what?" Ed asked innocently as he squirrelled the small jewel away up his sleeve just as Midori entered the room. "Honestly, Mal, you ask me the strangest things."

The Kitsune strode up to where they were standing and stared at Edgar, who took a moment to look her up and down before continuing his conversation with Mallory.

"So," he said softly, "I think Cecilia is the Dreamer, but there's something important about the rest of her family that I can feel but I can't quite figure out."

"Aren't you going to address your Mistress?" Midori asked sharply.

"Yes, hello," Edgar said dismissively before looking back at the Artist. Mallory had to stifle a smile. "The most relevant piece of information that I need to share with you is that we've made her aware that there's something wrong with Galaxy, but we've not explained the time slippage; at this point, I feel that would be a mistake.

"Michaela did suggest that we shift her mind to a focal point, and she has latched on quite nicely to the Galaxy Applied Physics laboratory as the root cause of all the strangeness in the town."

"So what's our next move?" Mallory said, yawning as soon as he'd finished speaking. *I'm dead on my feet.*

"We rest," Edgar said, "and then we take our Dreamer to the Applied Physics building. If we're lucky, hopefully the dream will start to unravel from there. At least we don't have to deal with the Faceless Police Officers any longer; we seem to be in a new phase of this waking nightmare."

“What use will rest do if none of this is real?” Midori snapped.

“Our minds make it real,” Mallory said, “and we need to be on the ball for the end of this.”

“I think we should go immediately,” Midori countered, raising her voice slightly. “It's foolish to spin this out longer than is completely necessary.”

“It'll be over when it's over,” Edgar said gently. “We're entering the most dangerous stage of this; old tigers sensing their end are often at their most fierce.”

“Not to mention that we have no idea what to expect,” Mallory added. “We don't have time to rush.”

“But-” Midori began, however Edgar cut her off and shook his head firmly.

“He's better at this than you are,” he said as he placed a supportive hand on Mallory's arm. “The Ravenblade exam selects for combat ability and momentary cunning, but it neglects strategic planning and operational awareness. I'm not usually one for hierarchy, however in this instance, it would benefit you to just listen to your mission leader, Midori.”

“You are just humans,” Midori growled, her fingers twitching slightly. “You are fragile creatures that die easily!”

“Of course we are,” Ed said, cocking his head to one side, “but your immortality makes you arrogant and short-sighted. You're just a relic of a bygone era. The fragile, however, must work to endure; our weakness makes us into something that you can never be.”

“Which is?” she asked testily.

“Survivors,” Mallory said. He yawned again as Noor entered, followed by Patryk who carried Rusty in his arms. “Everyone get some rest, and we'll gather again to plan our next steps in the morning. Sleep well.”

He looked at Midori, who was staring at him defiantly.

"Go to bed," he said firmly. "That's an order."

Chapter Twenty Nine – The Road to Damascus

Ivy

"Here you go," Sissy said as she handed a steaming mug of coffee to Ivy.

"Thank you so much," Ivy said with a sleepy smile. She closed her eyes and felt the warmth of the afternoon sun on her face; the entire team had slept for almost twelve hours.

You know, if it wasn't a waking nightmare, this would be a wonderful place to live.

"How long do we have left?" Michaela asked. She was perched atop the kitchen worktop, and her face was the most worried Ivy had ever seen it. "Edgar?"

"I'm not sure," Edgar replied, "but definitely less than a full day. I don't think we're already dead, but we can't be doing too well."

"If we are doomed to die," Michaela said softly, "smash that fucking pearl first."

Fucking hell, Ivy thought as she took a sip of her coffee, *this place really is doing a number on you, isn't it?*

"She's good at what she does," Michaela said, glaring at the Kitsune, "but that doesn't stop her being an evil fucking bitch."

"Do you regret the training she gave you?" Edgar asked, and Michaela shook her head.

"No; I'm grateful for what she taught me. I still wish I hadn't been in Lamplight, though." She hopped down and walked over to where Midori sat silently, sipping at a cup of tea. "Every single person involved in that monstrous experiment is going to get what's coming to them, one day.

"I don't need to be a Seer to know that."

"Maybe we shouldn't dwell too much on the past, Michaela," Edgar said as he moved beside her and put an arm around her gently trembling shoulders. "This isn't the place nor the time for such thoughts; they could be dangerous."

She's right, Ivy thought, *and-*

She jumped when Sissy put a hand on her arm, spilling the hot coffee over her hands.

"Oh, honey, I'm sorry! I didn't mean to startle you!"

"That's alright," Ivy said as she dabbed her hands dry on the tea towel Mallory handed to her. "What's one more burn amongst friends?"

Nobody laughed, and she felt her face flush; this was clearly not the time for gallows humour. She saw Noor self-consciously hide her face behind her hair a little, and her stomach immediately knotted with shame and discomfort.

"Sorry, Noor," she muttered.

"It's okay, Ivy," the Fate replied softly. "I suppose I'm going to have to get used to it. Does the humour help?"

"Sometimes," Ivy said quietly.

"I find it does," Mallory said with a grin, "although I tend to be told that the delivery of my jokes is a touch... wooden."

Noor snorted and Ivy couldn't help but chuckle.

"You are some of the strangest people I've ever met," Sissy said, smiling as she finished mopping up Ivy's spilled drink, "and I mean that as a compliment."

"What's the plan?" Midori asked, seemingly

unmoved by the giggles of her allies. "Mallory?"

"We'll head out to the Galaxy Applied Physics building shortly," he said, steepling his fingers as he rested his elbows on the table. "We'll approach on foot; that seems the safest option. Sissy, how long will it take?"

"A few hours," she said, a hint of nervousness in her voice. "Do you want me to come with you?"

"Please," Mallory said. "We need a local guide, and it sounds like you have unfinished business there."

He added that last bit so casually, Ivy thought. *He's getting good at this.*

"Yes, I most certainly do."

"Then hopefully you'll find some closure there," he replied, giving her a warm smile. "We are mandated to minimise civilian involvement wherever possible, so I will have to ask Patryk to remain here with Rusty. I trust that won't be an issue, Dr Nightingale?"

"As long as you look after Sissy," he said, "that's fine by me."

"We'll protect her with our lives," Mallory said. "I give you my word."

"And mine," Ivy added.

"Me too," Noor said, raising her hand.

"Then I'm satisfied," Patryk replied, pushing up his glasses before folding his arms. "Are you sure you don't want to take the Lincoln?"

"I'd prefer to proceed on foot, but thank you all the same." Mallory turned to look at his Agents. "I don't expect resistance, but if we encounter any, who has had the best record dealing with these things?"

"They... um... they don't seem to be able to see me," Noor said, "but I think that only applies to me. Sorry."

"No need to apologise," Mallory said. "In fact, that's

good to know; you're not much of a fighter, no offence, so it's helpful to know that we don't have to protect you."

"None taken," Noor said with a quiet smile.

She's hiding something, Ivy thought, *but this isn't the time to go digging for the truth.*

"I managed to take down one of the bears," Midori said, "although I had assistance. I did manage to hide both me and Mallory from the Faceless Officers, however, but it was a close cut thing."

"Francis," Mallory said, "I'm assuming that you survived through hiding also?"

The bearded man nodded, before answering to the affirmative.

"Alright. So it seems that our offensive capability is severely limited. Ivy, did you also keep a low profile?"

"No," Ivy said, her voice flat. "I killed every Faceless that crossed my path."

"Permanently?" Midori asked, her eyes wide. Ivy nodded and the teacup began to tremble in the Kitsune's hand. "How is that possible?"

"I'm a monster," Ivy said dispassionately. "Born of monsters, raised in horror, and trained to kill; I did the only thing I know how to do."

"Could you do it again?" Mallory asked tentatively.

"Of course," Ivy said with a tired sigh. "It's what I'm for, after all."

"Hopefully it won't come to that," Noor said gently.

Silence hung over the table for a few moments, until Mallory got to his feet.

"Check your equipment, fill your water bottles, and get ready," he said firmly. "We leave in an hour."

"I don't like this," Michaela said, sticking close to

Ivy and Edgar as the shadows deepened and the day drew to a golden close. "Something about this forest feels really wrong."

"This entire place is trapped in a waking nightmare," Ivy muttered. "It would be strange if it didn't feel off."

"It's not that," Michaela replied, shivering slightly. "It feels like we're in two places at once; split in half, almost. Ed, do you feel it?"

He shook his head.

"Look, Kiki," Ivy said a little more loudly, "we're nearing the end of this thing and it's gonna start cresting like a wave; a tsunami only really gets big close to shore, after all, and it's natural for it to freak you out a little."

"Don't therapise me!" Michaela snapped.

"I'm not!" Ivy said defensively. "All I'm asking you to do is to realise that it's natural for you to get the willies in such a tense situation, and try to move past it. Please, Kiki; I need to keep as focussed as possible."

"Do you two really not feel anything at all?" Michaela asked, crestfallen and cowed.

"I'm sorry, but I don't," Ivy said.

"Me neither," Edgar said, attempting a consolatory tone.

"Maybe I'm just cracking up," Michaela said shakily. "Finally losing my nerve after too many close calls over the years."

"That's not true," Ivy said gently. "I trust you with my life. How many tight scrapes have you gotten us out of?"

"I guess so," Michaela said with a sad smile. "And I did correct your shooting stance in Wellington-"

She stopped speaking at the sound of someone

approaching from behind.

"Ivy," Noor asked as she trotted up to her, "who are you talking to?"

"My imaginary friends," Ivy said with a smile. "They make me feel better."

"Oh. Okay." Noor blinked in surprise, but let Ivy's strange comment go.

Ivy checked over her shoulder to make sure that Francis was keeping up with the rest of them, but thankfully Mallory seemed to be doing a good job in keeping his agoraphobic brother moving through the forest.

"You're more than just a killing machine, you know," Noor said as the two women strolled side by side along the deserted mountain road, slightly ahead of everyone else. "I mean it; you're more than what was done to you."

The wind moved the branches of the overhanging trees, sending the limbs creaking and rustling, dappling the early evening twilight. The sound mixed with their footsteps to create an eerie, lonely rhythm.

There was no birdsong.

"Do you really believe that?" Ivy asked after a minute or so of walking silently.

"I have to," Noor said enigmatically.

"Why don't you carry a gun?" Ivy said, looking the young woman up and down. "Or even a knife, for that matter?"

"I don't like violence," Noor said, wrapping her arms around her chest. Ivy sighed and pulled one of her knives from its sheathe, flipped it around so that she was holding it by the blade, and offered the handle to Noor. "No, I don't want it."

"Take it, damn it!" Ivy said firmly. "You might need

to cut yourself free of something or rough up some kindling to make a fire. I understand you have principles, but it doesn't have to be a weapon; sometimes a tool is just a tool."

"Thank you," Noor said awkwardly, tucking the blade into her boot.

"If you ever do want to learn how to fight with it, let me know."

"You'd teach me?" Noor asked.

"No, but I'd introduce you to someone who would." She smiled at the thought of Charity. "She's the most dangerous woman I've ever met, and one of the kindest too."

"Is this your girlfriend?" Noor had a wry smile on her face.

"Yes." Ivy chuckled slightly. "When we first met each other, we couldn't stop fighting."

"It's always the surprising ones that get you, isn't it?"

"You can say that-" Ivy trailed off as a tall woman in a white coat walked out of the trees towards her. Ivy blinked and rubbed her eyes, but the figure remained. When she spoke again, her voice was a whisper. "How are you here?"

"Come along, Kätzchen," the woman said, holding out her hand. A lollipop clattered noisily against her teeth as she rolled it around her mouth.

"Ivy, don't!" Michaela yelled, but Ivy couldn't hear her. "Edgar, pull her out of here, right now!"

"I can't," Edgar said, his voice already distant, as Ivy took the woman's hand in her own. "She's already going."

"Get away from her, you fucking monster!" Michaela screamed, her voice on the edge of hysterics. "Mother, leave her alone!"

It was too late, however. Both women were already gone.

Chapter Thirty – No Saving You

Noor

Ivy crumpled to the ground, startling everyone. Mallory was by her side in an instant, his face a mask of terror and panic.

"What's happening to her?" Sissy asked, clutching her hand nervously to her chest.

"It's taking her," Midori said, unsheathing her sword. "We have to end this, now."

Instead of speaking, Noor leant down to Ivy's unconscious form and placed a hand on her face. The Tangle rushed through them both, blending their separate timelines into one chaotic blur. Noor looked at Mallory, who awaited her verdict with bated breath.

"The town isn't taking her," she said firmly. "She's not becoming one of the Faceless."

"Thank fuck for that," Mallory said. "Do you know what's happening to her?"

"This town is overflowing with grief and despair," she said quietly, trying not to look at Sissy. "Ivy's more susceptible to it than most, and now she's drowning in it. Something terrible happened in her past and now she's stuck there."

"Do we just wait for it to pass?" Mallory asked.

"No," Noor said, kneeling on the ground beside her prone friend. "Even if I was sure that she'd come back on her own, which I'm not, we don't have time to wait for that."

"If we carried her with us-" Mallory began, but Noor shook her head.

"We need her help," she said, more certain of the

path to take with each passing second, "and if she doesn't wake up soon, we all die here."

"What can we do?" Midori asked.

"The rest of you can keep any threats away from me and Ivy." She took a deep breath and rolled up her sleeves. "I'm going after her."

"Alone?" Mallory said, but by that point Noor was already in a trance, her heartbeat slowing to a crawl as she plummeted into their shared timeline. The wind whistled in her ears as she sped through the air, and her nerves jangled as she grew ever faster.

I hope there's still somebody down here to help me, she thought as she stuck her left hand out into the rushing air.

There was a moment of terror as she fell, but then a strong hand closed around her wrist, almost wrenching her arm out of its socket as she was pulled to a sharp and sudden stop. She groaned in pain as she was hauled into a dimly lit room, lavishly decorated in pink and black.

"Thank you, Edgar," Noor wheezed as she finally caught her breath.

"That was a hell of a jump," he said with a grin. "I was worried that I wasn't going to be able to catch you."

He helped her to her feet, and then supported her as she staggered uneasily over to a chair. She tried to rise once again, mindful of the urgency of their task, but Edgar forced her back down into the seat.

"Just rest a moment," he said firmly. "Time runs differently in the Parlour, and you'll need all your strength for what you're about to see."

"Where's Michaela?" Noor asked, looking around the dark parlour for the stern woman. "We could use all the support we can get."

"She's gone ahead to help Ivy," Edgar said, although Noor sensed that he wasn't being entirely honest with her. She raised a questioning eyebrow and, after a moment of hesitation, he relented. "This is the day where we all came into being, Noor. Michaela has rejoined with Ivy to give her the strength to survive what is currently happening to her."

He handed her a cup of hot chocolate, which she downed in a single gulp. The warm, rich liquid suffused her body with light, power, and resilience; she had never felt so strong.

"That's a hell of a brew," she said with a smile as she got to her feet.

"My own special reserve," he replied, a crafty grin crossing his face. "Are you ready?"

"I think so." She thought for a moment. "Are we in the past, or just a memory?"

"In any other situation I'd discuss that with you all night," he said with a chuckle, "but right now the pertinent thing is that we can't change anything; all we can do is track down Ivy and guide her back out."

"Have you tried to alter the past before?"

"Yes."

"This memory in particular?" Noor asked quietly.

"All the time," Edgar said sadly. "If the unique circumstances that have arisen in Galaxy won't let me change it, then I have to accept that it's never going to happen. What's done is done, and all that remains are the nightmares."

"I'm sorry, Edgar." She put a sympathetic hand on his shoulder. "Nobody deserves to go through pain, least of all someone as gentle as you."

"That's kind of you to say," he said awkwardly, "but

I've done my fair share of evil. Nobody and nothing that you're about to see is innocent. We didn't have a choice, though, so please don't judge us too harshly."

"Where are we going?" Noor asked as he led her towards the only door in the room.

"Betony Island, on the Twenty Fourth of April, Nineteen Ninety Four," he said, and she notice a hint of fear in his voice. "The day that Project Lamplight went to hell."

The facility was in absolute chaos.

Fires raged, the sound of gunfire filled the air, and everywhere there were bodies; scientists, soldiers, and children. Noor felt her stomach turn over and she nearly vomited on the floor at the sight of one little girl, barely six years old, who had been shot over a hundred times.

There's barely anything left of her.

"Edgar, how could they do something like this?" Noor asked, and he pointed at several dead guards that were slumped against the wall. Blood streamed from every orifice and several of them had ruptured eyeballs.

"Subject One Two Six, Belinda Chestnut, Codename Popcorn," he said gravely. "She was a Shriek; she burst their brains and blood vessels like balloons."

"What?! She must've been awful!"

"She was a sweet girl," Edgar chastised, "who wouldn't say boo to a goose. This island made monsters of us all."

"We should keep moving," she said, picking her way carefully through the carnage.

"Agreed."

He followed her, occasionally guiding her left or

right when they came to a junction. Noor tried to ignore the corpses and the terrified screaming, but some sights were just too awful to shut out.

As they rounded one corner, a little girl sprinted past them, periodically scrabbling on all fours like an animal. She saw a man, probably in his early twenties with prematurely greying hair enter the room, deflecting stray bullets away from him as he did so.

The girl let out a feral growl before ripping a clear plastic muzzle from her face and charging headlong at the man. Thick, glistening saliva flowed from her dirty, twitching mouth and hung in sloppy strings from her moist chin.

She leapt at him, taking him by surprise, and climbed him like a rabid monkey until her face was level with his. She smashed her mouth into his, saliva mingling with blood as she savaged his lips and tongue. Still locked together, they both crumpled to the ground where the man began to twitch and convulse.

"What is she doing to him?" Noor asked, unable to hold back her disgust.

"That's Lola," Edgar said, "and the man is Gideon. Her saliva is addictive and toxic; she's enslaving him for the rest of his life. He'll never be free of her, at least not until he dies."

"Does he die?"

"Eventually," Edgar replied darkly. "Lola is still alive, though. She's back here, in fact; they turned this place into a prison when the fires finally died down."

"Can't we help him?" Noor asked, taking a step towards Gideon.

"This is just a memory," Edgar reminded her. "Besides, he wasn't a good man. He deserved his fate."

I'm not sure anyone deserves that, Noor thought, but she kept it to herself. *It's a miracle anyone got out of here alive.*

They pressed on, passing a rat faced blonde girl who killed an entire contingent of armed guards with a flick of her wrist, snapping their necks with seemingly no effort whatsoever. Noor remembered what Verity had told her, and realised that this girl must be a Fulcrum; a rare case of true telekinesis.

"Edgar," Noor asked quietly as the rat girl strode imperiously past them, "what were they trying to do here?"

"They wanted to train us to be soldiers," Edgar said, "and spies and assassins. We were to be the generation that would allow the Ministry to rule the world from the shadows."

"What went wrong?"

"If I'm going to be completely honest," he said with a weary sigh, "absolutely nothing."

"What do you mean?" Noor said, aghast. She gestured at the corpses and burning building. "How is this not wrong?"

"They trained us to fight, so we fought." He looked down at the bodies. "If you want a killer, don't be surprised when they decide to kill you too."

"But why today?"

"I don't know. I don't think anyone does." He continued down the corridor, towards the sound of mad cackling. "Maybe they pushed one of us too hard, abused us one time too many, or maybe we struck first; it doesn't matter in the end, though.

"Regardless of who started it, we finished it."

They entered a large dining room and at the centre

was a raging inferno. It took Noor a few seconds to realise that the conflagration was the source of the laughter; in the middle of the whirling vortex of fire was a little girl, disfigured and deformed by the heat.

"Subject Zero One Six," he said, anticipating her next question, "Madeline Gilbert, Codename Shirtwaist. I think the current estimate is that she is responsible for around forty percent of the total body count for today.

"I never got the chance to speak to her, so I can't tell you what she was like before she killed all those people, but I do know that what happened here drove her completely mad."

"A slave to the flames," Noor murmured, recalling Miranda Salt's words.

"We're getting close," Edgar said. "Ivy and Michaela won't be far away."

"At least we'll get there together," Noor said.

"I'm afraid not," he replied, and when she looked, he was fading away like some sort of translucent ghost. "I believe in you, Noor. You can save us."

The flames closed in around her as Edgar vanished, and Noor took off running. *I'm short on time,* she realised, *and I refuse to leave them in this place.*

I wouldn't leave anyone here.

A pair of guards were in the corridor ahead of her. They raised their weapons at her, but two knives flashed into view in the air before them, striking each man in the throat, killing them instantly.

Noor slowed down as a boy jogged past her, snatching up the knives and keys from the fallen bodies.

"Come on, Charity!" he said in a sing-song Welsh accent. "We're almost free!"

A second pair of footsteps raced down the corridor, although Noor couldn't see their source. *I guess there are invisible people out there too.* She shuddered when she thought of all the violence she'd witnessed; the fact that it was committed by children made it so much worse. *I don't think I'll ever feel safe again.*

"Michaela?"

Noor turned at the sound of a gentle boy's voice and followed it into a side room. She found two children inside; one was a boy who had been shot in the stomach, and the other was a girl with horrific burns.

"Michaela, are you still alive?" he asked, reaching out for her.

"Yes, Oliver," she replied, taking his hand in her own ruined and skinless one. "I'm so afraid though."

"You don't need to worry," he said weakly, with a smile. "I'm here."

"But you're going to die."

"Yes."

"Oliver, I don't want to be alone again." Michaela began to cry.

"I know," he said softly, "so I'm going to help you. You'll never be alone again, Michaela; I promise."

His eyes rolled back in his head and Michaela's burned body twitched and shivered on the ground. For a brief moment, she had three shadows instead of one, and then they all merged back together. Once she had stopped moving she looked at Oliver, who lay dead on the cold tile floor. Michaela let out a mournful wail, drawing Noor's attention back to her.

The Fate blinked, and the burned child vanished; replaced instead by the grown woman that she knew. Edgar and Michaela knelt either side of Ivy, stroking her hair and making soft, reassuring noises.

“Ivy?” Noor asked, reaching out her hand. “Ivy, I'm here to take you away from this place.”

“I can't,” she moaned, writhing on the floor now. “I'll never be free of it!”

“Of course you will,” Noor said, and the others murmured in agreement.

“You can't drag me out of the darkness,” Ivy sobbed. “No one can.”

“I'm not dragging you anywhere,” Noor said, remembering something her mother had once said to her. “I've come to join you on the ground not to pull you up, but to be by your side as we rise together. Will you come with me?”

“I don't think I can do it.”

“I know you can,” Noor said, taking Ivy's hand firmly in hers. “Of this, I'm absolutely certain.”

“You won't let me go?”

“I promise.” Noor closed her eyes and took a deep breath. “Let's go home.”

On the moonlit street of Galaxy, some hours after she had first departed, Noor returned, bringing Ivy back with her.

“You're alive!” Sissy said, awed.

“We are,” Noor said weakly, helping Ivy to sit up as she did so. “Sissy, will you help Ivy to walk?”

“Of course I will,” the DJ said, sliding a strong arm around Ivy's waist. “Up you get, Doc.”

Mallory hauled Noor to her feet, nodding proudly at her.

“You did well, Noor. I'm impressed.”

“Thank you,” she said, her shoulders sagging with exhaustion. “We aren't done yet, though.”

“Then let us end it,” Mallory said with a heaving sigh, “once and for all.”

Chapter Thirty One – The Keys to the Gulag

Mallory

There were a dozen dead bodies on the road towards the Applied Physics building, their outlines softened in the growing moonlight.

"Are they Faceless?" Midori asked, one hand on her katana and poised to strike.

They're all faceless to me, Mallory thought sadly as he waved her to stand down.

"They're dead, Midori," he said softly, "just like everything else in this town."

"What killed them?" Noor asked, looking around nervously.

"I don't know," he lied. He looked back over to where Ivy and Sissy were standing; the latter was supporting the former. "Are you going to be okay, Ivy?"

"I'll survive," she said weakly, with a grim smile. "Besides, I've got a three to one advantage over the rest of you, which isn't to be sniffed at."

Francis still hugged the edge of the street, both terrified of the forest and ready to flee into it at a moment's notice. Mallory walked over to him, slowly and carefully to avoid startling the agoraphobic man.

"We'll be inside soon enough, Francis," he said gently. He took his older brother's trembling hand in his.

"You should leave me behind," he said, his voice shaking with fear. "Down to Gehenna and all that."

"Don't make me recite Guest at you," Mallory said with a chuckle as he led Francis down the road. "Weary, wandering brother, et cetera, et cetera."

"Eddie Guest?" Francis said, a touch of mirth coming to his words at last. "Who are you; Father?"

"What on earth are you two talking about?" Ivy called as she stumbled forwards, with Sissy barely keeping pace with her. "Is this really the time to be laughing and joking?"

In the face of desolation and desperation is the only time to laugh, Mallory thought, but he decided to answer with a shrug. *Whistling as you pass the graveyard,* he mused, *or the hymns for the gallows; only in the darkness can you truly find the light.*

He clung to his brother; the only man who could ever truly understand the anguish of his gift. For Francis as well as Mallory, as each used their gift they grew more powerful but their curses worsened exponentially.

One day I might not even be able to see Thaddeus's face, he thought sadly. *I might completely forget who I am, just like Bert did.*

Mallory sniffled and wiped the tears from his eyes.

"What's wrong?" Francis whispered.

"It's this place," Mallory said, louder than he intended. "It's this fucking town! It's a black hole that just takes and takes and takes until there's nothing left of you, only to forget it all as soon as the sun rises. It's just sorrow and grief and emptiness.

"This is an evil fucking place, and I hate it!"

He screamed the last part, and staggered away from Francis towards Sissy. He grabbed her coat by the lapels, tears streaming down his face, and shook her violently.

"How can you fucking stand it?" His face was inches from hers, but it was no good; it was as blank to him as a virgin canvas. "How can you bear to live here?"

"Mallory, what's wrong with you?" Ivy asked.

"What's wrong with me?" he asked, incredulous as he was grief stricken. "What the fuck is wrong with *her*?"

"I've always lived here," Sissy said softly. "Everything I've ever loved is here."

"This place is dead!" Mallory howled. "Everything you think you have is just a lie; a dream cooked up around that fucking laboratory!"

"How could they even do that?" Sissy asked, stepping away from the frantic painter. "How is that even possible?"

"Who cares?" Mallory said angrily. "You're imprisoned here, Sissy."

"Mallory, don't." Ivy said sternly, but the warning in her eyes was lost on him.

"It's been almost forty years, Sissy," Mallory said as all the fight left him. "We've only been here for three days, but we're most likely already dead."

"Forty years?" Sissy said in shock, and he nodded. "But how can that be?"

"I don't know," he said, with a desperate sob, "but all I wanted was to rescue my brother. I just wanted to bring him home safely."

"Mallory..." Francis said weakly, but his brother shrugged him off.

"It's all fucked now, isn't it? I'll never get to see the people I love again." He wiped a tear from his cheek, but it did no good; they came fast and freely now, hot and painful. "I made a friend and then I killed him as he lay in my arms; how am I supposed to recover from that?"

"But how can I still be the same age?" Sissy asked quietly, and Mallory rounded on her once again, drawing his weapon.

"You're dead, Sissy!" The pistol trembled wildly in his grip as he wept. "Or you aren't real, but either way you're just a symptom of the madness of this town!"

"Mallory!" Ivy said sharply. "Mallory, fucking stop it! Get a hold of yourself!"

"We're never getting out of here," Mallory said quietly. He lowered the pistol and Sissy breathed a ragged sigh of relief, only to gasp once more as he put the gun to his own temple. "Better fast and on my own terms, than trapped forever in a dream."

"You're going to kill yourself?" Ivy asked gently. "After everything we've been through?"

"We aren't leaving this town, Ivy," he sobbed, "so why fight it?"

"The Master's victory seemed inevitable," she said, "but you still fought him with everything you had. Why is this any different?"

"You don't understand," Mallory said, crying even harder now. "You don't understand what's been taken from me; what I've lost. I can't do it all again, Ivy; I'm just not strong enough."

She put an arm around his shoulders and held him as he cried.

"Of course you are," she said tenderly. "Things just seem bleak right now because you're in the depths of it. This is just the extinction burst, Mallory; the death throes of the phenomenon that we're trapped inside."

She pulled him in tight, and let him weep uncontrollably.

"This too shall pass; I promise."

Sissy Sparrow stood silently at the side of the road, staring into the middle distance.

Mallory sniffled and handed the gun to Ivy.

"You better take this for now, at least until I start feeling a bit more myself." He looked at the dead Faceless that littered the street. "Somehow, I don't think guns are going to help us any longer."

"What makes you say that?" Noor said.

"Can't you feel it?" Mallory asked. The young woman shook her head, but Sissy spoke up instead.

"I can. It's like something has shifted; small and monumental at the same time."

Maybe there is hope after all.

"The passing of a mountainous cloud," Mallory said, "or the easing of a looming, oppressive shadow."

"What do you think it is?" Sissy asked as they began walking once again.

"It's the beginning of the end," Mallory said. "Something is in motion now, and all it will take to see this through to its conclusion is to keep moving."

"This town really is dead, isn't it?" Sissy looked at Noor instead of Mallory.

"It is," Noor replied, "but it's been that way for a long time, hasn't it?"

"I guess so," Sissy said, wrapping her arms around herself. "Fewer and fewer callers into the radio, and every year the population gets older; at some point it stops being a life and becomes..."

"A haunting?" Mallory offered tentatively.

"Yeah, that's exactly it."

She's almost there. He looked at her, smiling gently. *I wonder what she's going to find inside the Applied*

Physics Building?

"I think we're here," Ivy said as they reached a chain link fence; it seemed to loom up on them out of nowhere. "I'm surprised we didn't see this from further down the road."

"You don't sound surprised," Sissy said. She looked at Mallory, almost suspiciously. "Why am I alive when everyone else is dead, Mallory?"

"Are you so sure that's what's happening?" He gestured to the main entrance of the laboratory. "Do you want to go first?"

"What if it's locked?" Sissy asked, half-heartedly.

"You know it won't be," Mallory said. "You already know what's happening, don't you?"

"Yes," she said after a colossal pause, "but I still need to see it."

"We're here with you." Ivy put a hand on her shoulder. "Take as long as you need."

"I always imagined that this place was like some giant maze," Sissy said walking slowly forwards, "but now that I see it, I know that there are just going to be two rooms; a big foyer, and a strong room inside."

"What's in the strong room?" Ivy asked as they neared the door. Sissy put a trembling hand on the handle and pushed it open. Sissy didn't answer her question, instead choosing to walk into the room that she'd described as the foyer.

It was anything but.

Two rows of hospital beds, filled with withered, elderly women flanked the black carpet that ran up the centre of the room. The beeping of heart monitors and the gentle hum of machinery filled the air, along with the cloying scentless stink of imminent death.

This is Galaxy, at its very core, Mallory realised.

He looked and saw that Sissy no longer wore her casual clothes, but the uniform of a candy striper. *I bet she looks just like her mother,* he thought, although he had nothing to base that on. *How strange; things must be on the verge of total collapse.*

Sissy took a moment to greet each patient as she passed down through the foyer, and every single one flatlined as she moved on. Tears rolled down her cheeks as she moved closer and closer to the door at the end of the carpet.

There was a loud ding that reverberated through the air, ringing clear and true, as a call light was illuminated above the door. Mallory was now able to read the words printed in black on the pale door.

Palliative Care.

The bell dinged again, and Sissy quickened her pace.

The elderly patients died off faster as she trotted towards the pale door, then she finally broke into a desperate sprint as the bell rang a third time.

Mallory was hot on her heels when she finally reached the door and burst through it at full speed.

Instead of a hospital room, Sissy stumbled into her own home.

Patryk Nightingale, the love of her life, looked at her from his spot on the sofa, his eyes already misty with tears.

"Hi, sweetheart," he said, his voice cracking slightly. "I'm glad you came."

"How long have you known?" she asked him as Mallory handed her a cup of strong black coffee.

"I guess since it happened," Patryk said softly, "but it feels like forever and never all at once."

"Why didn't you tell me?"

“It would break your heart, darling,” he said, in the most tender tone that Mallory had ever heard. “Besides, you already knew, deep down.”

“It was both of you, wasn't it?”

Patryk nodded.

“Was it quick?”

“I barely noticed, same for Rusty, too.”

Sissy took a sip of her coffee, but spat it out as the sobs finally took her. She placed her cup on the table and rocked back and forth in her seat, keening shrilly. Mallory placed a hand on her shoulder, offering the only comfort he could give; he remembered the grief he'd felt at his Father's death and just how isolating and lonely it had been.

“It's not fair!” she screamed, pulling at her hair.

“I know, sweetheart,” Patryk said, almost too quietly to hear, “but sometimes these things just happen. I'm sorry.”

“What!?” she said, her eyes wide. “What do you have to be sorry about? You're the one that... that died.”

“I'm sorry that I left you, darling, even if I didn't mean to. I miss you all the time.”

“I miss you even when you're still here,” Sissy said, looking at him with wild, unblinking eyes. “I'll always miss you.”

“I know you will,” Patryk said solemnly, “but you have to let me go, Sissy.”

She was silent.

“You have to let yourself go,” he said quietly, “and you have to let everyone else leave this place.”

“No.” Her voice trembled as she spoke.

“You will, Sissy,” Patryk continued, “because you're a good person and it's the right thing to do.”

"I'm not a good person!"

"Of course you are." He smiled adoringly at her.

"How can you say that, after all I've done?"

"I know you're a good person, Sissy Sparrow, because I love you." He leant forwards and kissed her softly. "That's all the proof I'll ever need."

"I love you, too, Patryk." She nodded tearfully. "You're right; I have to let everyone go."

Sissy let out a quiet sob.

"But, I," she said haltingly, "but I don't know how."

Chapter Thirty Two – Signing Off

Michaela

"I'll help you," Michaela said quietly. She settled down next to Sissy and placed an arm gently around her. "I'll walk through this with you; you won't be alone."

"Ivy-" Mallory began, but Michaela shook her head.

"Ivy isn't here, Mallory." Her voice was tired, but the resolve in her heart had never been stronger. "Nor is Edgar. I've hidden them away, somewhere safe; they'll wake up at the end of this."

"But you won't?" Noor asked.

"No, I won't, but that's okay," Michaela lied as the tears threatened to spill over. "I never really had friends anyway, and one of us has to do this."

"I never meant to hurt anyone," Sissy sobbed, still held fast in Michaela's arms.

"No one ever does," Michaela whispered, "but it doesn't change what happened. You need to let everyone go, Sissy."

"But how did this even happen!?" Her voice broke slightly as she teetered on the edge of hysteria. "I'm not special!"

"But you are," Patryk said, taking her hands in his. "You are so fucking special, Sissy. I've never met someone who loves so deeply or cares with such reckless abandon; you're the most amazing person I've ever met."

"I'm a selfish person," she croaked out through her tears.

"You're a wonderful person," Patryk said, his tears

flowing freely too. “You're my *favourite* person.”
“Everyone makes mistakes, Cecilia,” Midori said. “I'm older than I look, and I have made hundreds; it doesn't taint the heart of you, though.”
“How many people have died because of me?”
“It doesn't matter,” Michaela said as her mind filled with images of Charity's face, smiling in the candlelight. “You loved someone enough to keep them here; I would've done the same.”
“Me too,” whispered Noor. “I would've let the world burn if it would've kept the people I cared for in my life.”
“Will you wake up?” Sissy asked, looking at the Ministry agents that surrounded her. “Will you still be alive?”
“Yes,” Mallory said. “We'll be weak, and we'll need looking after for a few days, but we'll be alive.”
“Maybe you'll see each other again,” Francis said quietly. “Who knows what happens next? Maybe you'll let everyone go and the three of you will just be left standing here, able to spend forever as a family.”
“That doesn't sound so bad, does it, Sissy?” Patryk asked.
“No, it doesn't.”
I wish that were true, Michaela thought sadly. *If only I could see her one last time.*
“Where do you want to be, Sissy?” Mallory asked. “Where will make this easiest?”
“The radio station?” Patryk suggested, but she shook her head.
“No,” Sissy said after taking a moment to gather her strength. “I know where I have to be; where it all started.”
“I understand,” her husband replied. “I'll get Rusty,

and then we'll meet you there."

He got to his feet and smiled sadly at her before bending down and planting a gentle kiss on her forehead. Sissy laughed softly as he swept a hand through his messy hair.

"You're too damn handsome for your own good, Dr Nightingale."

"I've got you, Sissy," he said after a pause. "I'll always be with you."

"Promise?"

"Of course I do, you brave, brave woman." He looked at Michaela. "There's no other way to do this, is there?"

"No, there isn't." Michaela's usually stern tone was gentle; soft as the moonlight that streamed through the curtains. "I wish that-"

"Save your wishes," Patryk said. "That's the one problem with life; nobody gets out alive. It's a downer ending, every single time."

"I'll see you soon, Patryk," Sissy said, her voice stronger than before. "Give Rusty a good night kiss from me."

"I always do. Miss you already, darling." Patryk lingered for a few seconds longer before walking through the living room towards the kitchen. Before they knew it, he was out of sight.

"I miss you too," Sissy murmured. "I always do."

"Should we go now?" Michaela asked.

"Not yet," Sissy said, wiping the tears from her eyes. "They'll come for me when it's time. All that's left to do now is wait."

The clock on the mantel had long since stopped, but it was sooner than Michaela expected when the flashing red and blue lights lit up the windows. She put her hand on the hilt of her sword and Mallory reached for his revolver, but Sissy shook her head.

She sighed heavily and stood up, smoothing out the creases of the house dress she'd changed into. There was a sharp knock at the door and she faltered, freezing in place for a few seconds. Michaela stepped forwards, moving her hand from her blade and into Sissy's.

“I'm with you,” Michaela said gently. “You don't have to do this alone.”

“Thank you,” Sissy said as they approached the front door. The knock came again, followed by a voice.

“Sissy, are you in there?” asked a man's voice, deep and gruff.

She stood at the front door and reached for the handle, her fingers trembling as she did so. Michaela gave her hand a squeeze and Sissy opened the door with a mournful sigh. Before them stood a great hulking bear of a man, with a wide brimmed hat atop his head and a sheriff's star pinned to his chest.

He had the same gentle eyes as Sissy, and the same soft curve to his mouth; it was buried beneath a greying beard, however. The look of sadness that he gave the young disc jockey almost broke Michaela, but she fought to stay strong.

“Hi, Daddy,” Sissy said, tears running down her cheeks. “I've missed you.”

“I've missed you too, honey.” He hesitated, but only for a moment. “Sweetheart, there's... there's been an accident.”

The words were barely out of his mouth when Sissy threw herself into her father's arms. He held her tightly, with the fierce love that only the grieving can muster. She began to weep openly, and he stroked her hair affectionately, tears moistening his own cheeks.

"Will you take me to see them, Daddy?" Sissy asked, knowing full well what the answer would be.

"Of course, sweetheart." He closed his eyes briefly, resting his head against hers. "Don't you dare feel guilty for all that's happened, Sissy."

"But, I-"

"I don't care," he said, his voice cracking with emotion. "What you did was out of love, and it wasn't like you did it on purpose, either. I'm just grateful to be able to hold you again, Sissy."

He opened his eyes and looked at the Ministry agents that were standing in the doorway behind her.

"Did you folks come here to help my daughter?" he asked quietly. They hesitated initially, unsure of exactly what to say. It was Mallory who spoke up.

"I came here to save my brother," he said, "but then we met Sissy and, well, how can you not help someone so kind?"

"She helped us first," Michaela said quietly. "We wouldn't have got through this without her."

"You wouldn't be here if it weren't for me," Sissy said.

"It's time to go," the Sheriff said to his daughter. He looked at the others. "Are you coming with us?"

"I am," Michaela said, "but they're not."

"We'll be waiting here when Ivy wakes up," Mallory said. "Goodbye, Michaela."

"Take care, Marsh. Stay on the straight and narrow." She looked at Noor. "Thank you for helping Ivy when we couldn't, Noor. Enjoy your life, as much as you can."

Noor nodded and Midori stepped forward, placing

her hand on Michaela's shoulder.

"You were my most talented and least disciplined pupil, but I am so very proud of you. Die well."

"I will, Mistress Midori. Thank you for everything you taught me."

"I apologise for none of it."

"I expected nothing less." She turned to face Sissy and the Sheriff. "Let's go."

The three of them climbed into the idling police car, belted themselves in, and drove on through the darkness. Overhead, the moon gleamed brightly and Halley's comet made its lazy way through the heavens.

"I'm glad that I got to see you," Michaela whispered to the celestial wanderer. "I was always worried that I was born at exactly the wrong time."

"What's your name?" the Sheriff asked after a few minutes of silence.

"Michaela Inglewood. Yours?"

"Samuel Sparrow. You got family back in England, Miss Inglewood?"

"I do," she said, smiling at the thought of the Night People. "They're a ragtag bunch, but I love them."

"No blood?" Sissy asked. Michaela shrugged.

"My parents are alive, but they don't know me, and that's alright by me. I do have a half brother though, and I regret not getting to know him." She looked at the window; for the first time in almost four decades, her reflection was alone. *Maybe Ivy and Edgar will be able meet him one day.*

"Nobody goes to their end with a completely clear heart," Samuel Sparrow said, not unkindly. "Take comfort in those that you did know and that when the time comes, you won't be facing it on your own."

"I'm glad to have known you, Samuel," she said,

"even if it was only for a little while."

"Likewise, Miss Inglewood." He gave her a solemn smile. They rounded a sharp bend, and Michaela was able to make out the glow of road flares further along. Samuel slowed slightly, and Sissy took a deep breath. "We're almost there, sweetheart."

"I-I can't do this!" Sissy cried out, shaking her head tearfully. "I'm not strong enough!"

"Of course you are," her father said, stopping a short way from the burning pink light. "Your mother would be so proud of you."

"But all the people I killed..."

"Don't dwell on it," Michaela said. "You gave some people much longer than their allotted years in this place; take heart in that if you can."

"You got a second chance with Patryk and Rusty," Samuel said, his lip quivering as he spoke. "Damn near forty years more than you were supposed to; I'd have done the same to hold on to your mother and then some.

"You get to say goodbye properly, Sissy." He took a deep breath as he unbuckled his belt. "Most folk never get more than a glance."

"I don't want them to go," Sissy muttered, unfastening her seatbelt nonetheless. "I don't want you to go."

"I know you don't, sweetheart, but you can't stay locked away in this town forever; you need to spread your wings and fly, my little sparrow." He left the vehicle and reached out a large hand to his daughter. She took it in hers and stepped out on to the moonlit asphalt.

Courage, Michaela.

Michaela joined them, slipping one of her hands into

Sissy's free one, and the three of them slowly walked towards the crash site. Their tears glinted in the luminous glare as they wept, but they drew strength from each other.

"Will it hurt?" Sissy asked.

"I don't think so," Michaela replied. "I think it will be like waking up from a dream; it'll just happen."

"So we might not even notice?" Samuel asked. Michaela nodded. "That's a comforting thought."

They slowed as they reached the mangled wreck, but Sissy kept on going when the other two stopped. She approached the car, her eyes never leaving the shattered bodies of Patryk Nightingale and Rusty Sparrow that were still inside.

She did not startle when she was joined by her husband and son, who stood either side of her, and regarded their long dead forms with respectful silence and a sense of absolute inevitability.

"Goodbye, Patryk," Sissy said, almost too quietly for Michaela and Samuel to hear. "Goodbye, my sweet boy. You two were my life, and I was so fucking lucky to have you as long as I did. Our time was stolen from us, but I took it back.

"I wanted my time with you, God damn it! I was promised a lifetime!" She dropped to her knees. "We were supposed to grow old together!"

"We did, Sissy," Patryk said as he joined her on the ground. "This will be my seventy third year on this earth. Look at our son, Sissy."

She peered up at him through her tears; Rusty was no longer a child, but a grown man in his mid-forties, handsome, just like his father. He, too, knelt beside Sissy, who was now an old woman. They held each other for a moment, and then she turned to look at

Michaela Inglewood.

"I'm ready."

"Keep talking," Michaela said as she walked carefully forwards, her heart racing with fear. She took even breaths as she approached the Sparrow family, who were gently whispering to one another. "It'll be done soon, I promise."

Michaela placed a hand on Sissy's shoulder, letting her power flow into the elderly woman's form. She filled her mind with images of ending; of closing doors, setting suns, and the snuffing out of candles.

Her vision began to darken at the edges, and she caught sight of the Lamplight tattoo on her arm; it too was fading.

"At last," she murmured, "it's done."

The darkness continued to deepen around them, dimming the light of the flares. Samuel was already gone when the blackness was near total, but just before the light faded completely there was a final flare of colour followed by a shocked gasp, as if someone had just awoken from a deep sleep.

On the snowy ground near an ancient wrecked car, surrounded by skeletal remains, Ivy Livingston opened her eyes.

Epilogue – The Land of the Living

The helicopters went into Galaxy less than eight minutes after the radio broadcast ceased and the shimmering sphere around the Easy collapsed. Their receiver operators were flooded with pings from the countless emergency beacons that had been carried across the event horizon since it first went up, almost forty years ago.

The Ministry ones were the easiest to locate; they were on a slightly different frequency to the Bureau's, and two helicopters were tasked with locating the agents. One landed a hundred metres or so from the Sparrow house, and was met by Noor Turner, Mallory and Francis Marsh, and Midori Aoki; all were dehydrated and exhausted, but alive.

The second helicopter could not find a safe landing zone, but instead directed an all-terrain vehicle to the other Ministry beacon's location. When the first responders arrived, they found Ivy Livingston sitting amongst the skeletal remains of at least four people, staring into the middle distance with tears running down her cheeks.

She wordlessly climbed aboard the vehicle, which brought her back to the Forward Command Post. After three days of intravenous fluids, medical examinations, and bed rest, the Ministry agents were permitted to return home.

Ivy Livingston returned to Oxford alone; more alone than she'd ever been, in fact. Edgar was still with her, but in his grief addled state all he could do was rattle around the recesses of her mind like a ghost.

She paid her taxi driver for the fare, insisting that he kept the change as a generous tip, and exited the vehicle. She looked up at the looming Jericho Folly, unsure of whether to enter or not. She'd not spoken to Charity since Michaela had died, and although Mallory had informed her of their approximate return schedule, there was no way for her lover to know for sure that she had returned.

I could just go, she thought. *I could just take a few days to hole up somewhere and drown in sorrow.*

Something made Ivy turn her head, and she glanced down the street towards the Night People's favourite pub, The Old Bookbinders; straight into the shaded eyes of the woman she loved. At the sight of her, Charity abandoned her table and sprinted headlong towards Ivy.

All thoughts of loneliness and isolation were driven away when the Ghost reached her and drew her into a tight embrace.

"I'm so glad you're back," Charity said, her words muffled by Ivy's heavy winter coat. "I've missed you so fucking much."

"Michaela's gone," Ivy whispered. It was the first time she'd said it aloud since leaving Galaxy, and the truth cut to the very core of her.

"Mallory told me," Charity said, still clinging to the now weeping woman. "I'm so sorry, Liv."

"She loved you," Ivy said tearfully, "in her own way. She thought of you at the end."

There were no more words between the two women for some time; only tender touches and the comforting reassurance of physical companionship. As they lay in bed together that night, Ivy had a single, heartbreaking thought just before she drifted into a dreamless sleep, safe in her lover's arms.

I hope I die first.

"Elsie?" Noor called out as she opened the door to the stylish Islington flat that her partner had picked out for them. "Elsie are you here?"

Only silence answered her.

Sissy's words echoed in her head.

I miss you even when you're still here.

She walked into the kitchen and ran her fingertips along the worktop, resisting the temptation to dive into the Tangle and see exactly what her girlfriend had been up to while she'd been away.

"Control is key," she said, remembering Miranda Salt's words. "I will not become a slave to the flames."

The rattle of a key in the lock made her jump, and she spun around to see Elsie entering the flat, a large bouquet of flowers in hand. She grinned when she saw Noor, and crossed the distance between her in a few large strides.

"For you!" she said giddily as she thrust the flowers into Noor's hands. The smell was wonderful, but it tickled the Fate's nose a little and she let out a dainty sneeze. Elsie's eyes widened, a heartbroken look on her face. "Oh no, please tell me that you're not allergic!"

"I'm not, Elsie," Noor said. She tried to smile at her strange, wonderful lover, but her lip began to quiver and tears beaded in the corners of her eyes. "I missed you."

Noor set the flowers down on the worktop and wrapped her arms tightly around Elsie.

"You want to talk about it?" Elsie asked softly. Noor nodded. "Alright then. Why don't you go and put your pyjamas on, and then we'll get cosy on the sofa; then you can talk for as long as you need. Go on, sweetheart, and I'll put the kettle on."

Noor nodded and headed towards their bedroom as Elsie filled the kettle. She turned as she reached the kitchen door and looked tearfully at her girlfriend.

"Elsie?" she said quietly.

"Yes, darling?" Elsie replied, kettle in hand.

"Is this real?"

"Yes, it is."

"Would you tell me if it wasn't?" Noor asked, her hands shaking slightly.

"In a heartbeat."

"Promise?"

"Cross my heart."

"I love you," Noor said.

"I love you too, sweetheart," Elsie said. She set the kettle boiling and looked at Noor. "You want me to come with you?"

"Yes, please." Her voice was small, but Elsie was by her side in a flash. "Please don't leave me alone."

"I won't," she said, "as much as I can help it."

Elsie gave Noor's hand a squeeze and they walked towards the bedroom. They only got about eight feet, however, before Noor collapsed to the ground, weeping uncontrollably. Elsie wordlessly put her arms around her and held her as she cried.

Is this what my life has become? Noor wondered as she wept.

Will it always be like this?

Nobody made it out of that town alive, Mallory thought sadly, *least of all those of us still living.*

Mallory's brush hovered over the canvas as he

hesitated, contemplating his next stroke.

"Still painting?" Francis asked as he walked into the studio. Mallory nodded.

"It helps me stay in the moment," he said. "I don't want to think about how far I've got to go."

"I'm with you every step of the way, old boy," Francis said.

Mallory smiled at him, looking at the disparate features of his brother's face; the shaggy beard was gone and his youth had returned. *I suppose you look like your old self,* Mallory thought, *although I'll never know for sure.*

"I don't want to be rude, Francis," Mallory said, "but I do paint better when just left to it. Is there a reason you're here?"

"Ah, yes; two actually." He put a hand on Mallory's shoulder. "The first concerns two of the Americans that went into Galaxy with you; an Agent Verity Lovage and a Captain Christopher Jennings, to be exact."

"They found their bodies?" Mallory asked sadly.

"After a fashion," Francis said, a smile in his voice. "They were found alive yesterday morning. Unconscious, but alive. They both woke up today and are, by all initial reckoning, completely unharmed. I thought you'd want to know."

"Thank you, Francis," Mallory said, gripping his brother's arm tightly. "I really needed to hear that today."

"I thought that might be the case." He patted Mallory's hand with his free one. "The other thing is more of a question; are you up to having visitors? I can send them away, if you like."

"No, please let them in. I'm a bit stuck on this

painting, anyway."

Francis nodded and strolled away, his shoes tapping sharply on the tiled floor.

Mallory smelled his guests before he saw them; the spicy scent of carnations and the rich sweetness of liquorice. He got to his feet as Jess and Teaser entered his studio.

"Hey, Mal!" Teaser said as she swept him up into her long, lanky arms. "I always forget that you've got such a swanky gaff!"

"Hello, Mallory," Jess said, greeting him with a tender hug and a long, lingering kiss. "It's good to see you."

"Thank you both for coming," Mallory said, almost shyly. "I'm sorry that I don't look like I normally do..."

"You don't need to apologise for that," Jess said, running her fingers through his hair. "I fell in love with you when you were a vampire, after all."

"You've always looked weird to me," Teaser said with a playful giggle, "so no change there."

"I've missed you," he said taking their hands in his. "I've missed you both so much."

"Likewise," Jess said, kissing him once again.

"Who's this, Mal?" Teaser asked, pointing at the portrait that Mallory was working on.

The canvas showed a smiling young man, dressed in a white outfit and standing behind a counter, as he handed a chocolate phosphate to the viewer. The little table next to the easel was covered in photographs, kindly sent from America, so Mallory could be absolutely sure that he got the man's face right.

"That's Agent Albert Gillespie, or Bert, at least to anyone that matters," Mallory said, fighting back the tears. "He was my friend."

"You're sure?" Finley asked excitedly as he looked at the results on the screen.

"Yes, Boss," Dylan Weiss said. "We checked, and then double checked before we came and told you."

"This..." Finley grinned and put a grateful hand on his friend's back, "this is absolutely fantastic. How soon can we get there?"

"Depends on how big a crew you need, but the advance team can have boots on the ground in three days, tops." Dylan couldn't help but chuckle. "This really is it, huh?"

"Yes it is, Dylan. We're about to change the world." Finley looked around and called over his shoulder. "Thaddy, come look at this!"

Thaddeus Thane, Finley's latest obsession, rose from the comfortable sofa where he was lounging and strolled over to the computer. Finley playfully stroked the tall man's beard and tapped the screen eagerly.

"What am I looking at?" Thaddeus asked, putting an arm affectionately around the eccentric billionaire.

"This," Finley said gleefully, "is an island in the Southern Ocean. It was previously buried by sea ice, but what with global warming being what it is, it's finally visible to the satellites I have in orbit!"

"What's so special about it?" Thad asked.

"I knew it was going to be there, Thaddy," Finley said with a grin. "I found several relics that all pointed to the same location, and there it is, exactly where it's supposed to be!"

"But what is it?" Thad said, getting a touch exasperated.

"Avalon," Finley said reverentially, "the island at the heart of Arthurian legend."

"Are you certain?" Thad asked, shocked.

"I am," Finley said with a sly smile. "I have more sources than anyone knows."

"What are you expecting to find there?" Thad looked at Finley who offered his hand towards him.

"Why don't you come with me and find out?" Finley said, giving the large man a coquettish smile. "Are you ready for the adventure of a lifetime?"

Thaddeus nodded and returned to the sofa in order to let Finley continue planning the expedition with Dylan Weiss. In the back of his mind, however, the Modern Midas was only able to focus on one thing.

This is the most important moment of my entire existence, he thought excitedly. *At last, a chance at life eternal.*

I won't let anything stand in my way.

Or anyone.

The madness continues in...

OUR FORBIDDEN FUTURE

Acknowledgments

This one got away from me a little, dear reader. Some of the plot points ended up writing themselves, often to my considerable surprise. I actually intended this book to be a stand alone drama novel, but it ended up being one of my favourite Ministry books so far.

It's also important to point out that I was diagnosed with Epilepsy in the course of writing this book. It was a rough time and it has been (and will continue to be) a long road to recovery and adjustment.

I would like to make a special mention to the paramedics, doctors, medical professionals, and my loved ones who worked hard to care for me during the depths of my medical emergency. Without you all, I would not be here.

There are others, to thank, of course, because such a book cannot be written in isolation.

Firstly and most importantly, I would like to thank my partner, Syd, for the love, support, and final proofreading of this story. She has listened to me talk about this for months, and has given me both inspiration and encouragement in spades. I love you, darling, and I am so lucky to have you in my life.

Likewise, I would like to thank my metamor, Ben Wright. Thank you for all the support and discussion that has helped this book become the nightmare that it finally grew into. I especially enjoyed bouncing around ideas for the cursed hospital with you.

I would like to thank you both for inviting me into

your life and your (now our) home; I feel loved, wanted, and cared for, which I am grateful for beyond measure.

I would also like to thank our guinea pigs, both for their reassuring presence and constant source of amusement. There will continue to be references to you scattered throughout my writing. I would like to especially mention Bert and the late, great, Mandelbrot; the original Bert and Uncle.

A big thank you goes out to my best friend, Dr Georgia Lynott. You are a source of light in my life and always a joy to spend time with. I hope you will enjoy this book, and the series as a whole.

I cannot write a horror novel without thanking my parents, Steve and Samantha Farrell, my grandparents, Frank and Lorraine Keeley, and other members of my family; you have all played a crucial part developing my absolute love of horror. From late night films to tatty paperbacks read in the car on long journeys; it all has culminated in this book, and all those that follow it. Thank you.

I would like to extend my thanks to my childhood friends, James Bullock and Colum Taylor, for all their support and all the horror films we watched together over the years.

Once again, I would like to thank my therapist, Zayna Brookhouse, for her help in turning my fear and grief into something constructive that I could share with you all.

I'd like to thank all the musicians, artists, writers, and cinematographers that have contributed to the horror genre. I write to music, so your help was invaluable in the creation of this work.

Of course, I'm sure that I have missed people off of

this list; it is not exhaustive, after all! So, to all the other Parrots out there who helped to make this work a reality, I thank you.

And, last but not least, you, dear reader, for choosing to read this book.

Thank you.

About the Author

Eleanor Fitzgerald is a polyamorous non-binary trans woman living in and around Oxford. Eleanor uses any and all pronouns, and is neurodivergent and disabled. Eleanor is hard of hearing, and completely deaf on one side.

They have a fascination for all things weird and wonderful, and have thoroughly enjoyed writing this work for you. Rest assured, it will not be the last!

Eleanor also paints, and created the base artwork that this book's cover illustration was based around, before editing it digitally to get the final piece. Their particular style is impressionism, which they love immensely.

If you have any questions or comments, they can be reached at the following email address:

eleanorfitzgeraldwriting@gmail.com

Printed in Great Britain
by Amazon

51422484R00182